SPECIAL MESSAGE TO READERS

This book is published under the auspices of

THE ULVERSCROFT FOUNDATION

(registered charity No. 264873 UK)

Established in 1972 to provide funds for research, diagnosis and treatment of eye diseases. Examples of contributions made are: —

A Children's Assessment Unit at Moorfield's Hospital, London.

•

Twin operating theatres at the Western Ophthalmic Hospital, London.

•

A Chair of Ophthalmology at the Royal Australian College of Ophthalmologists.

•

The Ulverscroft Children's Eye Unit at the Great Ormond Street Hospital For Sick Children, London.

You can help further the work of the Foundation by making a donation or leaving a legacy. Every contribution, no matter how small, is received with gratitude. Please write for details to:

THE ULVERSCROFT FOUNDATION,
The Green, Bradgate Road, Anstey,
Leicester LE7 7FU, England.
Telephone: (0116) 236 4325

In Australia write to:
THE ULVERSCROFT FOUNDATION,
c/o The Royal Australian College of Ophthalmologists,
27, Commonwealth Street, Sydney,
N.S.W. 2010.

Mary Street was born in Heanor, Derbyshire. Her interest in writing began whilst she was in hospital following a road traffic accident. She has written several romance and suspense novels.

SEE A FINE LADY

A handsome, impoverished baronet might well seek to restore his fortune by marriage. But Sir Justin St John Martin had engaged himself in a very different enterprise, which made it impossible for him to move in fashionable society. Miss Judith Tremaine had a fortune at her disposal and was well accustomed to being courted. So when Sir Justin showed not the slightest interest in her, she quite naturally became very intrigued by him. But could Judith be content with him in the remote country neighbourhood? What would happen if she went gallivanting off to town with his sisters?

Books by Mary Street
Published by The House of Ulverscroft:

DIAMOND CUTS DIAMOND
BETTER TO FORGET
THE GEMINI GIRL
A FRIENDLY STAR
A RELATIVE STRANGER

MARY STREET

SEE A FINE LADY

Complete and Unabridged

ULVERSCROFT
Leicester

First published in Great Britain in 1999 by
Robert Hale Limited
London

First Large Print Edition
published 2001
by arrangement with
Robert Hale Limited
London

British Library CIP Data

Street, Mary
See a fine lady.—Large print ed.—
Ulverscroft large print series: romance
1. Great Britain—Social life and customs
—19th century—Fiction 2. Love stories
3. Large type books
I. Title
823.9′14 [F]

ISBN 0–7089–4368–3

Published by
F. A. Thorpe (Publishing)
Anstey, Leicestershire

Set by Words & Graphics Ltd.
Anstey, Leicestershire
Printed and bound in Great Britain by
T. J. International Ltd., Padstow, Cornwall

This book is printed on acid-free paper

1

Although Sir Justin St John Martin had many difficulties in the matter of finance, he made no declaration of love to me. He showed not the smallest interest in me — or my fortune.

I had, I confess, been displeased when I first heard there was an impoverished baronet on his way to Brinsley Park, for I was accustomed to a particular kind of attention from such, which a vainer creature than myself might suppose had something to do with feminine charm.

I was out on horseback, when I met him. The November fog had descended rapidly, a thick, steamy mist, so my mount was reduced to walking pace and I chanced on the gentleman at the crossroads. He had a pair of matched greys with him, which betrayed his identity, and when he hailed me to enquire his direction, I was surprised to find myself liking what I saw.

He was younger than I expected, and handsome, very handsome indeed, with a good figure and a profile that was aloof and impenetrable, the jaw sharply outlined, the mouth straight and austere, the cheekbones high, and his brows level and strong.

I felt a most unaccustomed sensation of pleasure as I looked at him and said, 'Sir Justin St John Martin, I presume? We are to become acquainted, sir. Mr Wysall said you were expected.'

'You appear to have the advantage of me, madam.'

'Judith Tremaine of Bennerley, sir, at present visiting Brinsley Park with my brother and his wife.'

There was a hint of withdrawal in his voice, 'Indeed?'

He was looking at me, though he displayed no eagerness to be better acquainted, and he only said, 'I was not aware that Mr Wysall was entertaining visitors.'

'You will find us perfectly agreeable,' I said. 'You will like us, when you come to know us.'

His features relaxed a little and he permitted himself a brief smile.

I could easily comprehend his reserve, for there was scandal in his family. Last night, at dinner, five of us had picked over the details.

Occurring five years ago, it had been of little interest to me until now. Last night, I had been reminded that Sir Justin's father,

Sir Robert, had taken a gun to himself after gambling away all his fortune. Sir Justin had inherited a title, a sixteenth-century manor, and financial ruin.

Most gentlemen in Sir Justin's situation would seek to improve their fortunes through marriage. By Mr Wysall's account, however, here was a gentleman of sterner character, who had engaged himself in a very different enterprise.

'He is determined to keep Melrose Court and provide for his sisters,' we were told. 'The man knows about horseflesh and is putting that knowledge to profitable use. His income, these days, comes from breeding, training and trading in horses.'

'One cannot condemn a man for such an undertaking in such a situation,' said my brother. 'Though horse-trading is not an occupation befitting a gentleman.'

'He is no shabby dealer!' said Mr Wysall indignantly. 'Wait until you see my greys! I declare, never in my life have I seen such a sweet-stepping pair. Prepare yourself to be impressed, Hugh! I defy you not to be impressed.'

'If you say so, Charles, I am sure to be impressed.'

'Well, the world has need of good horses,' I said. 'He is to bring your greys himself, sir?

Why does he not send a groom?'

Humour crept into Mr Wysall's voice. 'I desired he should visit, and though he is a gentleman, he has been in business long enough to learn the wisdom of pleasing his customers.'

Sarah Wysall chuckled and revealed her husband had the kindest of motives: he had chosen this method of prevailing upon Sir Justin to benefit from a few days of leisure.

'He shall have good sport and good company,' Sarah declared, 'for there is little of either in his daily life, at present.'

Now I beheld the greys, fine beasts which vindicated Mr Wysall's expenditure. But it was Sir Justin's own mount which really caught and held my attention and which became the subject of conversation between us as we moved on together.

Here was a most noble lord of the equine world, a glossy liver-chestnut who stood at eighteen hands; a mettlesome beast I had no doubt, though he showed no sign of nervousness. Cool and superior, he knew we humans were lesser beings and looked upon us with aloof disdain.

'Have a care, sir!' I said. 'My brother will try to buy him.'

'Blue John is not for sale.' His tone was

mild and courteous, but I had no doubt he meant what he said.

We talked of horses, moving slowly, picking our way through the fog, myself leading him to Brinsley Park.

By the time we arrived, I was well pleased with him. He was quiet, reserved, certainly no rattle: but I felt he had intelligence and I suspected there was humour lurking somewhere beneath the austerity of his manners.

Here was a gentleman I could wish to know better.

My opinion did not change when I observed how he greeted and conversed with the others. And when I went upstairs to change I found myself dissatisfied with all the gowns I had with me.

I am not a lady given to adorning myself with fripperies and indeed, they do not become me for I do not have the elegant beauty of Sarah Wysall, or my sister-in-law, Helen. My figure is good, though I could wish to be taller, but my features leave much to be desired. I have a square jaw and a mouth that is much too wide. My nose, thank heaven, is unexceptional but my eyes are too big, dark brown and surmounted by a pair of straight, heavy brows.

After some deliberation, I chose the gown

I would have worn anyway. A cream silk, it was severely cut, and adorned only by a frill of lace on each sleeve.

Clean and changed, I seated myself at the looking-glass.

'Do what you can with my hair, Betty,' I told my maid. 'You have my permission to be quite ruthless.'

At dinner, I discovered my brother had seen the stallion, Blue John. 'I offered two thousand guineas for him and, do you know, this fellow refuses to sell!' Hugh did not look put out. 'I cannot wonder at it. Were he mine, I would refuse to sell.'

The gentlemen fell to discussing bloodlines and I heard that Blue John was by Peregrine Falcon out of a mare called Pharaoh's Queen. I knew nothing of sire or dam but my brother did and he was impressed. 'By heaven, man, he will make your fortune!'

'I have learnt to be cautious in my hopes, sir, though I will confess to some optimism. Nine of my own mares are in foal by him. I had a tenth, but she slipped.'

Hugh nodded: his mind had been opened up to another idea. 'I have a broodmare, good bloodlines. What do you think Judith? Shall we put Morning Star to Blue John? Such a foal would be a remarkable creature, do you not agree?'

'If it can be got,' I said. 'Certainly, it is an idea worth pursuing.'

Sir Justin looked surprised that my brother should seek my opinion. There was a time when he would not have dreamed of doing so, but Helen, my sister-in-law, had encouraged Hugh to share with me his passion for horses.

Helen herself knew little of horses and it was she who changed the subject. 'If you gentlemen wish to discuss withers and fetlocks and spavins and things,' she said reprovingly, 'you may do so when we ladies have withdrawn from table.'

She began to make some enquiries about Sir Justin's home county of Derbyshire and conversation turned.

'A very gentlemanly gentleman,' she pronounced when we ladies had left the table. 'Very civil indeed, but reserved! Have you noticed, Sarah? He does not speak of himself.'

'Perhaps he will, when he is better acquainted with us,' said Sarah. 'I cannot wonder at his present reserve for there are many in society who disapprove of his enterprise. Is it not strange, that some people approve more of the father who wasted his fortune than of the son who works to restore it?'

The ladies asked my opinion of the gentleman. 'Thus far, I am disposed to like him,' I said.

Perhaps it was my instinctive liking, or perhaps I had the design of drawing his attention to myself: whichever it was, I found myself hastening to smooth over a difficulty which arose later that evening.

Someone proposed we should play cards. Sir Justin flushed and looked awkward and begged to be excused. 'I am afraid I do not care for card games of any sort.'

My brother thought he understood. 'Come sir,' he said good-humouredly, 'there can be no possible objection. Here, amongst our friends, we play for amusement only. We do not propose to fleece you, you know.'

'Indeed, sir, I did not think it,' he said quickly. 'I have no wish to offend: I concede the fault is all my own, but I cannot bring myself to play cards.'

There was a most uncomfortable silence for we saw repugnance in him that went beyond reason. Recalling his history, I thought it not to be wondered at.

'Well,' I heard myself saying, 'I confess I have little inclination for cards, this evening. You gentlemen shall indulge your wives at quadrille and, with your permission, madam,' — I turned to Sarah — 'I shall amuse myself at the pianoforte.'

'My dear, that is an excellent scheme!' said Mr Wysall. 'Nothing could be more delightful! May I beg for the indulgence of some Mozart? He is quite my favourite composer, you know, yet so few of my acquaintance play his music with aptitude.'

Mr Wysall was grateful to me and, to own the truth, I was pleased with myself for I had the satisfaction of seeing Sir Justin's colour subside. If he was now obliged to listen to the others telling him all about my musical accomplishment, I hoped he did not think it too high a price to pay.

I remained at the instrument for an hour and a half, playing pieces requested by the others. Sir Justin sat gazing into the fire with a pensive expression and I know not whether he was listening to music or merely absorbed in his own thoughts.

Eventually, I made so bold as to enquire whether he had a preference for any particular piece.

He looked taken aback, but answered civilly. 'You are very kind, madam. May I request you to play your own favourite?'

I did so, moving into a Beethoven sonata. Having no score, I could play only the slow second movement which I knew by heart, but I think he was pleased with my choice.

I could not help wondering why he had avoided mentioning his own preference.

It was late when we retired, but despite the lateness of the hour I was restless. I found myself thinking of Helen with her husband and of Sarah with hers. Then I thought of Sir Justin, himself retired for the night in some other part of the house, and I wondered if he felt as lonely as I sometimes did.

I felt a pang somewhere deep within me, and I was not at all displeased by the discovery that I had, at last, met a gentleman with whom I could fall in love.

Some years ago, before he was married, my brother had set up for me an establishment in town, where I lived under the supervision of a chaperon and companion, a very wise lady. I still counted Mrs Armstrong as my most trusted friend and often I felt I knew the counsel she would give me.

It was she who had pointed out that my birth and fortune were recommendations which would attract the attention of suitors, and she was right. At the age of two and twenty, I had received ten proposals of marriage.

Once she had said: 'Being secure as to fortune, you need not marry, unless you choose. Be certain then, to make your own choice. Do not allow others to make determinations for you.'

She had taught me how to exercise my judgement and become critical in my observations. Perhaps it was because of her teachings that none of my suitors had pleased me. I did not repent my refusals: yet, observing the happiness of my brother and his wife, there were times when I felt wistful.

So, upon meeting Sir Justin, I was pleased to discover there was one gentleman in the world who had the power to attract me.

The next day, my hopes of knowing him better were frustrated by my brother. At breakfast, he reminded Sir Justin that he had a mind to put his mare, Morning Star, to Blue John.

'She is due to foal in March,' he said.

Because broodmares come into season very soon after foaling, Hugh arranged to send the mare to Sir Justin in February. She would have her foal in Sir Justin's stable, be mated with Blue John and remain in Derbyshire until her foal was grown enough to travel home with her.

At first, I was pleased to see my brother was easy and well-disposed to Sir Justin. But the gentlemen were engaged with a shooting party during the day and that evening, Hugh again monopolized Sir Justin and I had no opportunity to talk to him.

I am not often vexed with my brother, but I confess I was annoyed with him then, for Sir Justin was not a man who could spare much time for leisure, and I knew he would be leaving us again the day after tomorrow.

I need not have despaired, for a circumstance arose the next morning which put me in a very good humour indeed.

I was disposed to tease him, so at breakfast, I announced I had a most pressing need for pink ribbon. I must walk into the town of Underwood to procure some. I begged Sir Justin would be so good as to escort me.

The astonishment in his eyes told me he had perceived the blatant mendacity, and I think he saw also that the others were diverted, but he could not, with any civility, do other than say he would be very happy to escort me.

We set off and he listened to my remarks about the weather in silence. When I had exhausted the subject, he came straight to the point. 'Perhaps you would be so good, Miss Tremaine, as to inform me of your purpose in proposing this excursion?'

'Well, sir, I must have an escort, you know, and my maid does not enjoy walking at all, for she suffers with bunions. I do not care to put her to such pain.'

'Your thoughtfulness does you credit, madam,' he said politely. 'Yet I believe you have some design other than pink ribbon. Ribbon,' he added, 'I might believe, but not pink. Some ladies might wish for pink, but not you.'

'Why, sir!' I exclaimed. 'I had no idea you were so well acquainted with me.'

I was laughing at him and he knew it. He caught his breath and said, 'I have observed your style, madam, and I cannot feel that pink ribbon belongs with it. Come, you might as well tell me your true purpose, for I shall discover it, you know.'

I sighed, recalling that he had sisters and was, no doubt, well used to feminine guile.

'I had no unworthy aim,' I assured him. 'The others desired me to spare you the obligation of accompanying them on a morning visit. You would not enjoy the Hubbards, and you would prefer my company.' He looked at me quizzically and I went on, 'Do not imagine I am making large claims for myself! You do not know the Hubbards. The others are obliged to wait on them, for they are related to Helen and Sarah, but I assure you, they do not go with any expectation of pleasure.'

I began to describe the family, entertaining myself as much as him. 'The Hubbards will favour them with accounts of their ill-health, how concerned the doctor was and what he advised. Soon, they will detect alarming symptoms in their visitors, and no assurances will relieve their minds of anxiety. They will prescribe the most disgusting remedies imaginable.'

Sir Justin was chuckling now, a most delightful sound which came from the back of his throat. 'I confess, I wondered at your brother's pained expression this morning.'

I nodded. 'Hugh says the greatest danger to their health is the fact that they tempt him to strangle them.'

He laughed again. 'Is there a family connection then, between Mrs Wysall and your sister-in-law?'

'They are sisters, sir. Did no one mention it?'

'No, indeed, and I would not have guessed, the one so fair, the other so dark. They seem greatly attached to each other.'

'Yes, they are. I believe only Sarah could persuade Helen away from Bennerley, at present.' He gave an enquiring look and I went on to explain that my nephew, Christopher, was but nine months old and too young to expose to the journey in wintertime. 'Helen feels the separation, and so we return home soon. As a rule, we would spend Christmas with the Wysalls.'

I went on chattering about my family, hoping to encourage him to make disclosures about his own. Instead, he spoke of Helen and Sarah, remarking on their beauty, the sweetness of Sarah's disposition and his own suspicion that Helen was the more intricate character.

He was right. Helen was shrewder in her judgements, more penetrating in her observations, more forthright in her opinions than Sarah could ever be. Yet in his presence, Helen's conduct had been warm and friendly, nothing beyond the ordinary. I was interested to notice he had formed such an accurate opinion on such a slight acquaintance.

With a little trepidation, I understood he must have made some determinations about me. I recalled what he had said.

'*I have observed your style, madam, and I cannot feel that pink ribbons belong with it . . . Some ladies might wish for pink, but not you . . .* '

Thus far, he had been quite alarmingly accurate. Not wishing him to form the opinion that I was of a prying disposition, I postponed my intention of quizzing him.

I continued with inconsequential chatter until we reached the town. In the draper's shop, I purchased eight yards of pink satin ribbon, and was diverted by Sir Justin's astonishment. Letting him make of it what he could, I did not trouble to explain that, having no use for it myself, I had determined to present a length of ribbon to each of the housemaids.

The shopkeeper asked whether we wished to take it with us or have it sent. I thought it not beyond Sir Justin's powers to carry the parcel for me.

On the way back, felt I might now begin to enquire about his concerns and I began by making some remarks about Derbyshire.

'I have never visited within the county but I have passed through it and I was very struck by the scenery in the Peak District. I have observed some good pasture land also, in the lower lying areas. Since your concern is with horses, sir, I must assume your home is within reach of good pasture. Where exactly is it situated?'

He told me that Melrose Court was not far from Chesterfield and I was surprised to learn it was closer to Brinsley Park than I had hitherto supposed, a distance of less than twenty miles. He looked amused. 'Derbyshire and Nottinghamshire are neighbouring counties,' he told me. 'Had you not realized?'

'I had, sir, but Nottinghamshire is neighbour also to my own county of Leicestershire and our journey here is more than twice as far. Yes, I see. Here we are nearer the Derbyshire border.'

Sir Justin seemed to have a very easy way of deflecting attention away from his personal concerns. He did it again, by making enquiries about our estates at Bennerley. I answered, wondering if his avoidance was intentional and as soon as I could I spoke open enquiry.

'You have sisters, sir, as I understand?'

'Half-sisters, madam. My own mother died when I was four years old and my father later remarried.'

He seemed disinclined to say more, but I enquired their names and their ages and thus wrung from him that Blanche was sixteen and Amy fifteen. 'And their mother, sir? Does she yet live?'

'No, madam, she died soon after Amy was born.'

'That is unfortunate. However loving a nurse, however wise the teachers, they do not compensate for lack of a mother.'

'They have their aunt, madam.'

'I see. Well, perhaps that makes a difference. A relation is something more than a servant, after all. And they remain at Melrose Court with their aunt at this present?'

'They do.'

Something in his tone told me he was not happy with this inquisition and I determined to end it. I thought I might learn more from others, when he was not by.

So I said they were fortunate to live in such a beautiful part of the country, and went on to mention how I had heard about caves at Castleton. This might have provided an interesting and safe topic of conversation all the way home, had I not then chanced to see something which put an end to all polite conversation.

Our path sloped into a valley and, as I looked across to the hillside opposite, my eye was drawn upwards to the skyline. There, I caught sight of a loose horse.

And though there was distance between, and though I had caught only the most fleeting glimpse, there was no doubt in my mind that all that Sir Justin's hopes of future prosperity were now in very grave danger indeed.

The animal I had seen was Blue John.

2

'It is Blue John!'

Sir Justin stared at me in disbelief when I told him what I had seen, but the horse broke cover long enough for him to see for himself. White in the face, he thrust my parcel into my hands and set off at a run in pursuit of the animal.

He could run much faster than I could, but I lifted my petticoats and followed him, knowing all the dangers that could befall a valuable horse on the loose.

Any distressing circumstance can be greatly aggravated by memory. Now, and I knew it was because of something I had witnessed long ago, I had a sick dread of Blue John getting into a field where a farmer kept his bull.

I had once seen a horse that had been gored by a bull. I do not wish to describe it. I did not, then, wish to remember it, but I could not help myself. I began to run faster, frightened by my ideas about what could happen to Blue John and also the danger to his master.

Some instinct led me in the right direction:

I came upon a gentleman's hat lying upon the ground and knew that Sir Justin had but shortly passed this way. I picked it up and went on.

I came to a stile, clambered over it, and shortly thereafter I came upon his top coat. I picked it up and went on.

Another stile led into pasture with sheep, which taught me there was no bull. The ground rose and when I had breasted the rise I stopped short in astonishment.

I had expected, upon coming across horse and master, to discover Sir Justin slowly circling the animal, attempting to quieten him, attempting to corner him. Instead, I saw Blue John already docile, with Sir Justin waiting calmly beside him, one hand grasping his mane.

Even Hugh could not have quietened or captured a runaway beast so quickly and I felt a little thrill of admiration of the man's skill, for Blue John wore neither bridle nor halter.

The horse was not hurt, but there was still the pressing question as to how we were going to lead him home. Then my gaze fell upon the parcel in my hand and, to my delight, I found I had a most unexpected use for pink ribbon.

The speechless amazement on the gentleman's

face was all the reward I needed. I had doubled the ribbon, knotting it at intervals for strength, and now, as I approached, I fashioned the makeshift cord into a head-stall.

'Yes, a rope would be better,' I agreed with his unspoken comment, 'but we have none, and ribbon is stronger than you might think. It will serve long enough to lead him home.'

I approached the horse cautiously, ready to stop short if he showed any sign of alarm, but he did not. It was the work of a moment to slip the cord over his nose and ears.

I handed the free end of the ribbon to Sir Justin, who took it speechlessly. 'Have a care, sir,' I said, 'for satin is slippery material and he could pull away.' He nodded, and I watched him take a secure hold.

I was very pleased with myself indeed. 'I knew I had a pressing need of pink ribbon,' I said smugly.

Arriving back at Brinsley we parted in the courtyard, myself going into the house, Sir Justin leading his captive towards the stables. Mr Wysall, upon learning of our adventure, was angry to feel there had been neglect on the part of his stable lads, and took himself off to castigate the culprits.

He was indoors again when I came

downstairs after shedding my outdoor clothes, but I was a little piqued to discover Sir Justin was nowhere to be seen.

That evening, we were to attend a dinner party, given by the Merryweathers. I was in my room, having my hair tortured with curl-papers, when there came a knock at the door. Answering it, my maid returned with a small brown-paper parcel. 'With Sir Justin's compliments, miss.'

The parcel contained another length of pink ribbon. 'Bless the man,' I exclaimed. 'He must have gone back to town expressly to procure it. What on earth possessed him? He knew I had no real need of it.'

I confess I was diverted, and rather pleased too, though I could not have said exactly why. After a moment or two, I gave into temptation and asked my maid what they were saying in the servants' hall about Sir Justin.

'They find him a pleasant gentleman, miss, very civil. They do say he is quick on the uptake, if you get my meaning.'

'Yes, that I have discovered for myself. Have you learnt no more about him? Does his manservant say nothing?'

'Very little, miss. It is difficult to converse with him, him being hard of hearing.'

Servants, usually the most curious of creatures, had learned even less than I. Recalling his reluctance to reveal even the most commonplace facts about himself, I thought it likely he had brought that particular manservant by design.

A gentleman in impoverished circumstances might well choose to conceal the extent of that poverty, especially when visiting a house where he would be in company with those who, if they did not flaunt their wealth, made no secret of it, either.

Sir Justin carried himself well and, walking out with him that morning, I had cared not at all that his coat was out of fashion: but later, picking up after him, I had seen how worn it was, with patches and mends to the lining.

Now the foolish man had spent shillings he could ill spare on pink satin ribbon, a frippery he knew I did not wish for.

'Betty,' I said suddenly. 'Bring my red gown.'

It was a wine-dark red, the colour of burgundy, and when I laid the pink ribbon against the heavy silk it made a very pleasing contrast. And so, wishful of teasing him or wishful of pleasing him, when I went downstairs later, I was wearing a burgundy-coloured gown and no ornament other than a length of pink satin ribbon threaded through my curls.

When we arrived at the Merryweathers' that evening, their girls, Frances and Louisa, no sooner set eyes upon Sir Justin than they began to behave in the most giddy way imaginable, smiling and fluttering their eyelashes and simpering and offering him every possible attention.

I had no opportunity to rescue him from their importunings for my attention was claimed by their grandmother, old Mrs Merryweather. This lady was mischievous: she took advantage of her age to behave in a most outrageous manner, with the design of causing embarrassment.

She addressed me with loud familiarity, asked me how old I was, and said it was time I was married. 'I heard you refused Viscount Saxondale,' she bawled at me, thus telling everyone in the room of a circumstance which I thought was best kept private. 'After leading him a merry dance, too! What do you mean by it, miss? Is not an earl's son grand enough for you?'

I wished the old lady had not chosen to remark on that particular information in Sir Justin's presence. I dreaded to think what impression of me he must now be forming. I did not dare look at him, but I caught a glimpse of his reflection in a looking-glass. He stood impassively, staring into his wine glass, and whatever he was thinking was very well concealed.

Since I was obliged to answer the old lady, I murmured I had found the viscount limited in his powers of conversation.

For all her loudness, I knew she was not deaf, and I had kept my answer deliberately low, rather than draw further attention to myself.

My design was defeated. 'Conversation?' she barked. 'Is that what you want from a husband? Ha ha! In my day we had different ideas!'

I heard a few stifled gasps and I knew my own complexion must now match my dress. Mr Merryweather sought to smooth over the embarrassment, and spoke to his mother in a bantering tone. 'You are a wicked old lady to tease Miss Tremaine so. Come, madam, allow the lady to know her own business best and stop this prying into her affairs!'

The old lady was enjoying herself too much to pay any heed. 'Aye, well,' she said, 'I suppose you mean he did not flatter you with pretty speeches.'

'You are mistaken, madam,' I said coldly. 'He flattered me excessively — with many pretty speeches.'

I hoped this would discompose the old lady, but it did not. Her eyes gleamed, and she opened her mouth to make another of her salty comments, but before she could do so, I curtsyed to her and excused myself, already regretting having said as much. I was most careful not to look at Sir Justin. I knew not whether he had heard me or, if he had, what he made of it.

I sought refuge with my brother. 'How did she know about Saxondale?' asked Hugh. 'It is not like you to boast of your conquests, Judith.'

'Whatever she has heard, sir, and however she came by her knowledge, you can be certain it did not originate with me.'

The giggling Merryweather girls left Sir Justin with no alternative to escorting them in to dinner.

They contrived to seat themselves one on each side of him, and never have I seen such a silly smirk as the one I observed on Louisa Merryweather's countenance that evening. I was glad I was seated far away from Sir Justin for there was little pleasure in watching his valiant attempts to be courteous in the face of such designing arts and allurements.

When we ladies withdrew from the dining-room, Frances and Louisa descended on Sarah, Helen and myself and it was clear there was only one topic of conversation which would interest them. They wanted to know all about Sir Justin. I had no intention of gratifying their curiosity and I was pleased that Helen and Sarah gave them only the most trivial information.

Old Mrs Merryweather was not so nice. She repeated the scandal about his father, but the only fresh information I received was that Sir Robert, having no interest in his offspring, had left the upbringing and education of his son to the boy's maternal grandfather.

The old lady was less interested in supplying information than in being spiteful to her granddaughters. 'It is not the smallest use setting your caps at him, my dears,' she jeered. 'He is a very pretty young gentleman, but he has not a penny to his name: you cannot afford him. Judith could: what say you, Judith? If you wish to purchase yourself a husband, you might as well make sure of a handsome one.'

The old witch had provoked me once that evening and I had learnt my lesson: I displayed only indifference as I said, 'I will give the matter my consideration, madam.'

I think I had not betrayed my own interest in the gentleman: she was merely tormenting her granddaughters by promoting the notion of our future union. 'I cannot answer for his powers of conversation, of course,' she told me sardonically, 'but you may depend upon it, he is a man who knows very well what he keeps hidden inside his breeches — and what it is for!'

I will not repeat the rest of what she had to say. She was indelicate, she was salacious and she was vulgar, and the more Frances and Louisa tried to quieten her, the worse she became.

No one had informed Frances and Louisa of Sir Justin's aversion to card games. Later that evening, they seated themselves at one of the tables, saving a place for him, inviting him with their eyes to join them. He seemed not to notice. The girls were joined by Sarah and Mr Wysall and two other gentlemen. Sir Justin talked with Hugh, and those two soon joined Helen and myself.

Which did not please Frances and Louisa. Tiring of cards, they requested me to entertain the company on the pianoforte.

I declined to do so, for I saw their design. They would listen to one piece and then demand airs to which they could dance. I had no inclination to remain seated at the pianoforte whilst they flirted with Sir Justin.

They found someone willing to play: dancing was suggested, and a few couples formed a set at one end of the room. I hope I did not look as indecently triumphant as I felt when Sir Justin requested me to dance with him. The Merryweather girls were obliged to accept other partners.

We danced for some little time in silence. Then he said: 'I believe I owe you an apology, madam.'

'Do you, sir? I was not aware of it.'

His teeth gleamed as he smiled. 'I doubted your wish of pink ribbon,' he reminded me. He glanced at the frippery I wore in my hair. 'I now perceive that was very wrong of me.'

I felt laughter bubbling inside me. 'Indeed it was,' I agreed. 'But I believe I may pardon you.'

Our conversation throughout the dance was equally agreeable and nonsensical and my pleasure was tempered only by the fact that I knew he was planning to return to Derbyshire tomorrow.

Since Hugh was clearly taken with Sir Justin, I thought he would invite him to visit us at Bennerley, but that was not likely to happen before the winter was out.

There was nothing I could do about it. I must resign myself to the separation, but I was forming an idea which would make certain he remembered me, which would make certain we met again and which would also give me an excuse to visit Melrose Court.

When the dance ended, I indicated that I wished him to sit beside me. 'I believe I have heard you say, sir, that you have mares in foal by Blue John. Should one of your foals prove to be a nice little filly, would you give me the opportunity to buy her? I can promise you, she will be well cared for.'

'Why, certainly, madam, if you wish it. Though it will be some time before she is ready for you. Well, of course, you know that. Would you wish me to break her and train her, or would you prefer your brother to do that?'

'No, I believe I may trust her training to you,' I said, smiling. 'Provided you have no objection, of course.'

'It will give me great pleasure, madam. And what would you have her called?'

'Pink Ribbon, of course.'

He laughed. 'Of course! And I — '

Louisa Merryweather interrupted our conversation at that point, determined to make Sir Justin ask her to dance. Another gentleman partnered me and I had no further opportunity for private conversation with Sir Justin.

I did not let this trouble me. I wished to

know him better and had taken pains to ensure that I would, but I did not care to be as obvious as the Merryweather girls.

The next morning, he sought me out before he left and there was a serious look in his eyes when he spoke. 'I have not yet thanked you, madam, and indeed I know not how I can thank you adequately for the valuable assistance you gave me yesterday.'

'Sir,' I protested. 'Really, I did very little.'

'I knew you would say that. But you know very well how much I am indebted to you. You understand the value of Blue John.'

I did indeed. He was a valuable animal in himself. More importantly, he could procreate and his progeny would be numerous and likewise valuable. Those that Sir Justin could get with his own mares would bring him a handsome profit, and besides that there would be other gentlemen, like my brother, who would pay well to get their mares in foal by him.

'I have spoken to your brother, madam, and he agrees that it would not be improper, in the circumstances, to express my gratitude by offering you a gift, if you would be so obliging as to accept it.'

'Sir, I — '

'It is little enough, madam. Small recompense indeed for the service you have done me. This is something I have with me: a gentleman's thing, but perhaps it will please you.'

He pressed into my hands a small but heavy tissue-wrapped parcel. When I opened it, I discovered it was a paperweight.

'A mere trifle, madam, a trinket of little value, I fear.'

I stared at it. 'Of little value perhaps, to those who measure worth by pounds, shillings and pence,' I murmured. 'But I think I have never seen a thing which pleased me more.'

From the rim of a circular metal base sprang a circlet of silver horseshoes, each about an inch high. Within the circlet, held by it, was a smoothly polished ornamental stone, deep blue in colour, with one marbled streak of brown and white.

'How beautiful it is! Never before have I seen a stone such as this. What is it; do you know?'

'It is a fluorspar, madam, and quite rare, for it occurs only in certain parts of Derbyshire and, I believe, nowhere else in the world.'

He paused, and when I looked up at him, he smiled and added, 'They call it Blue John.'

3

His departure left me with much to think about.

His gift encouraged me to wonder if it had been given with any hope that it would remind me of him. Displaying it to my friends, however, I was a little perturbed.

'Beautiful and strange,' murmured Sarah, touching the stone with one delicate fingertip. 'And so appropriate, do you not agree?'

'Hmm.' Hugh regarded it in some perplexity. 'Odd, though.'

'How so?'

'Does it not strike you?'

'I see nothing strange,' said Helen. 'Blue John is local to Derbyshire, do you wonder he should have such a thing, or he should so name his horse?'

'Indeed, I see no mystery there,' agreed Hugh. 'I do not, however, comprehend his motive in bringing here with him an object such as a paperweight. It makes no sense at all. What would he want with it?'

'He found a use for it,' pointed out M Wysall. 'He gave it to Judith.'

'That could hardly have been his d

in bringing it,' I said. I had not thought of it myself, but Hugh was right: a paperweight was indeed a strange object to carry with him.

'Perhaps,' I said lightly, hoping to disguise the hollowness I felt as the notion occurred to me, 'perhaps he has a ready supply of such things, as gifts for ladies.'

'I do not read him as such a man.'

I confess to a rush of relief at Hugh's judgement. I had not read him as such a man, either, but I knew that my sex could not always discern a philanderer. Gentlemen usually could, and Hugh was no fool. His opinion could be trusted.

'I expect,' said Sarah, still attempting to explain the paperweight mystery, 'it was simply brought along by accident. You cannot deny that such things happen.'

No one could think of a better explanation. I was not wholly satisfied: it was a very convenient kind of accident indeed that provided him with such an appropriate gift.

Other reflections gave me unease: I quickly discovered Sir Justin had volunteered no information about himself to the Wysalls. Having less reason than I to be inquisitive, they had been too polite to pry. Sparse as it was, my own information was more than my companions had learnt.

These uncomfortable reflections were made more disagreeable by the most unwelcome knowledge: calculating when I might reasonably expect to see him again, I realized that from February onwards he would be busy with mares and their foals: not until July could we invite him to visit us at Bennerley.

Scheme as I might, I had not the smallest hope of seeing him again for many months.

In Sir Justin's company, I had been happily enjoying all the delightful sensations he had excited in me. Though I was vexed by the distance between our homes and the knowledge that we must be separated, I had been content with the pleasing prospect of future meetings. Now, I perceived that future meetings were likely to be few and far between.

My mind had been opened also to the possibility of rivals. The flirtatious behaviour of the Merryweather girls had taught me what my own sentiments had not: many ladies found that gentleman pleasing. In Derbyshire, there would be others, who had better opportunity of attaching him.

I now had doubts about the wisdom of my inclination, and resolved to temper all my wishes with strong common sense. Afte all, my partiality for Sir Justin was the wo of but a few days, which was far too short a time for me to consider myself seriously in love.

We returned to Bennerley and in my daily life I had many friends for company and other matters to interest and occupy me. I would not wish to give the impression here, that I spent seven months wholly preoccupied with Sir Justin.

There were, however, a few occasions when I learnt more.

Over Christmas, we were often in company with our neighbours and it was natural to mention our meeting with Sir Justin. Everyone knew the scandal about his father, and there were some who had been acquainted with that gentleman.

'Robert St John Martin had but little interest in anything besides cards,' Sir Matthew Hargreaves said. 'He did not speak of his family. He seemed even to forget they existed.'

I was recalled to the way Sir Justin had been reluctant to speak of his sisters. I could not accuse him of having little interest in anything besides cards, quite the reverse, but I wondered if he shared his father's attitude to his family.

'That was after his wife died, of course,' id Lady Hargreaves.

'Which wife was that?'

'Oh, his first, Dorcas Metcalfe.'

'But he married again?'

'A tradesman's daughter, from Sunderland!' sniffed Sir Matthew. 'She was wild for him — or for the title — and she had some little fortune to make it worth his while. It gave her little joy, if you ask me.'

They expressed disapprobation that Sir Justin had taken to 'soiling his hands with trade', an opinion which received little sympathy from Hugh. 'He chooses hard work and honest measures to restore himself. I confess, I admire the man.'

'Indeed?' Sir Matthew raised his brows. 'And what of you, Judith? How did he strike you?'

'I liked him very much indeed,' I said. I spoke more frankly than I would have done to most, though I confess it was with mischievous design, for Lady Hargreaves had determined on a certain future for me with their son, which I did by no means intend.

In February, as he had agreed, Hugh sent Morning Star into Derbyshire. He questioned the groom who took her, but only about th[illegible] stables and provision for the horses. W[illegible] discovered that Sir Justin's enterprise [illegible] larger than we had supposed.

March brought Hugh a letter fr[illegible]

gentleman. It was very brief and to the point. All was well with Morning Star, who had dropped a fine colt: also, would Hugh please inform Miss Tremaine that he had her 'Pink Ribbon'.

'What is this about, Judith?'

I realized, to my consternation, that I had never told my brother of the arrangement I had with Sir Justin. I did so now. 'I cannot imagine how I never came to mention it.'

Hugh regarded me with approbation. 'An excellent scheme,' he said. 'Very shrewd, Judith. Why did not I think of it for myself?'

Just after Easter, I received a letter from my dearest friend, commanding my presence in town. Miss Sophia Burton was to be united with His Grace, the Duke of Flamborough.

Sophie was a popular girl and was well liked by all her acquaintance. She was, however, selective about her intimate friends and only two people shared that honour: I was one of them; the other was a rather serious girl, Isobel Townshend.

We two were to be bridesmaids. Isobel was already in town. I was to join them and, for the duration of my stay, I would reside with Sophie's mother.

I went to town. I know not what impulse [illegible]d me, but I took my Blue John paperweight with me.

Very soon after my arrival, Mrs Burton made a personal visit to my rooms to ensure that everything was exactly to my liking, and stayed to converse with me about Sophie's young man and the forthcoming wedding. For half an hour we enjoyed a comfortable chat on this matter, which was, naturally, close to her heart and occupying her thoughts a great deal.

So I was surprised when she noticed the paperweight. She broke off in mid-sentence and exclaimed, 'Good heavens, the Blue John! Judith, dear, is this yours? How on earth did you come by it?'

Her words and tone told me she had seen the thing before and I was instantly alert. 'It was given to me,' I said, and I told her who the giver was.

'Sir Justin St John Martin?' She repeated the name before she placed the gentleman. 'Oh yes, of course. His grandson.'

'Madam, I am all bewilderment! Do you know about it?'

Mrs Burton picked up the paperweight, holding it to the light, turning it in her hand before revealing it had once belonged to a gentleman named George Metcalfe, who had been Sir Justin's maternal grandfather.

'You knew him, I take it?'

'His wife, Dorothea, was cousin to

father,' she explained.

I stared at her. 'So you are *related* to Sir Justin?'

'Second or third cousin, I suppose,' smiled Mrs Burton. 'Not that I can claim acquaintance with him. But I met Dorothea, of course, and her husband.'

'And this paperweight?'

'The stone is called Blue John, did you know? Yes, I see you do. George Metcalfe kept it as a kind of talisman; he took it with him wherever he went. Yes, it is only natural that it should be passed on to his grandson. I confess, I am surprised to learn he has parted with it.'

I was more than surprised; I was wholly astonished, and, I confess, a little ashamed of the suspicions I had entertained about that paperweight.

All these doubts were at an end. Mrs Burton's intelligence had taught me the reason for Sir Justin having the thing with him at Brinsley. I knew not whether he saw it as a talisman, as his grandfather had, but something had moved him to follow that example, to take it with him wherever he went.

And he had given it to me!

' . . . *a trifle, madam, of little value, I am* *aid* . . . '

A thing of infinite worth to him, however. He had given it to me, at some cost to himself. Yet he knew not how I would value it. I confess, I was shaken: distressed, too, that I had accepted such a gift without knowing its history.

I questioned Mrs Burton more about Sir Justin and his family.

She could recall the Metcalfes' daughter, Sir Justin's mother, as a tall, striking woman, but no more.

'My dear, we saw them very rarely: they lived so far northwards, you see, and we had but few occasions to meet.'

Left alone, I indulged myself in a review of all that had occurred at Brinsley Park, sighing at some memories, chuckling at others, smiling as an image of his face rose in my mind.

My own observation had taught me much of his character: he was reserved but civil; he seemed accurate in his perceptions of others; he was, as my maid had put it 'quick on the uptake'; he was not without generosity and he was not without humour.

All of which pleased me.

And he had given me the Blue Joh[illegible] Certainly, he would not have done so [illegible] he not liked me and held me in some est[illegible] I was encouraged to hope that I migh[illegible] some advantage over any other ladies, and I was determined to persuade Hugh that Sir Justin should be invited to Bennerley that summer.

Whilst I was in town, I took the opportunity to visit some of the fashionable dressmakers, ordering gowns suitable for the summer, and if I considered how they might assist me to captivate a certain gentleman, I make no apology for it.

From Sophie, Isobel and I heard all about the duke's amiable disposition, and endured some teasing on the subject of our own suitors.

'I have fallen in love with a chattering idiot,' said Isobel gloomily. 'I cannot tell you how it pains me! I, who have always prided myself on my discernment and good sense, am now wholly mortified to discover myself harbouring tender feelings towards a gentleman who cannot speak one word of sense in ten. Have you ever been in love with a fool, Judith?'

'I confess I have not,' I said, with some amusement. 'I believe I am too inclined to chatter away myself, and two chattering idiots are not at all likely to suit each other, you know. Have you determined what is to be done about it?'

'There is nothing to be done about it: he

is wholly beyond redemption. He is trifling and silly and nothing will teach him sense. I must tolerate his foolishness, or I must forget him.'

'Who is this foolish gentleman?' cried Sophie, excessively diverted. 'Do we know him?'

Isobel, however, refused to divulge his name and we spent half an hour happily recalling all the foolish men we knew in the hope of persuading Isobel to betray herself.

'Upon my soul, my suitor is not to be despised, after all! He has advantages over the gentlemen you have named!'

I was not spared: both girls wanted to know whether any gentleman had claimed my heart, and clamoured in delight when Sophie detected my blush.

'I could be in love,' I admitted, 'were I to be given a little encouragement. Unfortunately, the gentleman contrives to be absent. I have not seen him since November.'

Isobel gave me a sharp look. 'That cannot be agreeable.'

'There are some awkward circumstance
I said. 'And I have no reason to sup
— and I am not yet certain — the r
is complicated. I have hopes of see
in the summer. No, I shall n

his name, and I think you will not guess it.'

'Well, my dears,' said Sophie, 'I wish you both great joy with the gentlemen of your choice.'

The days progressed. Sophie's wedding took place, and I returned in due course to Bennerley, settling into my usual pursuits. No one mentioned Sir Justin, which did not surprise me: my relations were occupied with the present.

Not wishing him to be forgotten, I ventured to enquire of Hugh whether he had sent any news of Morning Star.

'No, but I do not expect it,' said Hugh absently. 'It is a busy time for him; he will not write unless there is something amiss. No news I take as good news.'

'Morning Star's foal will be old enough to travel soon. Will Sir Justin bring them to Bennerley himself, do you think?'

'He will send them next month, with a groom.'

'Could you not write and suggest he keeps Morning Star and her foal in Derbyshire [illegible]til such time as he is free to bring them? [illegible]r all, a groom can be as ill spared as [illegible]lf, during the busy time.'

[illegible]' agreed Hugh, apparently unsuspicious [illegible]sign. 'Well, we are at home in July, so we may prevail upon him to visit. I will write to him.'

We were to go to Scarborough in August. We extended our invitation to Sir Justin until then, for Helen pointed out that he would take the same route on his return journey and we could all travel comfortably together.

Reflecting upon it later, I thought Sir Justin would not consent to spend a whole month at Bennerley should such an invitation separate him from any lady who was dear to him.

Had he formed an attachment, he would not come. Acceptance of our invitation, therefore, would be proof of his freedom.

Should he come and should I continue to find him as pleasing as I had done previously, I might then begin to encourage him, myself.

4

His response to my brother's invitation left me none the wiser. He would bring Morning Star but regretted that matters of business left him with only a few days at his disposal.

'One would suppose he could arrange his affairs to remain with us,' grumbled Hugh.

'Should he wish to do so,' I agreed. 'But perhaps there are matters elsewhere, which are closer to his heart. It could be, you know, that he has been captivated by some lady.'

I spoke lightly, desirous of concealing my disappointment and desirous also of prompting my relations to quiz the gentleman on this subject when he arrived.

Whatever the situation concerning his attachments, his stay was to be of such short duration that I could not suppose he entertained any great ambition to attach me. I would, however, display whatever charms I had to the best of my ability.

We knew when to expect him. The weather [illegible] hot and sultry and I had Jupiter saddled [illegible] set out with the intention of intercepting [illegible] r I could show him a pleasant short [illegible] ugh green and leafy shade.

My scheme was successful and I could not help smiling as we approached each other. He did not look displeased to see me. I could have wished, however, that he had displayed as much admiration for myself as he did for my horse.

'Oh, yes, Jupiter is a very fine fellow,' I agreed, leaning forward in the saddle and patting the horse's neck. 'He is out of Morning Star, you know, as is this little fellow here.' I gestured towards the foal, and addressed Jupiter. 'Well, sir, and what do you think of your brother? And should you not pay your respects to your mama?'

Jupiter displayed scant interest in the foal, but he knew his dam and greeted her with equine snorts. Sir Justin and I fell in side by side and headed towards Bennerley, talking about horses, Morning Star and her foal, Blue John, and my own little filly, Pink Ribbon, still at Melrose Court with her dam.

'A chestnut, with a white star on her forehead and a very kind eye,' he said. 'I think you will be pleased with her.'

I intended to see her very soon, to use h as an excuse to visit Melrose Court on way to Scarborough, but that was some I kept to myself for the present.

I spoke of the arrangements we h

for his stay with us. 'We ladies are to be deprived of your company, tomorrow,' I told him. 'For my brother has made up a fishing party. Our river is very good for perch and chub, and Hugh will supply you with rods and tackle. Do you care for fishing sir?'

His face lit up with genuine pleasure. 'I do, indeed, madam, whenever I have the opportunity.'

I had been vexed when I discovered Hugh's intention, for this would take up the greater part of a day. Now, I could not resent it, for I could see he was tired. I could imagine no better way of easing him than a day by the riverside.

Fearful of seeing all the days pass by with the gentlemen engaged in their own pursuits, I had been quick to suggest that one day, if the weather held fine, we should take an excursion, perhaps a picnic, to Brecon Hill and Stamford Park. This scheme had found favour, and some of our neighbours had been invited to join us.

I was about to mention it, and the summer ball which Helen had, after a few hints om me, planned for his last evening. He stalled me, pleasing me utterly when aid; 'May I hope to be granted the ence of some music, whilst I am here? recall with pleasure that evening at

Brinsley Park when you were so obliging as to play for us.'

And I, delighting in the pleasing sensations his words and his smile provoked, could only beam at him and say, 'You shall have music this very evening, sir.'

He did: I played for over an hour and would have continued longer had not the majestic music of nature intervened. I declared I could not compete with the thunder that was rumbling in the distance, so I closed the instrument and walked to the window to watch the firework display of lightning and the dark clouds rolling towards us.

'I do so enjoy thunderstorms,' I said absently.

'Would you like to take this one and enjoy it elsewhere?' said Helen, who did not.

'It will be of short duration. Storms such as this seldom last long.'

The rain began, great heavy single drops which evaporated as soon as they touched the heated flagstones in the courtyard. It ceased briefly, then the heavens opened and let fort[illegible] a downpour that curtained the windows i[illegible] great stream of water.

Helen, though she tried to contain he[illegible] winced at every flash of lightning, cr[illegible] every roll of thunder. Hugh slippe[illegible] around her shoulders to comfort her.

The light died into dimness, a torrent of rain fell, fiery streaks of lightning flashed across the sky and hot thunder gathered and roared. Whilst Helen sobbed into Hugh's shoulder, I felt only a wild exultation as I stood at the window watching the raging elements.

The storm was following the course of the river, and somewhere upstream there had been rain earlier, for the waters were rushing down and, at the place where stepping stones were set, a white foaming waterfall had gathered. Now the downpour was so blinding that I could see little, except in the brief flashes of lightning.

There was one great shock when lightning and thunder came together and on the river-bank a black twisted shape flamed and flared and leapt and a great fiery thing threw itself aloft and arched into the river and went black again.

'One of the willows has been struck,' I told Hugh. 'Uprooted, too, I believe. It may be [illegible]olding back the water, for certain I am it [illegible] into the river. There will be floods in the [illegible]r meadows unless it is soon removed, I [illegible]'

[illegible] another ten minutes the rain slackened [illegible]hunder rumbled away downstream.

We exchanged our house shoes for boots, and slipped capes around our shoulders. By the time we went outside the sky had cleared and the rain had ceased altogether, although puddles lay in the courtyard and water still streamed off the roofs and down the guttering into the butts. As we drew closer to the river, we ladies were obliged to lift our skirts to cross the heavy and sodden expanse of grass.

My brother's steward was already out in the park; meeting us, he reported the fallen willow.

'Half the roots gone, sir, the other half still clinging in the ground, and the trunk and a great tangle of branches and leaves blocking the river. We need to get chains round it and horses to pull, and men with axes to cut it free from the roots. It may take some time.'

My brother gave his orders and men came, gardeners and grooms together, and a pair of carriage horses, ready to draw their unusual burden. Men chopped away at those roots remaining in the ground: other men waded into the water, attaching chains to branches. Hugh strode around making sure that all measures were taken in the best and safest way, for one slip could mean danger and we were all sensible of it.

Sir Justin stood a little aside, perceiving my brother knew his business and needed no advice. Watching the men in the river but making no comment, he unobtrusively divested himself of his coat, waistcoat and stock, not interfering but preparing himself to lend assistance should there be occasion for it.

I smiled, enjoying the sight of him in shirt sleeves, shivering with new sensations as I became conscious of powerful muscles in his shoulders and arms. I wondered what it would feel like to be held within those arms, close against that strong body. I felt a quickening in my own body, a heat centred somewhere deep within me and I found myself half excited, half embarrassed by the very improper thoughts I was entertaining.

There came a shout, a flailing and a splash and a white shape launched itself head first into the river and struck out towards the spot where nothing could be seen but churning water. A head surfaced briefly, shouted something, then two heads submerged at once, seeking a third. Twice they surfaced, twice went down again, then they brought up with them another head, lolling senselessly on Sir Justin's shoulder.

It was one of the under gardeners, a boy, no more than fourteen years old. While Sir Justin struggled to keep the head above water, others dived again, for the boy had somehow got his foot entangled with branches and chain.

They sought to release him, did so at last, brought him to safety, pummelled at his back and the boy stirred and coughed and vomited water and shook and wept. His father ran up, scolding the boy, thanking his rescuers.

I had gone to lend what assistance I could to Hugh, who had seen at once how necessary it was to hold back the horses, for one of the chains had already been attached to the harness and, should the confused animals have exerted the least pull, the accident might have had more serious consequences. As it was, the boy suffered no more than a fright and a sprained ankle and the others, though wet, had taken no injury.

Work progressed without further mishap and the tree was eventually heaved from the water.

As we walked back to the house, I spoke to Sir Justin. 'When you have changed, sir, you must allow me to lend the services of my maid to mend the tear in your shirt. Betty is an excellent needle-woman, every care will be taken.'

'Is there a tear? I was not aware of it.'

'Done whilst you were in the river helping

that poor boy. My maid will be happy to set it to rights.'

Indoors, Hugh directed our servants to prepare a bath for our guest and I was left alone with Helen. I spoke of the way the storm had freshened the atmosphere, expressed the opinion that the morrow would be another fine day and the gentlemen would enjoy some good sport by the river.

'A day by the river will be of benefit to Sir Justin, no doubt. He looks very tired.' I spoke lazily, determined to show no more interest than was proper. 'A consequence of keeping irregular hours, I suppose. Such a pity he must leave so soon, for certain I am he should take more leisure. He must have some particular reason for going.'

Helen regarded my words as no more than idle speculation. But I had succeeded in my design, for her own curiosity had been aroused. When Sir Justin returned to the drawing-room, her civil concern for his comfort gave way to persuasions that he would extend his stay.

Sir Justin remained polite but steadfast in his refusal. 'Well then,' said Helen, 'I shall tease you, for I believe your pressing business bears the name of a pretty lady.'

And though she teased him, Sir Justin neither confirmed nor denied it. I was vexed, for I had to make such deductions as I could from his demeanour. I looked for a hint of self-consciousness, and saw none: I looked for signs of aloof withdrawal, and saw none. His smiles were not the lingering kind which might indicate pleasing thoughts of a dear one, rather they seemed no more than polite responses to Helen.

Sir Justin displayed none of those aspects I had observed in Hugh when he first became attached to Helen. I knew this was not a conclusive argument, but I allowed myself some optimism.

The next morning the sky was soft and blue and the river had settled again and the only remnant of the storm was the scar in the earth where the willow had been torn from it. Nothing was to prevent the gentlemen from spending the day by the river. Helen and I saw them off with smiles and spent the day at our own pursuits, and smiled again when they returned.

Their talk was of the sport they had and the fish that had escaped capture and we ladies laughed with them and teased them and I had never been happier.

Sir Justin excused himself when it wa time to change for dinner. On my way my own rooms, I recollected something I meant to ask Hugh, and I turned back t saloon, meaning to mention the subject I had thought of.

I found myself accidentally witnessing a private moment I had no right to witness: Helen and Hugh were together, their arms around each other. Hugh's head was thrown back, his eyes were closed and Helen's mouth was in the hollow of his throat.

His head came down, his mouth fastened on hers and I whisked myself smartly away, shaken by their intensity.

My brother's marriage had convinced me against accepting any of my former suitors. Hugh had met Helen when I was sixteen, married her when I was seventeen, and I had become increasingly aware of their deep love, their respect for each other, their delight in each other. I knew I wanted nothing less, would accept nothing less for myself.

I did not repent any of my refusals, yet I had often been aware of my own needs, of what I was missing, and the scene I had witnessed brought my loneliness home to me in a great agony of longing.

There was a particular young man at the centre of this longing. There was impatience also, for I was sensible of the any circumstances which kept us apart of how little time I had to engage his tions.

That evening, at dinner, the talk was of the excursion we had planned. Among those joining us were a couple named Glover and we told Sir Justin a little about them.

Helen went on to speak of Sir Matthew and Lady Hargreaves. Now I learnt some trouble with their carriage had caused an alteration in our travelling arrangements. To leave room in our landau for our neighbours, Hugh was to drive Sir Justin in the curricle.

This arrangement found no favour with me, but I said nothing. Then Helen surprised me by saying, 'Richard will have to accompany us on horseback.'

'Has Richard come home?' I asked. 'I had thought him in Essex with his regiment.'

'He returned on Monday and called here yesterday to pay his respects,' said Helen. 'He seemed quite put out that you were not by,' she added teasingly. 'He said he had a particular matter about which he wished to speak to you.'

'Which means he is in a scrape of some kind,' I said. 'What is it this time, I wonder?'

'Must he be in a scrape before he may speak with you?'

'Certainly not, but I have found it is usually the case, when he is seeking me out. You may depend upon it, he is in need of assistance in some matter.'

'He did speak of resigning his commission,' said Helen with some emphasis, 'of returning home and settling down.'

'That should please Lady Hargreaves, at all events,' I said blandly. 'She has long wished for Richard to settle down.'

Lady Hargreaves entertained the hope that Richard, her son, would settle down to a prosperous marriage, and I knew who she wished him to take as his wife.

Her matchmaking activity had troubled Richard more than me. At length, bored by country life, restless and unsettled, he had chosen to join the militia, but Lady Hargreaves had not yet given up her hopes.

Now, it seemed Helen shared her hopes and I was displeased, for her hints of an attachment had not been lost on Sir Justin. I hoped my own remarks had dismissed any ideas she might have begun, but I would have liked to be more certain of it. I had so little opportunity to pursue my interest: I could not afford to be patient with the meddling of others.

Alone with Helen, after dinner, I let it be known that her attempts to arrange my destiny were most unwelcome.

She laughed. 'Come now, Judith! We know you too well to be deceived. You cannot deny you are fond of Richard.'

'I am fond of him,' I said. 'I am not, however, inclined to take him for a husband.'

'Do you doubt Richard's affection for you?' asked Helen in some concern. 'Is that the reason for this evasion? Judith. I can assure you, Richard has a very sincere regard for you.'

'I know he does, but matrimony is not his design, neither is it mine.' And when she gave a disbelieving smile, I felt my temper rise. 'I am not being evasive, madam, I am being very direct, and I wish you would believe me sincere. When I take a husband — if I take a husband — it will be a gentleman of my own choosing.'

'Well, of course, but Judith . . . '

'And it will not be Richard.' I said with finality. 'So please, I beg you, abandon this scheme, for there may be consequences which I shall find hard to forgive.'

Helen confessed to disappointment, her reason being that such a marriage would keep me in the neighbourhood.

'With Richard I could have nothing approaching the happiness you have with Hugh. Helen, dear, do not wish for me something less than you have yourself.'

This argument struck Helen more forcibly than any other. At last, she accepted it.

I was not wholly relieved: I could not help

wondering how many hints on the subject had been conveyed to Sir Justin.

No one requested music that evening. Hugh challenged Sir Justin to chess, Helen picked up some needlework and I took up a book. I watched Sir Justin, sulked because Hugh was again monopolizing that gentleman, and now regretted Sir Justin's aversion to card games which we could have played together.

As I took my place in the landau the next morning, I was in a better frame of mind. Before me was the happy prospect of securing Sir Justin's company for at least part of the day.

When we arrived, the Glover children were desirous of paying their attentions to Christopher, my nephew. Helen was happily receiving compliments on her son from Mrs Glover and reciting the litany of his accomplishments.

Hugh, to my vexation, continued to monopolize Sir Justin. And, by the simple expedient of lagging behind, Sir Matthew and Lady Hargreaves contrived to leave me alone with Richard.

5

I swallowed my vexation.

I reminded myself that the day was hardly yet begun and there would be later opportunities to fall in with Sir Justin.

I reproved myself for my ungracious feelings towards Richard: his mind was occupied with some business of his own and he was in no mood to detect any ill humour on my part.

We were separated from the others: Sir Justin and Hugh had now joined Helen and the Glovers and halted to allow Sir Matthew and Lady Hargreaves to catch up with them. I stopped, too, in the hope that I might soon find myself with another companion, but Richard said testily, 'Oh, come on, Judith!'

It was not the moment for feminine protests at this cavalier behaviour. Richard wanted to talk to me. I knew he would not leave me in peace until he had his say.

'I hope,' I said, 'you are not thinking of proposing to me, Richard?'

Once before, pressed by his mother into believing I wished it, Richard had proposed to me. His words, 'Shall we be married soon,

Judith, or would you rather wait a year or so?' had shown me very clearly that he was by no means an eager suitor.

His proposal had given me the opportunity to talk frankly, about his mother's expectations, my feelings and wishes and his own. Now I could make such a bold statement with no fear of being misunderstood.

He gave a reluctant grin. Then, to my astonishment, he said, 'The thought had crossed my mind, and why not? It would be a very suitable match. We are good friends, we could be happy together, and please our families at the same time. It would be so easy, would it not, to take the line of least resistance?'

I knew not which was the more flattering of his proposals. 'There is but one thing you have forgotten to mention.'

'You know my situation in life, what is to be explained?'

'You can explain why you are proposing to me when it is perfectly clear you are in love with some other lady?' And then, since he had seemingly been struck dumb: 'You cannot deny it, sir. Everything about you proclaims the distracted lover.'

'Indeed?' he said stiffly.

'Yes, indeed!' I mocked. 'Do not imagine I am pleased to receive your proposals, sir.

You seek only to divert yourself and that is no compliment to me. You had better mend your differences with the lady.'

'Oh, Judith, you wretch!' Richard looked as though he would deny it, but honesty would not allow it. 'There is little prospect there, I assure you. I do not seek to divert myself, Judith.' His pause gave some weight to his words. 'I am persuaded our marriage would answer very well. You and I, and why not?'

'I do not wish it.' I laughed. 'Come now, enough of this nonsense! Tell me about the lady.'

He was silent. I plucked a few blooms of wild scabious, twirling them in my fingers and when I had waited long enough for an answer, I said, 'If you do not wish to confide in me, sir, may I suggest we now rejoin the rest of our party?'

It was too much to hope. There was some feeling in him, which he had not yet been able to express to anyone: he now sought the relief of doing so.

'I have nothing agreeable to tell you about her,' he said resentfully. 'She is aloof and disdainful of ordinary mortals. She prides herself on superior judgement and good sense and presumes to instruct the rest of us on our moral duty. She has not a grain of humour, not a shred of wit. I confess I allowed myself to become attached to her, but why I did so is more than I can fathom. She is wholly pretentious and dreary.'

'Dear me.'

'Now, I suppose, you are laughing at me.'

'No, not at all.' I knew that such people existed though it was hard to believe Richard had fallen in love with such a creature. 'I suppose she must be very beautiful?'

'Not even that,' he said gloomily. 'I do not say her looks are displeasing, but even my affection for the lady could not blind me into calling her beautiful.'

I slanted a quizzical look at him.

'It is true, Judith! Even the most ardent lover could not call Miss Townshend beautiful. Although she does have the most expressive eyes.'

'Miss Townshend?' I turned to stare at Richard, my mind illuminated by a new and excessively diverting idea. 'Is it possible . . . ? Richard, do you mean Isobel Townshend?'

It was Richard's turn to be surprised. 'She is an Essex lady, how is it possible that you know her?'

'I have not spent all my time in Leicestershire.' As I explained my acquaintance with Isobel, my mind was occupied with new perceptions. I recalled her comments on her suitor:

'I now discover myself harbouring tender feelings for a gentleman who cannot speak one word of sense in ten . . . He is trifling and silly . . . Nothing will teach him sense . . .'

'Since you know her,' Richard was saying, 'you will comprehend how absurd it is! You could not find two people less likely to suit.'

A match between Isobel and Richard was not an idea which had occurred to me, but I only said, 'I find your reading of her character quite excessive. Isobel is not frivolous, but neither is she without humour. And I know she does not take a high moral tone unless there is something she finds particularly offensive. So what have you done, Richard, to offend her?'

Richard was brooding, trying to determine how far he wished to confide in me.

My thoughts were occupied in a different way. The cautious information I had received from Isobel gave me better intelligence than he knew. 'I expect,' I said at last, 'you have been making yourself ridiculous!'

'If my attempts to divert her, my wish to lighten her eyes with a smile can be so construed, then I must plead guilty,' he said loftily. 'I confess I made some exertions to persuade her that life has its lighter moments.'

Having experienced the delight of bringing smiles to Sir Justin's countenance, I could easily comprehend Richard's desire to divert the serious-minded Isobel. But Richard could be irksome and I was persuaded that in his anxiety to please, he had gone beyond what was pleasing.

'Certainly you have been making yourself ridiculous.'

Now I learnt of Richard's follies. None would have been serious had it been the only one: taken altogether, a picture presented itself which Isobel would find alarming.

He had spent money foolishly on foppish clothes, more to divert her than from any conviction of his own.

He had lost heavily at cards and shown impatience with her disapproval. 'I would not have joined the card table had she not been so cold to me,' he complained.

On another occasion when she had been cold to him, he had sought solace in drinking too much wine.

He had compounded these follies by paying attentions to other ladies in an attempt to make her jealous. This had decided Isobel: she was convinced he was not to be trusted.

I shook my head and sighed. 'Richard, had you been determined to set her against you, you could not have found a better way of doing so! You do not know her history.'

Her father had been a philanderer, and caused pain to all his family by the manner of his death, for he had been taken by a seizure whilst in company with his mistress. Certain circles in society had found merriment in this situation.

This had taken place years ago and the scandal had died, but Isobel had been affected by it. I told Richard, 'She would have no confidence at all in a gentleman who had a roving eye.'

He groaned. 'How was I to know?'

'You could not, of course.' I was unwilling to betray Isobel's confidence, but I knew she cared for him. At length, I said, 'You will not win her easily, but show a little sense and determination and you might prevail.'

He shook his head. 'I will not! It is hopeless. She has no good opinion of me, at all.'

'Then you must establish yourself as a responsible character.'

I discovered new significance in something Isobel had said:

'*Have you ever been in love with a fool, Judith*?'

I recalled certain words of my own and Isobel's sharp look.

'*The gentleman in question contrives to be absent. I have not seen him since November.*'

'There is another matter,' I said slowly. 'Richard, does Isobel know of your mama's ideas? For in my ignorance of your situation, I said something which might have suggested I had hopes of you. Well, it is unfortunate, but now you know, so you must remedy the situation as best you can. And now, sir, if you please, I wish to rejoin the rest of our party.'

We had been within sight of the others and I was vexed, for the lady who wished to promote a match between Richard and myself was looking very satisfied.

'I would be obliged, Richard, if you would refrain from making demands on my society for the rest of the day. There is nothing to be gained by encouraging your mama.'

I separated from Richard and joined the children, seating myself on one of the rugs, and playing cup and ball games. There would have been no impropriety in Sir Justin joining me: to my vexation, he showed no inclination to do so.

When he went to talk with Hugh and Helen, I hoisted Christopher into my arms and went to join them. Nothing could have seemed more natural. Sir Justin was all civility, but he moved away as soon as he could.

I concealed my displeasure and talked with Helen. Hugh was silent, and when I glanced in his direction, I saw him wince.

I forgot my vexation. 'Sir, are you hurt?'

'I confess, I feel some discomfort in my wrist.' Hugh looked puzzled. 'Almost like a sprain, although I can recall no accident to account for it.'

Helen insisted he should show her, and when he removed his coat and turned back his shirt sleeve, we detected a swelling.

'Certainly, it would seem to be a sprain,' agreed Helen. 'How did you come by it?'

Hugh repeated his assertion that he had no recollection of his accident. 'I noticed it only half an hour ago.'

Richard, with the benefit of regimental experience, declared that a pad of cloth soaked with cold water and pressed against the affected part was the most effective way to ease a sprain.

Other suggested remedies required ingredients we did not have, but it was easy to soak a handkerchief and apply it and Hugh, though accepting this assistance, became rather testy with those who continued their fussing.

'It is nothing of any great moment,' he

declared. 'It becomes easier already.'

We sat down to a collation of pigeon pies and cold mutton and cake and fruit. For the next hour I was separated from Sir Justin and, unless I wished to betray myself entirely, it seemed I was destined to remain so.

I had no difficulty in avoiding Richard who had his mind occupied, but Lady Hargreaves was anxious and made several attempts to discover how matters stood. I parried her questions as politely as I could.

Sir Justin made no approaches to me. I endured this as long as I could, and eventually moved towards him, attempting to engage him in conversation with some remark about the view. Sir Justin responded civilly. I made another remark, this time about the great beacon, received another civil response, after which he found some reason to excuse himself.

Now I could be in no doubt. He was avoiding me, deliberately. And I, who had entertained such hopes of this excursion, found my vexation increasing to the point where I had to exercise all my self-command in order to be civil to anyone.

An exclamation from Helen once again turned everyone's attention to Hugh. The swelling of his wrist had now increased to a monstrous size extending from his knuckles to a point mid-way between wrist and elbow.

It was mottled and inflamed and Hugh complained of the most vexatious itching.

'This is no sprain,' said Helen in some bewilderment. 'Never have I seen such an injury.'

'Something of the kind I have seen before,' said Sir Justin. 'This, I fear, is the result of an insect bite.'

Hugh wanted to know what insect could create such an effect, and was mortified to learn he had fallen victim to an ant.

'How could such a small creature cause such damage?'

Sir Justin assured him it could. 'I understand there is some substance in an ant's bite, a poison of some kind. Do not be alarmed, madam. It is of no serious consequence: your husband will improve tomorrow and recover within a few days.'

Little could relieve his present suffering; Hugh declared that only coldness would ease the burning irritation. We soaked his handkerchief again, spreading it against the swelling.

I had been toying with a daring idea. When it was time to be going home, I said, 'Clearly, sir, you cannot drive. You must take my place in the landau: I will drive the curricle.'

Helen accepted my offer with a gratitude it did not deserve and no one seemed to remember that Sir Justin was himself perfectly capable of sparing Hugh the necessity of driving.

I looked to see how Sir Justin took this alteration: his features remained impassive and whatever he was feeling was very well concealed. Unable to resist, I said, 'I trust you have no fear of being driven by a lady, sir?'

'I have no doubt you drive as skilfully as you do every other thing, madam.'

His bow was polite, his words gallant, and this might have pleased me had I not been aware of distance in his manner. As it was, I was too cross with him to be pleased.

Once, I had been obliged to witness another lady's attempts to captivate my brother: I had sworn then that never would I make such an embarrassing spectacle of myself.

I reviewed my own behaviour and was comforted to know I had not. I could not feel my attentions had been excessive: no more, in fact, than was courteous to a guest in our house. I had been friendly enough to show him I enjoyed his company, but I could assert that I had not demanded too much of his notice.

There were so many prohibitions in our society, so much protocol to be observed. This was all very well if a lady and gentleman had the opportunity to meet frequently, but in a case such as this, it was a cause of the most painful difficulties.

Now, I felt there was little merit in being guarded if it lost me the opportunity of attaching the only man to whom I had ever felt myself partial.

Driving him home, I would be alone with him. I could, at least, take this opportunity to discover the cause of his displeasure.

6

I shook up the reins, urging the horses to a moderate pace and made inconsequential chatter about the excursion, the company, the weather, the view, my brother's unfortunate mishap and my own enjoyment of the outing.

All this, he heard in silent indignation.

I kept my tone mild, as I added, 'I believe I would have enjoyed the day more thoroughly had I not felt a very strong persuasion that someone was taking pains to avoid me. Tell me, sir, how have I happened to offend you?'

Most gentlemen would parry such a question with a polite disclaimer. My companion scorned to do so and spoke with some displeasure. 'You might be wiser not to ask, madam, for I am in no humour to be trifled with. I do not care for being used.'

My mind was now in some perturbation. I perceived he had a mistaken notion, although the nature of it was not clear. 'I am sorry,' I said, 'that any conduct of mine should give you cause for uneasiness. I know not how you have come to this misapprehension, sir, but you may believe I had no design of using you — or trifling with you, either.'

'Do you claim I have misunderstood you, madam? I think not. I saw all your displeasure with Captain Hargreaves. Your avoidance of him and your subsequent attentions to me can have only one explanation. Well, I do not choose to act the suitor for the purpose of causing anxiety in another gentleman.'

There was an anger in my companion which would have been justified had I truly had such a design. Before I could deny his accusation, he went on, 'Neither do I believe I could succeed, for that young man is very secure in knowing you have rejected many other suitors on his account.'

I knew instantly how he had come by that intelligence and I was most indignant. 'How dare Lady Hargreaves make such a vulgar boast!' I exclaimed.

'She could not make such a boast were it not generally known.'

I sucked in my breath. Here were causes for Sir Justin's disapprobation! Were I better known to him, my character established, he would not accuse me of betraying any gentleman who had failed in his suit. I considered it a point of honour to remain silent on the subject.

It is a perverse fact, however, that where a young lady has fortune, many gentlemen will press their attentions too eagerly to escape the observation of others. However silent I remained, it was known I had refused several gentlemen.

I only said, 'People will gossip.'

'Indeed they will. Some, madam, take care that they do. Do you betray all your suitors or merely the illustrious ones?'

'You are offensive, sir, and quite ridiculous.'

'Not so ridiculous as you have made Viscount Saxondale. I cannot imagine that gentleman enjoys having his name bandied around as one of your conquests.'

Viscount Saxondale could not be accused of any mercenary motive, since he is the heir to an earldom and a fortune far greater than my own. And Lady Hargreaves had actually had the impertinence to name him, as though that refusal had anything to do with her ambitions for her son! I could almost hear her foolish prattle: 'But then, dear Judith has always been excessively fond of Richard.'

Sir Justin knew nothing of the circumstances. The viscount had pressed his suit most vigorously, not understanding the differences in our dispositions which would make us irksome, each to the other, should we marry. He flattered me with an offer of great wealth, great consequence and the prospect of becoming a countess. My coolness and discouragement had been disregarded, considered a manifestation of maidenly modesty. It had not occurred to him that any lady would refuse.

I recalled it was not the first time Sir Justin had heard the viscount's name linked with mine, not the first time I had been held accountable for that gentleman's indiscretion.

'We all have our crosses to bear,' I said, too angry to hold my tongue. 'I did not enjoy having my name bandied about, either. Certainly, it did not please me to learn that some, who call themselves gentlemen, were taking wagers on the outcome of that affair.'

Sir Justin gave a gasp and it was some time before he could speak. When he did, his tone had altered. 'I cannot deny there are some who will act in that way,' he said. 'The viscount betrayed himself, I take it?'

I said nothing. Sir Justin could determine the rest for himself.

'Poor fellow. He must have been very much in love with you.'

'I think not.'

Saxondale was, quite simply, a gentleman conscious of what was due to his own rank and importance. My connections (I am related to the Earl of Ramsgate) had recommended me as a suitable lady.

'My greatest comfort,' I said, 'is knowing he was not in love with me. His vanity was wounded. His heart was not.'

Nothing more was said. As we approached the turnpike, I felt there was still some uneasiness in Sir Justin and I recalled his first accusation, that I had been using him to make Richard jealous.

When the toll was paid and the gate opened, I allowed the horses to amble through at a walking pace. 'Lady Hargreaves does me no service by her foolish parading,' I said, brooding a little. 'I take it Hugh was not by to hear her prattle?'

'I do not perfectly recall, but I believe not.'

'No, she would not dare. Well, I will not deny that lady has ambition of her own. She will be disappointed. Richard and I understand each other very well, sir, but the nature of that understanding is not the one she has led you to believe.'

'Pray do not trouble yourself to explain, madam. I am not one of your suitors. Your attachments are no concern of mine.'

'Certainly, they are not,' I said, too angry with him now even to wish it were otherwise. 'But I like to be as open as possible in all my dealings and since I have been accused of using you to make Richard jealous, then I will claim the right to defend myself. You judge without proper knowledge, sir, and without understanding. However, it seems I must explain my . . . my . . . what did you call them? My subsequent attentions to you.'

I was thankful I had reviewed my own behaviour, even more thankful that I had nothing with which to reproach myself.

'Quite apart from any goodwill of my own,' I continued, speaking with some emphasis, 'you are a guest in my brother's house and, as such, entitled to my notice. Later attentions were testing my suspicion that I was being avoided, and my purpose in driving was to discover the reason for that avoidance. And now, I will not scruple to tell you that you have placed a great strain upon my aforementioned goodwill. However, that is unlikely to trouble you, since you dislike my attentions so much. We may continue the journey in silence.'

We were on a stretch of good road and I whipped up the horses to speed, all my attention given to driving. We covered the last two miles to Bennerley without speaking.

We arrived first, for Hugh and Helen were to take home the Hargreaves. Sir Justin leapt down from the curricle before it had properly halted. As a groom came to take the horses, he was by my side, waiting to help me from the carriage.

I fussed with my skirts and raised my parasol. A sideways glance taught me that his complexion, which had been heightened at the conclusion of my speech, had faded to an alarming degree. He was so pale I thought he must faint.

The reflections which had caused this alteration were made known. He spoke painfully: he recognized his position had been false, he was very conscious of having trespassed upon matters which were no concern of his, and of abusing all the kindness and friendliness I had shown him.

He was clearly distressed and the amends he made, his words, his voice, his expressions, all moved me. He then alarmed me by saying he would leave immediately.

I urged him not to, insisting that Hugh would be displeased with me if I allowed it. I told him we could be friends again, shook his hand, and if there was something self-derisory in my smile, I believe he was too embarrassed to take note of it.

Seeking to overcome the awkwardness, I was relieved when the others joined us, and knowingly incurred my brother's displeasure by becoming very concerned to discover the best method of relieving the discomfort of his swollen wrist.

When I went to change for dinner, I did not immediately ring for my maid, allowing myself a few minutes of solitude for reflection. I seated myself by the window, looking out beyond the park to the farmland, where the reapers were still out with their scythes, gleaning the last of the corn from the long strip. From this distance they appeared no larger than ants.

Now I had cause to be grateful to an ant!

Never would I wish my brother ill, but there was no denying his injury had given me an opportunity to discover and dispel all the mischief Lady Hargreaves had caused. Without it, Sir Justin might have continued for ever in his ill opinion.

There was much I had been unable to say, but I thought he would comprehend how improper it would be to reveal everything. He had penetration enough to determine some parts for himself, should he be inclined to do so. For the moment, it was enough that my character was secured from blame.

I could not blame his misapprehensions. Never having seen me discouraging a gentleman, he had only my behaviour to himself by which to judge me, and to him I had not been discouraging.

'*I am not one of your suitors.*'

That remark had been designed to sting, and it had.

I felt an ache in my throat. For however much Sir Justin might regret his suspicions, however much he might wish the words unsaid, that remark, stripped of any intent to wound, was nothing less than the simple truth.

It would be pleasant to deceive myself, to attribute his misapprehensions to jealousy over Richard, to believe his disapprobation had been due to some feeling of disappointment.

But I could not. I had to face it: I was merely part of Hugh's family, and it was my brother's friendship which he valued.

I had initiated most of our conversations, most of our dealings with each other. Particular attention from him had occurred after recapturing Blue John, but that could be attributed to gratitude as could the gift of the paperweight.

' . . . *I confess, I am surprised he has parted with it* . . . '

I started, recalling what I had learnt, and paused in my reflections, knowing it must have cost Sir Justin much to part with it. My spirits began to rise again, for I felt he would not have given such a thing had he not held me in some esteem.

Time was passing, and I was obliged to abandon my thoughts and prepare myself for dinner.

Conversation at table was made easy, because whilst we had been out, the post had brought Helen a letter from Sarah Wysall. Knowing the Wysalls, Sir Justin was interested in their news.

One item concerned Mr Merryweather, who had been fortunate to escape injury when his horse had taken fright and bolted.

'The beast must have caught sight of the old lady,' I said, and this wicked comment succeeded in making Sir Justin laugh.

So it was a puzzle and a grief to me that, when I looked at him directly, I saw him staring at his plate with such sadness in his expression, there was no accounting for it.

After dinner, the gentlemen soon followed we ladies into the drawing-room. As Helen poured out tea, Hugh enquired of me what I knew about *Water Music*.

When I had my own establishment, living in town with Mrs Armstrong, we had attended many concerts, and I had heard it.

'Handel,' I said. 'I seem to recall there

was a large part for the french horns. Why do you ask?'

Sir Justin had mentioned hearing the work praised by an acquaintance. Desirous of pleasing our guest, Hugh now wished me to play it on the pianoforte.

'I am unable to oblige you, sir,' I said, 'for I have no copy of the score.'

'There may be a copy in the library,' said Hugh. He turned to Sir Justin. 'Judith has inherited her musical talents from our grandmother,' he explained. 'Some manuscripts were put away after she died. I have been meaning to give them to you, Judith. You would like to have them, would you not?'

'Indeed, I would,' I said. 'I had no notion there was any music here, other than my own.'

In the library, a footman brought down several tooled leather boxes from a high shelf, placing them on a table. We looked through the contents. I found several manuscripts that would be valuable additions to my own collection of music.

Hugh was still looking for *Water Music*. 'It is an orchestral work,' I warned him. 'We may not have a score transcribed for a single instrument.'

'I believe I have found one,' he said

triumphantly. 'Do play for us, Judith. Sir Justin is most impatient to hear it.'

Sir Justin reddened. 'Sir, I must beg you not to importune your sister so. I swear I had no — madam, please believe this was not my design. An idle remark, made quite by chance . . . '

'Well, I do not object to trying it,' I said. 'Though I doubt I shall do it proper justice upon a first performance.'

I confess my performance was weak. Occupied with the intricacies of the work, stumbling here and there, I spared little attention to interpretation and expression. Sir Justin, however, seemed to feel it necessary to congratulate me.

'Well, I shall work on it,' I said. 'I hope when you visit us again, sir, I shall give a more polished performance.'

'I found the airs very pleasing,' he said innocently, but his colour rose when he saw my grin, comprehending the reason.

'You have found me out,' he complained. 'It is true, I am a simpleton! I have not — it is a rare pleasure to hear any music, and my introduction to music of real merit took place only recently, when first I had the privilege of hearing you play. I confess, I was amazed at such richness. Until then, I had heard only country airs and dances.'

'I do not despise country music,' I assured him. 'If you have a favourite, command me, sir, and I will play for you.'

'No. If I may make a request, I would beg you to repeat a piece I heard you play before, though I never heard the name of it.' He stopped, his colour rising again. 'Once before you asked whether I had a preference. I had nothing to say, being wholly ignorant. Unwilling to confess that ignorance, I asked you to play your own favourite. Madam, I know not what it was, but I will swear, never in my life had I heard anything to equal that music. Do you recall? Can you tell me what it was?'

I stared at him, too moved by these admissions to recollect. I wondered if Sir Justin understood himself, if he realized how rare it was for someone in his situation, for someone who had more pressing concerns — very different concerns — for someone not used to hearing music and not at all conversant with the composers, for someone like himself to come instantly to such appreciation.

At the Wysalls' I had played only part of Sonata 'Pathetique'. I told him what it was, explained the sonata form, found the score and now played the whole.

I knew by heart the slow second movement

and when I came to it, I watched him. It was late, the candles had been brought in and the moving shadows gave emphasis to the angles of his face. I saw the austerity in his expression, the intelligence in the tilt of his head. Something was there: ignorant he might be, through no fault of his own; simpleton, he was not.

Hugh asked Helen to sing and my sister-in-law chose to accompany herself, so I yielded my place at the instrument and seated myself in a chair close to Sir Justin's.

'I warn you,' I said, 'Herr Beethoven is a most prolific composer, responsible for many sonatas, concertos, minuets and symphonies. Now I am determined to inflict all of them on you.'

He smiled at me and I returned his smile, glad that he was easy with me, pleased because he had talked to me, happy because I felt he was beginning to trust me.

Later, having retired for the night, I did not immediately snuff out the light. I sat on the edge of my bed, smiling in anticipation of tomorrow's summer ball, knowing I would dance with Sir Justin. I picked up my paperweight, turning it in my hand, watching the play of candlelight against the silver surround, drawing my finger over the blue polished stone.

I gasped, recalling tomorrow would be his last day with us and I had yet to secure another meeting. So far, I had done nothing about procuring an invitation to visit Melrose Court.

7

In the morning I ordered Jupiter saddled, was dressed for riding, and discovered the gentlemen already in the stable yard. I joined their inspection of the horses, offering carrots, and making a great fuss of Morning Star's foal.

'The storm that followed him has given him his name,' said Hugh. 'I am calling him Thunder.'

'There is a mighty name for a little fellow,' I said. I nuzzled my face against the foal, stroked his mane, and observed that my Pink Ribbon must be grown to his size adding, very wistfully, how I longed to see her.

Neither gentleman took the hint. But Hugh obliged me in another way, by recalling a pressing matter of business and telling me that Sir Justin would accompany my morning ride.

My delight died when I saw a trace of uneasiness cross Sir Justin's countenance. It was gone in an instant, but there remained a set look to his mouth: he came unwillingly, which was enough to cause me distress.

It was not the time to venture another hint

about visiting Melrose Court.

As we set off, I took surreptitious glances at him. His expression was unsmiling. I could not help wondering if he disliked me until I recollected the previous evening, and how warm and appreciative he had been when I played for him.

Puzzled, I looked again: this time, I surprised him taking a sideways glance at me and when he looked away quickly, with a heightened colour, I came to a possible explanation. Perhaps he had been troubled by a recollection of the quarrel between us?

I would not refer to that subject. Instead, I smiled to show I meant no harm and offered a vague remark about returning in time for breakfast.

'We had a very fine crop of strawberries, this year,' I went on, 'and I have heard a rumour that our cook intends us to sample her famous strawberry preserve, this morning. I hope your appetite is equal to it, sir, for I can assure you it is like no other! She claims to have a secret ingredient: I suspect it is brandy-wine, but you shall give me your opinion.'

Such inconsequential chatter has its uses. I saw the tenseness in his jaw relax and he smiled and made some answer and, as I continued chattering, I contrived to make mention of our proposed holiday in Scarborough.

He answered amicably enough, but it did not occur to him that we might easily take in Melrose Court on our journey.

I sighed and changed the subject as I led the way across an open meadow towards a long expanse of turf which now covered what had been an old road built, some say, by the Romans. There were bushes on one side and woodland on the other and it ran wide and straight and true for almost two miles.

There was dew on the grass and the air was fresh and cool and the sunlight threw gilded ripples through the trees. We urged the horses into a gallop. I let him draw a little ahead, enjoying the sight of him, the speed, the wind in my face and the steady pounding rhythm of my mount.

Something long and green slid across the track, darting almost under my horse's hooves. Jupiter let out a scream of alarm and bucked and plunged and I slipped out of the saddle and landed face downwards in an undignified heap on the turf, jarred and breathless, and unwilling to move until my various pains subsided.

I saw the cause of the commotion disappearing into longer grass at the edge of the gallop. Letting out a mutter of exasperation, I began to pick myself up.

'Judith!' He was on his knees beside me, alarm in his voice and when I moved his arms came around me. He lifted me and I found my cheek pressed hard against the dark cloth of his coat.

'Thank heaven you are alive! For a moment I thought . . . I thought you had broken your neck! I . . . oh dear! Are you hurt?'

'I think not. What of Jupiter?'

'He scampered away, the rascal. Do not fret for him, he is sound. What of yourself? Did he kick you?'

'He did not. I am quite well, sir. I shall have bruises, I know, but nothing more serious.'

'You lay so still! I confess, I feared the worst.'

I was beginning to savour the pleasure of finding myself so unexpectedly in his arms. Held tight against his chest, I could feel his heartbeat racing and I lifted my face, wonderingly, to look at him. His face was pale, his eyes closed and his breath came in ragged gasps.

I hastened to reassure him. 'Truly, I am quite all right.'

Sir Justin recollected himself, relinquished his hold, and returned to his usual reserve. 'Can you stand?'

'If you will be so good as to assist me.'

He steadied me until I was on my feet and not one second longer. For some reason, I found myself unable to look at him and instead I began to brush away the debris which clung to my riding dress, clucking a little upon observing grass stains.

Blue John waited patiently nearby, blinking as though experiencing some mild surprise at these human activities. Jupiter was nowhere to be seen.

'He will find his way home, I expect. What startled him so, do you know?'

'A snake.' Then, as his brows rose, 'A grass snake, sir, and almost under his hooves or he would not have taken such fright, for he is not easily alarmed.'

This brought a quick smile and bright appraising look. 'Then I suspect he is much like his mistress. No other lady of my acquaintance would take such a tumble in so matter-of-fact a way.'

I felt my colour rise. I had, in fact, been upbraiding myself for not having thought to behave in a more feminine way, clinging to him and making much of my distress. But perhaps with this man it would have been a mistake, for he was smiling, and regarding me with some approval and I had won myself a compliment of a sort.

I said, 'My brother will take alarm when Jupiter returns riderless to his stable. We should return now, to set his mind at ease. May I ride pillion?'

'I had no thought of leaving you to walk, madam.'

So I was mounted behind him on Blue John, slipping my arms around his waist and, I confess, smiling with satisfaction at the pleasure of being so close to him.

'Judith!' A jingle of harness and a man's voice, not my brother's, but raised in anxiety, all the same.

I swallowed my vexation. 'Richard,' I told Sir Justin. 'And he has found Jupiter, by the sound of it.' I called back, 'I am here, sir, and perfectly sound. I am with Sir Justin.'

We came upon him, mounted, as we emerged into meadow-land, and when my accident had been explained and I had thanked him for recovering Jupiter, I declined to remove myself from Blue John on the grounds that Jupiter had lost a stirrup.

A lady's saddle is designed with more in mind than the elegant appearance of riding sideways on a horse. There is a device which ensures the stirrup comes away, should the rider be unseated: a lady may fall from a horse, but she will not suffer the fate of being dragged along the ground with her foot caught in the stirrup.

Richard looked surprised. 'Did you not retrieve it?'

I felt my colour rise. 'I completely forgot about it. I must have been thinking of something else.'

I spared myself from further questioning when I saw that his saddle-bags were full and he was dressed for travelling.

'Are you going somewhere, Richard?'

'First to Bennerley to take leave of you all and to apologize to Mrs Tremaine for I shall be unable to attend her ball, after all. I am setting out for Essex.'

I laughed. 'Urgent business calls you back, no doubt?'

It was his turn to flush. 'As you well know.'

Later, when we could speak privately, Richard made me acquainted with the situation. Lady Hargreaves considered herself very ill used upon learning her favourite wish had been thwarted. Her stream of reproaches convinced her son to be gone as soon as may be.

'It is all my fault,' he said cheerfully. 'I am selfish and obstinate. I take no heed of parental counsel. I am foolish and ungrateful. I should not have joined the militia: had I continued to press my suit, none of this would have happened.'

I shook my head and tut-tutted. 'It is indeed too bad of you, Richard.'

'Mama will not listen to reason, and I am in no humour to bear with her repinings. Besides, I have reasons for wishing to return to Essex, as you know. Judith, may I beg you will say nothing of my hopes, at present, to Mama?'

'I would not dream of mentioning such a matter.'

He refused Helen's invitation to breakfast, saying he wished to set off straight away. The company at table thought it such a pity Richard was to miss the ball. I said it was fortunate the weather was set fair, for he was travelling on horseback, and added my hopes he would have a safe journey.

I made but short mention of my recent accident, for I had a design, and the matter was pressing, now. I contrived to turn the conversation to horses: Jupiter, Blue John, Morning Star's foal, and my wistful longing to see my own little filly-foal, Pink Ribbon.

Helen regarded me quizzically, her eyebrows suddenly very mobile. Smiling, she put forward the very scheme I had in mind. 'You may see her very soon, Judith. When we travel to Scarborough, next month, we can take in Melrose Court on our journey. It is not so very far out of our way, after all.'

'Why, Helen, that is a capital scheme!' I turned to Hugh. 'You would not object to breaking our journey, would you sir?'

'Since my son is to accompany us,' said Hugh, 'we shall be obliged to take frequent breaks, for we cannot subject so young an infant to prolonged carriage rides. We might visit Melrose Court, providing it will not inconvenience Sir Justin.'

I used a looking-glass to observe Sir Justin. I reached for a slice of plum cake, appearing to notice little, though I was intent. I could have sworn I saw alarm flicker in his eyes.

If so, it was quickly concealed: he contrived to appear delighted by the scheme.

Perhaps his alarm had been self-consciousness, for Melrose Court could not be as grand as Bennerley. I confess I felt some compunction at putting him to the expense of entertaining us.

It could not be helped. I was determined to learn more about him and discover if there was any lady to whom he was partial. I also wished to know of his sisters.

Not once, in three days, had he mentioned his sisters and I had formed some suspicions: he had cause to mistrust ladies, and I thought his mistrust had begun with them. Moreover, his confession that he rarely had the pleasure of hearing music told me neither girl had troubled to learn an instrument.

It is possible to acquire some degree of musical skill even as an adult. A few months of learning and practice would allow them to please their brother with a few simple airs, and I thought it quite shocking that they made no attempt to do so.

I was angry, for he had the burden of providing for them. Common gratitude should have been enough to govern their behaviour.

'We do not know all the circumstances,' said Helen when I ventured to remark on this. 'Let us not be too hasty in our judgement. It could be, you know, that they do not wish to put their brother to the additional expense of engaging a master.'

I was silenced. But I determined I would take musical scores with me, and play for him when we visited Melrose Court.

No more was said, for Helen and I were busily directing the servants in all the arrangements for the evening ball.

The long saloon on the north side of the house was perfect for dancing. The floor shone with polish, the great chandeliers had been lowered and furnished with new candles. A dais for the musicians had been raised at one end, little gilt and brocade chairs placed along one side of the room and more chairs with tables set opposite. Supper would be served in an adjoining room, and card tables had been placed in another. Now, it was a satisfaction to know that one gentleman would not disappear from the ballroom to occupy himself at whist.

Sir Justin had done what good manners required of him and engaged me for the first two dances. I hoped this duty would also be a pleasure for him and that later in the evening he would find an opportunity to go beyond his duty and request me to stand up with him a second time.

Never had I taken such care with my appearance! I had a new gown, a peach-coloured gauze, simply styled but decorated with lengths of silver thread which gleamed as they caught the light. I had silver brocade slippers, and scattered at random in my hair I wore little silver flowers.

Even though my bruises were covered and I was satisfied I looked my best, I could not help feeling nervous as I pulled on my gloves and picked up my fan.

Helen brought a blush to my cheeks by demanding that both Hugh and Sir Justin should look at me and admire.

I bridled when Sir Justin confessed himself

disappointed: but he shook his head mournfully and said: 'Not one pink ribbon to be seen,' teasing me, and I was pleased that he remembered.

Sir Justin himself was plainly dressed in a black coat and cream-coloured waistcoat. He had a lace neckcloth, tied in the style known as Waterfall, and fastened with a plain gold pin. Elegant he was, and I could not help feeling there were gentlemen of means who would do well to emulate his style.

For half an hour we were kept busy greeting our guests and introducing Sir Justin. At last, the company was assembled and Hugh and Helen took the floor to open the dancing. Sir Justin claimed my hand, and bowed as we took our places in the set.

I considered myself a robust lady, but when Sir Justin took my hand, I experienced some feelings of feminine fragility. I was astonished to discover how pleasing were such sensations.

Our conversation, at first, was mere general civility. Then I saw that he was looking about him in a most puzzled way, and I ventured to enquire the reason.

He had noticed that several of the ladies were wearing damp muslins and found himself at a loss to account for it.

'At first, when I saw Miss Moore, I

thought some accident must have occurred, but I have since noticed other ladies in the same case. Is it a fashion? It seems very strange.'

Never had I been so diverted. Were Sir Justin accustomed to balls and assemblies, he would have known the reason.

'It is for the purpose of captivation, sir,' I said. I had to pause and bite my tongue to prevent myself laughing. 'Observe, if you please, how the damp material clings to the body, outlining the female form. I am told it is a most effective way of inflaming a gentleman's passions.'

The movement of the dance separated us: peeping at him, I was delighted to see the colour in his cheeks.

'I wish I had not asked,' he said, and looked rueful when I chuckled. 'You must think me a dreadful bumpkin, madam.'

'Not at all,' I said. I slanted an arch look at him as I passed beneath his arm. 'No bumpkin could dance half so well.'

'I am out of practice, I fear. I have few occasions for it.'

'That is a pity,' I said, 'for however many gentlemen are at a ball, always some ladies are obliged to sit down without a partner. A gentleman who enjoys dancing would be welcome at any assembly. Do you not attend balls in your own county, sir?'

'Very rarely, madam.'

I had to suppose he had not the inclination, for there must be opportunity. There were subscription assemblies even in country towns, and I could not feel that Chesterfield, the nearest town to Melrose Court, would be without a monthly ball.

'My particular friends are quiet people, more disposed to find pleasure in conversation and small dinner parties. I am so circumstanced — I go into society but rarely. I am more inclined to stay at home.'

I was watching him more closely than he knew and I saw a shadow cross his features: I thought I had reminded him of some worry, and I was sorry for it.

I only said, 'Well, staying at home can be agreeable: in the wintertime, especially, one's own fireside has an irresistible lure. But I hope you are not one of those stern moralists who believe every scheme of pleasure to be an irredeemable sin?'

'No, madam, I am not one of those.'

'I am glad. I believe little gatherings and parties are necessary for the refreshment of the spirit.'

'I am sure you are right, madam.'

He was unhappy and I indulged him in light-hearted banter, pleased to see him looking easier when we were obliged to part.

During the course of that evening, it was borne in upon me that I had two new suitors. I knew Mr Fielding and Mr Cross in a general way: now they seemed to be vying for my favours.

I danced with both gentlemen: I refused to dance with either a second time. But in an interval between dances, when Mr Fielding went to procure a glass of lemonade for me, Mr Cross remained by my side and paid me some very pretty compliments.

Discerning I was not impressed by his praise of my beauty, he recovered adroitly by saying, 'Ah, my dear Miss Tremaine, I see you have been influenced by the dictates of society in such matters. I scorn such insipid notions! Your countenance shows character, madam, which, to a gentleman of taste, must be more pleasing than regular beauty.'

I smiled, but only wished that one, who had said no such thing, might entertain the same thought.

Mr Fielding returned with lemonade, glowered at Mr Cross and said he hoped his friend had kept me tolerably entertained.

The gentlemen contrived to sit by me at supper, and I confess I could hardly keep from laughing when they both seized upon a dish of strawberry tartlets, each struggling to gain possession before presenting it to me.

All this was watched with distress by one lady, with indignation by Lady Hargreaves, with exasperation by Mr Fielding's sister and with amusement by others. How Sir Justin felt, I know not. I had not the courage to look at him.

When the dancing recommenced, I was claimed by another partner. Later, I asked this gentleman to escort me to my brother's side. It was pleasing that Sir Justin was with him, for I merely wished Hugh's proximity to dissuade my new suitors from pursuing me across the room.

Hugh slanted a sardonic eyebrow. 'Two conquests in one evening,' he murmured: 'My dear sister, you surpass yourself. Pray, when am I to wish you joy?'

'You shall be the first to know,' I promised him.

Hugh shook his head sadly. 'I fear you are a hard-hearted woman, Judith. You see how devoted they are. Have you no compassion for their plight?'

'Well, sir, however many gentlemen press their suits, I can, in the end, marry only one of them. So tell me, which of those two are you desirous of accepting as your brother-in-law?'

'As always, you go to the crux of the matter,' admitted Hugh. 'I take it you wish me to remind our company that you have a stern and forbidding guardian?'

'If you would be so obliging, sir.' I smiled at Sir Justin, inviting him to share the secret. 'You may be surprised to learn, sir, that in his role as my guardian, my brother can be quite the tyrant — when it suits me!'

Sir Justin looked amused. 'Fraternal tyranny would not be regarded as an advantage by many ladies, madam. Your brother is more fortunate than he knows.'

I turned to Hugh. 'I must give some thought to that remark,' I said. 'It sounds like a compliment, but I have misgivings. What say you?'

'I have not the smallest notion,' said Hugh. 'You go too deep for me. But I doubt not Sir Justin will be willing to assist us in discouraging those two puppies. Take the wench away, sir, and dance with her again. Since you must leave, you might as well give our neighbours something to gossip about.'

Sir Justin bowed politely and smiled at me. 'Well, madam? Do you obey your brother in this?'

'Most willingly, sir.' I made a curtsy, disconcerted that my second dance with Sir Justin had been so contrived. I would have preferred him to make the request of his own accord.

I would also have preferred him to keep his gaze fixed on me when we took our places, but he looked over my shoulder and seemed diverted by what he saw. He informed me that Hugh had been favouring Mr Cross with a very haughty stare.

'Have you known those two gentlemen long?' he asked.

'Something over a twelvemonth,' I answered thoughtfully, 'although they have not been so particular in their attentions until this evening. Which leads me to some strange ideas.'

'Am I permitted to know what they are?'

'I think Lady Hargreaves did me some service after all, when she was promoting the idea that I was attached to Richard.'

'Ah! You are quite right, of course. I have heard that he is the latest of your failed suitors.'

'Oh dear! Well, that piece of gossip is more likely to distress Lady Hargreaves than Richard. He has other matters to concern him, at present.'

Sir Justin did not answer this, neither did I expect him to. After we had turned across the dance, I changed the subject. 'Must you really leave us tomorrow? I am sure my brother and Helen would be delighted if you could prolong your stay.'

'As they themselves have been obliging enough to tell me,' he smiled. 'I regret I have matters of business requiring my attention.' He paused, and there was a flicker of pain in his eyes and a change in his expression: 'We horse dealers,' he said with a lightness which did not deceive, 'cannot afford to be idle for long.'

I felt myself flushing and said, 'I beg you will not speak of yourself so. Whatever business you may be employed in, you will always be a gentleman.'

'You are all kindness, madam.'

'You may believe me sincere, also.' I spoke with some energy. 'It seems I must apologize for the bad manners of someone in our company, tonight. I hope you will value my opinion more than his!'

When the dancing ended, he said quietly, 'You would disapprove of bad manners, of course, but I cannot feel you whole-heartedly approve of a gentleman engaging in trade?'

I smiled at him. 'Well, I will tell you, sir, that no one will persuade me to disapprove of honest endeavour. I am sorry, however, that it will deprive us of your company so soon.'

Hugh came to join us and I said, 'I

am trying to persuade Sir Justin to delay his departure. Can you think of some inducement that will tempt him, sir?'

'Indeed, I beg you will not try, for already I am tempted beyond bearing. Never have I met with such kindness. I fear I must resist, though I confess it goes against my inclinations.'

'Well then, I shall insist you pay us another visit very soon,' said Hugh.

Having danced with Sir Justin twice, I had nothing more to hope for, but I was sorry when the evening drew to a close.

He was to set off very early in the morning before the rest of us would be about. Unknown to him, however, I was awake and watched him go from the window of my bedchamber.

As he rode out of sight, a deep tremor ran through me and I began to shake. I am persuaded the only thing that sustained me then was the certainty of seeing him again within a few weeks, when we made our proposed visit to Melrose Court.

8

Melrose Court had a fair prospect. Situated on a rise, with a wooded hillside behind, it was not as large as Bennerley, but certainly larger than I had supposed. Built of local grit, it had wide pleasing windows and slate roofs with tall chimneys.

There were many acres of pastureland, divided into paddocks and occupied by horses, among them, I supposed, my little filly-foal, Pink Ribbon. And though I longed to see her, I had an even greater longing to see a certain human countenance.

He had seen our approach and came outside to greet us: he led the way into a wide hall with a stone-flagged floor. The only furniture was an oak chest which flanked the stairway.

A sound from above made Sir Justin pause. 'Blanche? Is that you? Come downstairs and pay your respects to our guests.'

A feminine form descended the stairs and we beheld a girl of seventeen, slightly taller than myself, a little too thin, but pretty enough. She had very fine, very pale hair, some of which had escaped whatever had been holding it in place, leaving one tress to dangle against her ear.

We were introduced and Sir Justin said, 'Where is Amy?'

'I believe she is with our aunt.'

'I see. Find her then, if you please, and tell her our guests have arrived.'

Blanche resumed the stairs and as we followed Sir Justin, he told us that Miss Fox, the girl's aunt, had been very shaken by a recent fall and begged us to excuse her. 'She sends her compliments, but prefers to remain quietly in her room.'

We were conducted into a small saloon, facing south, with a pleasing light coming from the windows. Someone had arranged white roses in a brass ewer, but this attempt to brighten the room could not disguise the overall dilapidation. The wallpaper was dark and old-fashioned and the fireplace was a hideous monstrosity, a great carved oaken affair, with vines and serpents and grotesque figures. From the brackets supporting the mantle leered carved human heads, reminiscent of Henry VIII: it was enough to give a child nightmares.

The furniture was arranged in the old-fashioned way against the walls, to be brought forward when needed. Sir Justin did not ring for a servant, but brought up chairs himself.

All the time we were talking. The fine summer, our journey, the scenery and the pleasing quality of the Derbyshire air.

Now Hugh was anticipating autumn fruits. 'The pippins look exceptionally well, never have I seen such abundance . . . '

Not being required to talk, I fixed my gaze on the beloved face, and happiness bubbled inside me with the joy of being close to him again. Intent on studying his features, I did not look round when I heard the door open to admit his sisters.

I saw him blink, I saw his eyes widen, I saw his colour rise and a look of extreme mortification cover his countenance. I heard Helen's sharp intake of breath and the strangled sound in Hugh's throat which was hastily turned into a cough. All this in the instant it took to rise from my chair. When I turned, I was struck by the full personality of Sir Justin's sister, Amy.

It was her apparel which commanded attention: sober-hued muslins were not for Amy. Amy wore crimson satin, ruched at the bodice and covered with a layer of gold net. She wore gloves, she carried a fan, there were bracelets at her wrists and pearls at her throat. There was a crescent-shaped patch on one cheek, and from her head sprang a tall ostrich plume.

Had not good manners forbidden laughter, concern for Sir Justin would have produced the same struggle. I bit my tongue very hard, cast down my eyes to hide the merriment in them, and did my best to control the muscles of my face.

We managed the usual civilities, and servants bringing in refreshments spared us the immediate necessity of making conversation.

When we were settled, Hugh talked with Sir Justin. Helen — and I know she did it purposely — began to converse with Blanche, leaving me to talk to Amy.

I expressed concern for her aunt's indisposition; I made observations about Derbyshire and enquiries about the house. My remarks met with little interest. At length, I fell silent, determined to leave the trouble of finding a subject to her.

'I expect,' she said at last, 'you think I am very foolish to have myself dressed up like this?'

I did think her foolish, though I could hardly say so with any degree of civility. At a loss for an answer, I simply murmured that it was, perhaps, a trifle unusual.

'I am told this fashion is all the rage, in London.'

'For a ball, perhaps. Do you like London?'

'Oh, yes! indeed. That is to say I have never been, though I may be going down this winter. For the season, you know,' she added airily. 'Shall you be in town yourself, this year?'

'I think not. I go but rarely.'

'But you must have had a London season?'

'Oh yes, several.'

'And were you presented at court?'

Receiving affirmation, Amy wished to know all about it. 'For I am not perfectly certain what to expect, you know, and one cannot be too well prepared for such an important occasion.'

Amy, I was persuaded, wished me to describe the grandeur of St James's Court. Some instinct warned me against doing so. I said, 'I found it a very uncomfortable occasion. There was a great press of people: I could scarce hear myself speak and I could not walk anywhere without bumping against someone. There was too much light from too many candles and consequently the atmosphere was excessively hot. Several ladies fainted.'

Her eyes widened at this slighting description of the great occasion. After a pause, she went on to ask me about the subscription balls at Almacks.

'I went occasionally,' I admitted. Wishful

of punishing her a little for causing her brother such embarrassment, I went on, 'I do not much care for public assemblies. I always think private balls are so much nicer, do not you?'

'Oh — er — yes! Undoubtedly,' said Amy, nonplussed.

Poor Amy! It really was too bad of me. Her brother had revealed that balls and parties were rare occasions. She was young and clearly her disposition was one which chafed against being obliged to remain at home. One could not wonder that she wished to engage in schemes of pleasure.

Feeling sorry for her, I would have relented and engaged her in talk of fashion had not Blanche excused herself and Amy, saying they had promised to take some tea to their aunt.

'I will carry the tray.' Her voice held a hint of contempt. 'It would not do to spill tea on your finery, would it?'

With their departure, it was time for me to make the acquaintance of my little filly-foal, Pink Ribbon.

Sir Justin led us to the stable yard.

All was neat, tidy and exceptionally clean. The cobblestones were steaming slightly, having recently been sluiced down.

'I insist upon cleanliness at all times,' said

Sir Justin. 'I employ a couple of simpletons for the work, lads who are of little use for anything besides, and they are happy because I insist on their importance here. Some say I am foolish and some say I am charitable, but I am persuaded that cleanliness is conducive to good health and events seem to bear me out for I have lost fewer beasts to infection than most.'

Hugh was regarding Sir Justin with a respect which delighted me and was possibly determining upon following this example at Bennerley. Our own stables were by no means dirty, but we did not make exertions such as this.

There was a second stable block, adjacent to the first, which had recently been built on, to give accommodation for visiting mares. I could comprehend the need for it, but I knew the cost of building work and I became curious about how Sir Justin conducted his finances.

I had not time for speculation, for now he was leading us towards the paddocks. There were several of them. We saw some fine yearlings and two year olds, a black stallion called Jericho, another stallion called Captain, a solid-looking grey with his own mares and progeny.

Hugh stood admiring and making enquiries,

monopolizing Sir Justin again. 'You gentlemen may talk all you wish,' I told them, 'but I am impatient to see Pink Ribbon.'

Sir Justin smiled, just for me. 'Come then.' He led the way to the furthest paddock: and though Pink Ribbon could not have known she belonged to me, it was pleasant to indulge my fancy, for she seemed pleased to see me and left her dam.

She was a beauty. Young as she was, she moved with supple grace: a chestnut, with a white star on her forehead, she regarded us with a very bright eye. I nuzzled my face against her and declared myself wholly captivated.

For a long time I could not tear myself away, even when Helen insisted. 'Come, Judith, we must go back to the house.'

With Hugh monopolizing Sir Justin, I became occupied with arithmetic, excusing my calculations with the reflection that Sir Justin's interests were very close to my heart.

I thought of the debt which was Sir Robert's disgraceful legacy to his son: I thought of the cost of that new stable block: I thought of three stallions and some thirty broodmares and calculated their value. I thought of hiring grooms and other expenses, such as farriers, and tack and fodder.

I thought of time: eleven months from conception to birth of a foal, a year before it could be broken and trained, and almost another year before schooling was complete. Monies had accrued from stud fees and sales, but I could not understand how Sir Justin had brought the enterprise to its present size.

I suspected that he lived frugally, and my maid confirmed it. There were very few servants for a house of this size, and she had learnt from the housekeeper that half the house was shut up, windows bricked up to avoid window tax, rooms unfurnished, and all in a state of dilapidation which had begun in Sir Robert's time, before Sir Justin became master.

'What of the servant's quarters?' I asked.

Betty sniffed. 'They are not what I am used to, miss. Though I have seen worse, and they do say the gentleman does his best for them. He bought new blankets, last winter.'

'It seems a pity to let such a house deteriorate,' I said.

'It needs money, and it will be years before he can set the place to rights. He could marry,' she added. 'There is one who has some wealth at her disposal, but he does not like her.'

'Indeed?'

My fear that Betty was warning me gave way to relief when she added, 'Neither does Mrs Payne, if it comes to that.'

'Mrs Payne?'

'The housekeeper. She says the master has more sense than to be taken in by her scheming.'

'Is there any lady he and Mrs Payne do like?' I enquired.

'She says gentlemen who have daughters are careful to keep a certain distance, the master being distressed for money.'

That had not occurred to me: now I felt hopeful.

I was encouraged by my reflection: I looked well in my green sprigged muslin. So I was smiling, as I stepped out of my room.

'Oh, Amy!' I heard Blanche's voice tinged with exasperation. 'When will you learn that Aunt Agnes is not the fount of all wisdom? In fact,' she added, 'she is a very silly woman!'

'You are jealous!'

'Because she likes you better?' Blanche sneered. 'You may believe her preference does you no service!'

Their voices carried very clearly indeed. I made a noise of shutting my door, coughed to tell them I was within hearing and allowed my footfall to sound more heavily than usual.

The girls, wherever they were, took the hint and fell silent. Intrigued by the fragment of conversation I had heard, I found myself regretting my own scruples about eavesdropping.

At dinner, Amy still wore the crimson, but the fripperies were removed and I could observe her better. She was a pretty girl, her hair deep gold and her eyes a bright cornflower blue.

I had expected dinner to be a plain but serviceable meal, and I was right. Pains had been taken, but no one had set out to impress. There was brown soup, three meat dishes with side dishes of vegetables, two puddings and a blancmange.

Were it not for Amy, I would have made a fool of myself, for when I tasted the beef I was persuaded something was wrong. I hesitated, unwilling to cause distress by mentioning it, though I do not, in general, hold with consuming suspect meat.

'Our cook,' Amy said, seeming all innocent of my dilemma, 'flavours our beef with rosemary. I think it is nice, do not you?'

'Yes, indeed,' I managed to say. 'Although I confess it is a new departure for me. Yes, I agree, it is very nice.'

And it was: knowing I could safely eat, I enjoyed the subtle flavour imparted by the herb. But I stole a few glances at Amy, suspecting that she had some of her brother's penetration.

That penetration was not much in evidence after we ladies had withdrawn from table. I had intended to pay some attention to Blanche, but Amy carried all before her and the subject of her conversation was, once again, the London season.

In her own eyes, Amy was destined to become all the rage, exciting the admiration of gentlemen and eventually bestowing her hand upon the noblest and wealthiest of her suitors.

To do her justice, she expected to fall in love with her illustrious suitor. Her motives were not entirely selfish, for she also meant to ensure the financial comfort of her brother and sister and to gratify the dearest wishes of their hearts.

'The dearest wish of my heart,' said Blanche ungraciously, 'is that you would rid your mind of these nonsensical ideas.'

I was quite in sympathy with Blanche, although I could not help smiling. There was something innocent and childlike about Amy and, a moment later, I had a clue to that snatch of overheard conversation, for she added brightly, 'Aunt Agnes says I will take London by storm!'

'You could not take Chesterfield by storm!' muttered Blanche.

Thankfully, a change of subject was occasioned by nurse bringing in Christopher, and the girls were happy to play with him. Amy began singing, a comical little ditty, and this was the scene which the gentlemen beheld as they joined us.

In Sir Justin, I saw anxiety give way to relief. Clearly, he had been apprehensive in case Amy had been exposing her folly.

He seated himself by me as we drank tea, enquiring after the acquaintance he had made in Leicestershire and, upon my expressing admiration of his enterprise, he went on to tell me a little about his daily round, working with the horses.

Once again the girls excused themselves to attend upon their aunt. I recalled my own design of pleasing him with music, only to learn there was no instrument at Melrose Court. Our evening was spent talking together and very agreeable it was, for both Sir Justin and Hugh had a fund of amusing anecdotes.

My feelings for him grew stronger and several times during that evening I fell silent, overpowered by deep tremors, almost afraid of the strength of my longing. Indeed, it was something of a relief when the time came to retire for the night.

I placed the floor of my bedchamber, considering my position. I felt he liked me and held me in some esteem: I was sure he knew I liked him. Yet whilst he had been friendly and agreeable, there had been none of those little attentions which a lady can encourage or discourage, nothing which suggested to me that Sir Justin had any thought of advancing his suit.

'*I am not one of your suitors . . .* '

My throat ached: I had tried to ignore the remark, knowing it had been uttered in some bitterness, hoping my manner would persuade him to reconsider.

I could spend only one day at Melrose Court and after that, unless something could be contrived, there would be several months, perhaps as much as a year before we would meet again. In such circumstances, a gentleman could be excused for pursuing his interest with some haste.

Sir Justin was not pursuing his interest at all: he seemed not to wish it.

I was confused. Had he not liked me, I could understand; had he formed an attachment for another lady, I would find it hard to bear, but I could understand. But there was no previous attachment; there was mutual liking and esteem, so surely the notion must have crossed his mind?

I sighed, coming to the sensible but dismal conclusion that I would know the truth before long. The day after tomorrow, I must go away. Should there be no sign from the gentleman before then, and I had only the smallest hope of there being such a sign, then I must accept that he had no inclination for it.

With a mind so filled with pain, sleep was impossible. I took a chair by the window, staring out over the moonlit hillside, reflecting that distance and separation would be no evil, should I be obliged to conquer my feelings for him. Yet so wretched was the prospect, I scarce knew how I would support myself.

Tears filled my eyes. When I reached for a handkerchief I found that my robe was twisted, the pocket somewhere behind my back, so I had to stand to let the garment fall into place.

From my window, the stables could be seen if one looked to the right. Had I not stood when I did, I would not have seen the lantern, or the figure crossing the stable yard. I dried my eyes, watching him, assuming he was a groom, assuming this night-time visit to the stables was for the purpose of attending a sick horse.

I saw him open the stable door and venture inside: then I saw him emerge, running back the way he had come. Now I was really attentive, for if he was in such a hurry, I thought he must have urgent need of assistance.

I watched him out of sight, returned my gaze to the stable and clucked in disapproval as I saw the door had been left wide open. Then I blinked and looked again, not quite knowing what to make of the flickering light I saw.

Even as I watched, the light brightened and flared into life and the stable was lit from within, as flames took hold.

9

My first attempt to raise the alarm was a pitiful failure. Instead of screeching to wake the household, my voice emerged as a half-whispering croak.

I used my slipper, banging on the door of my bedchamber, and this produced a hollow sound, satisfyingly loud. 'Fire!' I screamed. This time my voice had regained its power. 'Fire in the stables!'

A thudding sound told me that someone had been roused. I banged again, screamed again, and took my candle, mercifully still lit, to rekindle the candles in the wall sconces. All the time I was screaming, 'Fire in the stables!'

Sir Justin dashed past me, I heard my brother's voice, cursing, and sounds from below indicated others were about.

When I reached the stable yard, two women were working the pump, and water was already being thrown over the blaze.

I took a pail and joined the crowd at the pump. Becoming impatient with the waiting, my gaze lit upon three rainwater butts, which stood at intervals along the stable wall.

'The butts!' I dashed to the nearest and threw off the lid, thankful to see a quantity of water within. I lowered my pail.

My exertions to raise it were a waste of time for my strength was not equal to it: I heaved and strained and wept and groaned, and succeeded only in spilling water on myself.

'Eh up, missy, gizzit 'ere!' The incomprehensible speech belonged to a broad man who took the rope handle and lifted the pail with astonishing ease. He thrust an empty pail into my hands, removed a bung from the side of the butt, said, 'Theer yar miduck!' and disappeared in the direction of the blaze.

I kept busy holding pails beneath the flow whilst others directed them to the fire. Helen was at one of the other butts and someone, I think it was Blanche, had broached the third.

When my butt was empty I straightened and looked round, saw that others were still now, watching as the last few pails of water were thrown over the smoking remains.

'How bad is it?' I asked fearfully. 'Is there much damage?'

'I think not.' That was Hugh. 'The fire did not take hold of the roof, thank heaven. We have indeed been most fortunate.'

Sir Justin emerged from the stable. His hair was tousled, his face blackened and his nightshirt scorched, but he was smiling. Hay and straw and rope had been consumed, and a few of the wooden panels dividing the stalls, but that was all. He thanked everyone for their exertions and invited anyone who wished for it to partake of a mug of spruce beer before resuming their rest.

I was about to follow the others when a whinnying sound reached my ears. On this fine August night the horses were out in the paddocks, and the sound had carried from that direction.

Recalling how the fire had been started, I turned to Hugh. 'Sir, I am uneasy. I beg you, come with me to the paddocks. I must satisfy myself that all is well with the horses. You hear them? They seem disturbed.'

'I imagine they are,' agreed Hugh. 'They can smell the smoke and hear our activity. They will settle down, soon.'

I could not wholly believe it, much as I wished it. 'I must be certain,' I insisted. 'Please come with me, Hugh.'

'Oh, very well,' he grumbled, and was not pacified to discover all was well. He recalled how I had raised the alarm. 'How did you come to notice it?'

'I could not sleep. I was looking out of the window.'

'I do not wonder you could not sleep,' said Hugh. He was in a surly mood, which surprised me for his disposition is usually a cheerful one. 'If your bed is at all like mine, I would say it is impossible to sleep. I am persuaded there should be laws passed against mattresses such as that.'

I laughed. 'Should that be all you can complain of in your prosperous life, you will do very well indeed,' I reproved him.

'Judith, you wretch! Why do you always — you do, do you not? You always go straight to the heart of the matter. You are right. I should not complain.' He paused, then added, 'I am more blessed than he: I have fortune, a beautiful wife, a fine healthy son and, indeed, a sister whom I can be proud of, which is more than he can say of his sisters. Those girls! Dear heaven, Judith, why should I have such bounty when better men than I are so beset?'

'Indeed, there is no accounting for it at all,' I agreed.

Back at the house, the servants and grooms had retired to their quarters: only Helen and Sir Justin remained in the hall, waiting for us. 'Where have you been?'

'To the paddocks. The horses were

disturbed and Judith was anxious, but I think it was only the smoke.'

'You could have mentioned you were going.' Helen sounded quite sharp. 'No one knew where to look for you.'

'I beg your pardon.' Hugh made an ironic little bow. 'Next time the stables catch fire. I will endeavour to remember.'

'Let us hope there will be no next time,' I intervened, to prevent what might have become an open quarrel. 'Once is quite enough.' I turned to Sir Justin. 'Sir — '

'Madam. I am deeply indebted to you. Had you not raised the alarm — ' He stopped abruptly. 'Er — madam, you are soaked!'

I looked down at myself: my mind had been so occupied that I scarce noticed the clinging discomfort of my wet gown. Now I recalled how I had spilled half a pail of water down my person.

Sir Justin seemed embarrassed. 'I — er — I beg you will excuse me if I defer my thanks until morning. You should change, madam, dry yourself. I — er — I bid you goodnight.'

'Oh, Judith, I did not realize!' That was Helen. 'And I sent Betty back to bed! Well, no matter. I will help you.'

'It is of no consequence,' I said. 'I

believe I can dry myself.' But Helen insisted on accompanying me, and looked wholly bemused when, as soon as we were safely within my bedchamber, I collapsed into helpless laughter.

'What is it, Judith? What is so funny?'

I shook my head and refused to tell. But later, when I was alone and settled into bed, I laughed again, and thumped my pillow, and gave a little crow of triumph.

For though the dampening of my gown had happened by accident rather than design, I knew the material had clung seductively against my body, outlining my female form. Now I understood the gentleman's embarrassment: for I had seen, had I not? that his manhood had been aroused, his passions inflamed.

I fell asleep with a smile on my face. I slept deeply, awoke late and looked around in confusion, unclear where I was, and which was dream, and which was reality.

This was not to be wondered at: oddly at variance with events, the dream had been quite ordinary.

I had dreamed I was on horseback, waiting at a crossroads, near Bennerley. The gentleman who rode into sight was not the one I had been waiting for.

'Which way are you going?' he asked, and

I answered, 'I am waiting.'

And he had shook his head, and smiled, and said simply, 'He will make no declaration.'

He will make no declaration.

My dreaming mind had attributed the words to Hugh, but they came from within myself, a knowledge not consciously perceived.

I shook off my confusion and determined to consider the matter with all the reason at my command.

He will make no declaration.

I could not lose sight of the possibility that he had no inclination for it.

Other words came to me then, words spoken a long time ago by the vulgar, salacious Mrs Merryweather:

'*You may depend upon it, he is a man who knows very well what he keeps hidden inside his breeches, and what it is for . . .* '

Yet I was convinced Sir Justin was too fastidious to take his pleasures outside marriage. Another man's wife would not tempt him and, in his situation, it would be expensive and difficult to set up a mistress. I could not feel he would use servant girls, or any of the villagers, and certainly he would not purchase the services of a harlot.

If secretive liaisons were not to his taste, and I thought they were not, then Sir Justin, at this present, remained celibate. I was persuaded he would rather be married.

He will make no declaration.

I fell to wondering if there were reasons, other than a disinclination for me, why he would make no advances.

He knew I had refused many suitors. Yet though his pride might rebel at the prospect of becoming one of their number, if he really liked me, I could not feel this would deter him. Besides, I had shown how I liked him.

Melrose Court was, at present, in a state of dilapidation. Yet it was by no means unsuitable: and since I would bring fortune, I felt he would allow me to make improvements.

Could he be deterred by my fortune? He would not set out to marry for money: but should he like a lady who had fortune, then scruples on that account seemed a little nonsensical.

Then I recalled his own words:

'*We horse dealers . . . I cannot feel you would wholeheartedly approve of a gentleman engaging himself in trade . . .* '

There is a malicious tendency in our society to look down upon people engaged in trade. Sir Justin himself certainly felt some degradation in his necessity and it now occurred to me he would have scruples about asking me to make a connection society might frown upon.

I nodded, satisfied I had hit upon an argument which would weigh heavily with Sir Justin, the more so, perhaps, because of those other matters.

'Judith, it is close upon ten o'clock!' Helen put her head round my door. 'Do you not wish for breakfast?'

Setting aside my reflections, I followed her downstairs, noting she was softer, gentler, this morning. Discord between herself and Hugh had been resolved.

At table the talk was of last night's fire. Sir Justin was warm in his appreciation of our endeavours, and particularly grateful to me for having raised the alarm. 'So swiftly, too! We were upon the fire before it had taken a serious hold.'

I disclaimed any credit and said it was mere chance that I happened to observe it. Recalling how the fire had been set, I lapsed into silence, brooding over the matter.

Sir Justin would have to know. I was reluctant to speak of it at this present for there were servants in the room who might themselves know more than they should. In any case, they would gossip and, in so doing, possibly give the miscreant warning that he had been observed. I must find occasion to speak privately with Sir Justin.

Amy was subdued, and when I saw the tight-lipped glances of her sister I thought there must have been some quarrel between the girls. It did not surprise me: I suspected Blanche rarely agreed with Amy.

'You are very quiet this morning, Judith,' said Helen. 'I hope you are not feeling ill?'

'I am quite well, I thank you.' I roused myself, saying I had slept heavily and had some strange dreams.

The events of the night were held to be accountable. Blanche suggested that a stroll in the fresh air might be of some benefit to me, and offered to show me around the garden.

I was pleased by this approach, for I had not yet had opportunity to converse with Blanche. I collected my parasol and joined her in the hall.

The garden, enclosed by a wall and divided by a broad central path running down the length, was highly artificial, but pleasing for all that. Following a strictly symmetrical formal design, with elaborate patterns and geometric walks, with box hedges, with fountains and statuary and topiary, it was designed to show man's mastery of nature rather than the present fashion of harmony with nature.

'It is very old, you know,' said Blanche. 'It was begun in the reign of King Charles I and fashioned after the Italian style, originally. But I fear it is not kept as it should be.'

I could see it was not. Clearly, attempts were made to keep it tidy, but to flourish properly the place needed an army of gardeners.

'One of the fountains does not work,' said Blanche absently. 'I think a pipe is blocked, or broken.' She then surprised me by changing the subject in a very abrupt manner. 'Amy is not such a fool as she sometimes appears.'

Persuaded that Blanche did not like her sister, I was rather touched by this attempt to defend her. I looked at her, smiling a little. 'I know.'

'If you do know I am glad of it, though how you have discerned it is more than I can fathom. Her behaviour yesterday was quite intolerable.'

I permitted myself a quiet chuckle. 'Certainly, she made her presence felt.'

'Well, and I am glad you are come. Justin told Amy she should not give herself such airs and that if she wanted to know how a great lady behaved, she could learn by observing your style and manners. I hope she does.'

I felt colour rise in my cheeks. 'Your brother's approbation is indeed gratifying,' I said, 'but I have lapses, as he knows: are you certain he was not speaking of *Mrs* Tremaine?'

'She is a most agreeable lady. I believe Justin likes her, too. But you were the one he was speaking of.'

I was silenced, a little moved by his representing me in such terms, though I could not feel Amy would warm to anyone who was held to be a shining example.

Indoors, I learnt that Sir Justin had excused himself for half an hour and had gone to look at the stables. Hugh was reading the newspaper and Helen was conversing with Amy.

' . . . a paste of oatmeal and milk, made thick, not runny, can be most beneficial for brightening the complexion. Just cover your countenance with it and allow it to harden . . . fifteen minutes is quite long enough. Then rinse it away.'

Hugh hid his countenance behind the paper: again I had to bite my tongue to prevent laughter. 'Only take care that no gentleman sees you in such a mask,' I said. 'For it is indeed a ghostly sight, and can excite the most violent palpitations.'

Blanche seemed just as interested as Amy and we ladies spent some time discussing recipes for the preservation and enhancement of beauty, coming at last to the dressing of hair.

Helen discovered the girls did not have their own maids, but only the limited services of one of the housemaids. Offering Amy her own maid for the afternoon, Helen also gave a very strong hint that I should offer Betty's services to Blanche.

Having arranged for the girls to spend the afternoon in their rooms with their hair in curl-papers, I wondered how Helen would contrive to dispose of myself and our host.

I saw her design: something had been amiss between herself and Hugh yesterday, and there remained some ragged feelings to be soothed away. She wanted her husband to herself.

So I was not surprised to learn, when Sir Justin rejoined us, that I had often expressed a great curiosity to see the famous crooked spire of St Mary's church, in Chesterfield.

Sir Justin offered to escort me. I smiled and accepted his invitation. He followed me from the room and said, 'That was contrived, was it not? What does she mean by it?'

'It was no design of mine.' I spoke absently, for this was not the matter uppermost in my mind. 'Helen wishes her husband to herself. But, sir, there is a matter of some urgency! May we speak privately? I must make you acquainted with it.'

He was regarding me in some curiosity. 'Can you not tell me on the way to Chesterfield?'

'You may wish to remain here,' I said fretfully. 'Sir, this matter is of the utmost importance.'

He took me into a library, and watched my agitation in some astonishment. I spread my hands and could only say helplessly, 'Sir, it pains me to tell you so, but you have an enemy. That fire last night was no accident. It was set, deliberately.'

He heard me with only a momentary narrowing of the eyes. 'Can you be certain of this?'

'I saw it done,' I said, and told him how I had at first presumed the stable visitor to be there for no unworthy aim. 'It was dark and only his lantern and the moonlight to see him by, and never can I point to anyone and say for certain it was he. But some little, I can tell you.'

'Go on.'

'He was agile, there was a look of youth about him. He was slim and I think he was not very tall. I believe he cannot be a patient youth either, for had he waited to ensure that people were asleep, his mischief might have been more successful.'

Sir Justin was regarding me in curiosity. 'You seem to have given the matter some thought, madam.'

'Indeed I have, and I am very sorry I can tell you no more.'

'Have you spoken of this to anyone other than myself?'

'I have not.'

'Not to your brother?'

'No one. It is your business, not Hugh's.'

He gave a sigh and it seemed to be one of relief. 'Then I am more obliged to you than you know. I would be yet more obliged if you would undertake to maintain that silence?'

'Well, certainly, if you wish it. Surely you do not imagine my brother, or any of our servants here, could wish you ill?'

'And all of you so swift to lend assistance?' he exclaimed. 'No indeed! No such notion had crossed my mind, I assure you.'

'Some notion has crossed your mind,' I said. 'I believe you know the culprit.' Since he made no denial, I went on, 'I hope you mean to bring the felon to justice, sir. Should there be need of it, I will gladly bear witness.'

'I thank you, but that will not be necessary.

Well, madam, I am obliged to you. Be certain the culprit will be dealt with. Now, which mode of transport do you favour for our visit to Chesterfield? I can find a mount for you if you prefer to ride, or I can drive you in the gig. Which is it to be?'

'But sir, is there not some urgency in the matter of apprehending our felon?'

'I shall do that when I so choose. Not this afternoon.' His expression changed and he smiled. 'This afternoon, I will satisfy your great curiosity and take you to look at our famous crooked spire. I think you will not be disappointed.'

'Well, then,' I said, 'I confess I would like to see the spire.'

For his sake, I had been prepared to sacrifice the pleasure of having him to myself for a whole afternoon. Now, I could no longer argue against my own inclinations.

Since the weather was set fair, we thought it would be agreeable to ride. Changing into my riding dress, I saw myself smiling into the looking-glass, enjoying the sensations of excitement and anticipation.

He will make no declaration.

The dream words returned to me as I was halfway down the stairs. I stopped, wholly appalled at the idea which had crossed my mind.

From somewhere below a clock chimed the half-hour and I had a confused sense of time gathering speed, of events taking over. Were anything to be done, it must be done today.

He will make no declaration.

As my own intentions became clear to me my insides lurched and I will swear my very bones were shaking.

10

I struggled to regain command of myself. Ignoring the thudding of my heart, I found my way to the stable yard and I believe I showed every appearance of composure.

There was some joinery going on, men putting right the fire damage: all the wet straw and hay had been cleared away, the smoke-blackened walls had been whitewashed and the only trace of untidiness now was a pile of sawdust on the cobblestones.

Here was a subject for conversation and as Sir Justin came towards me, I said, 'You work quickly.' Encouraged by my own rational tone of voice, I went on, 'I think you have some good men, here.'

'I am very sensible of it, madam.' He was leading a grey mare, saddled for me, and she looked to be a sprightly lady, not at all discomposed by the sound of sawing and hammering. Sir Justin regarded her with affectionate approval. 'I believe you will find Calypso a comfortable mount.'

Calypso took a carrot from me and made no objection when I mounted her. Blue John, who had been skittering a little whilst the groom held him, quietened at once when Sir Justin approached and swung himself lightly into the saddle.

We set off, and Sir Justin directed our mounts to a grassy track, wide enough for two. The land rose and fell, but there were no really steep hills. 'Here we are east of the Pennines,' he told me. 'But not very far away.'

We passed through a village and on the outskirts he directed my attention to a handsome, stone-built house, small by comparison with Melrose Court, but clearly a dwelling of some importance.

'This is where I lived as a boy,' he told me.

'Here?' I was all astonishment. 'Not at Melrose Court?'

'This was my grandfather's estate. My father spent much of his time in London after my mother died.' His eyes were shadowed. 'My grandmother would not allow me to be left alone at the Court with only servants. I was brought here, and lived here until I was eighteen, when Grandfather died. Now it belongs to Colonel Makepeace.'

'I see. Well, I can sympathize with your grandmother's point of view. It is fortunate you were not far from Melrose Court. Were you happy?'

'When I could escape my masters and run around the stables,' he grinned. 'My grandfather was good with horses, at doctoring them as well as training them. He taught me what I know. It was not a bad life for a boy. But I never saw much of my father.'

'That was his choice, Justin, and no fault of yours. Had he wished it, he could have spared time for you.'

He scarce noticed I had taken a liberty with his name. His eyes flickered with some remembered pain and I now regretted my words for I saw they had opened an old wound.

As we rode on, I said, 'I would not wish to pain you by speaking ill of your father, but no account I have heard of him meets with my approbation. Perhaps he did you good service by leaving you to the care of your grandparents.'

'I take it you have heard of the scandal?'

'Yes,' I said. 'I have.'

'Cards.' The word was spoken with no expression of any kind. 'Had he enjoyed his games, I could understand it, but he did not. And when all was lost, he returned to Melrose Court to put an end to his existence. I thank heaven I was the one to find him, for it could so easily have been one of my sisters.'

I winced. Sir Robert had not improved in thoughtfulness, even when facing his Maker.

'He had taken a pack of cards, broken open a new pack and spread them, face downwards, on the table and only one card turned over. Can you guess what it was?'

'The Ace of Spades?' I hazarded.

'Not so. It was a Jester.'

I swallowed, unable to speak. 'It is believed,' he went on, 'that my aversion of card games is because my father lost his fortune thereby. In truth, I can scarce bear to look upon a pack of cards, for I cannot help but recall that scene, and I am visited again by that same horror.'

I had no great opinion of Sir Robert: now I was filled with consummate anger against the man who had left his son with debts and the responsibility of providing for his sisters, and who had caused abiding distress in the manner of his death.

He saw my expression and recollected himself. 'Madam, I beg your pardon! What kind of creature am I, to burden you so?'

'Do not make yourself uneasy, sir.' I was distressed on his behalf, and yet rejoicing he had seen fit to trust me, for he was not a man to confide easily in others. 'There is value sometimes, in talking over distressing matters.'

'I should not have done it: already I am indebted to you, and for more than raising the alarm last night. I do not forget the assistance you once gave me with this fellow, here.' He gestured towards Blue John.

'I did only what anyone might in such circumstances.'

His confidences were at an end, however, and his conversation became more general. I made no attempt to question him further.

All the time, there had been fluttering at the back of my mind that shocking notion that had so forcibly struck me at a most inconvenient moment, when I had no time to examine it.

Could I bring myself to abandon all delicacy, could I bring myself to go against all the proprieties and dictates of society? Could I be so brazen as to propose marriage to him?

What would he think of me? At present, he held me in some esteem: that esteem might well be forfeit should I proceed with such a daring plan. Certainly, in the eyes of the world, I would be sunk beyond reproach.

The eyes of the world, however, were unlikely to behold the spectacle. Whatever the outcome, I could depend upon his discretion. It was a consoling reflection.

Whatever the outcome, my own uncertainties

would be settled. Should he wish for me, we would marry. Should he not, I would, in any case, leave tomorrow.

And it seemed to me that, should I be leaving with all hope gone, I would at least replace my present confusion and uncertainty with clear understanding. I would leave and, if I must, I would bear what I had to bear and recover in my own good time with none but our two selves any the wiser.

He had been talking, pointing out aspects of the countryside and though I had been much occupied by my thoughts I believe I made sensible answer. When we breasted a rise I saw, in the distance, the strangely crooked shape of the famous spire.

'How odd it looks,' I exclaimed, thankful to be diverted from my preoccupation. 'How did it come to be so twisted, do you know?'

'Some say,' he smiled at me, 'that when the devil flew over Chesterfield, he caught his tail in the spire and twisted it as he pulled himself free.'

I was surprised into a laugh, for I had expected a more rational explanation telling of faults in the construction.

The ride into the town was pleasant, a gently sloping stretch of green and we took it at a swift canter. After I had looked my fill at the spire, he found a boy he knew to hold the horses, assisted me to dismount, and we strolled through the churchyard and into the streets, Sir Justin exchanging brief civilities with chance met acquaintance, myself pausing now and again to examine some article in a shop window.

At length, it was time to be going home and I was silent, attempting to quell my uncomfortable feelings of apprehension, and wondering, for the first time, if any gentleman felt as squeamish before declaring himself. I felt it unlikely, however, since proposing was a gentleman's prerogative.

Part of me was demanding conformity to the expectations of society, urging me to abandon the notion, insisting it was better to lose him than to so far demean myself. For I was by no means certain of my suit being successful, and to propose and be refused would be of all things the most dreadful!

Almost, I reached the point where this craven argument carried more weight than any other. I told myself I needed time to strengthen my resolve, but now I fancy that delay would have weakened it still further.

After some time, I wondered that he had not remarked on my silence. I looked and saw he was occupied by his own thoughts and on his countenance I surprised a look of deep unhappiness.

I urged Calypso forward, forging ahead. I knew not what particular trouble was occupying him, only that he had little to make him happy. And though I had no conscious thought, I knew I must now learn whether I had power to make a difference.

I reined in and wheeled round to face him as he approached. He came towards me slowly and his expression had changed now to one of enquiry. 'Is something wrong?'

'Do you think — ' I paused and swallowed. 'Do you think we could be happy together, you and I? Because I would like to marry you, Justin, if you will have me.'

His mount began capering and prancing in the most peculiar way and he was obliged to give his attention to bringing the animal under control. As I watched, my nervousness vanished and I felt amazingly calm. When Blue John quietened at last and his rider turned an astonished countenance towards me, I was able to regard him with cool amusement. 'Which have I frightened the most,' I asked, 'you, or the horse?'

'Judith, are you proposing to me?' he demanded.

'Should you not wish it, sir, then I beg you will tell me so. In fact,' I went on, painfully determined, 'I must insist upon that. I would have no reluctant husband.'

'I — er — I — ' For the moment he was incapable of speech. He looked down at his hands resting lightly on the reins and there was a strange little smile playing at the corners of his mouth. His vanity, if nothing else, had been gratified, and even if that were all, I would not begrudge it. Yet when he looked up, I saw there was a trace of shyness in his expression, and he said, 'Do you mean it?'

'We have not time — we are so much apart — '

'My dear, what have I to offer you? You are accustomed to living in the style of elegance, accustomed to fashionable society. It would mean giving up so much.'

'What do you mean by this? Do you think to let me down gently? Should you not wish it, do not scruple to say so.'

'You know I do wish it,' he said absently. 'Somehow, I have betrayed myself. Never would I have presumed . . . no thought had I that you . . . well!'

He paused to gather himself and said quietly, 'You do not know all my circumstances. I must — I have to impress upon you that I am by no means secure. All you have seen is forfeit, should I fail to pay back what I have borrowed.'

'I do know.' My calculations had taught me there could be no other explanation. 'I can do arithmetic.' But I was pleased by his admission, and I laughed, all my doubts at an end. 'Well then, you had better marry a rich woman,' I said. 'I am pleased to inform you, sir, that I shall bring some fortune.'

For the first time, a trace of hauteur crossed his features. 'I do not want a fortune.'

I laughed again. 'Were I to believe that, I should think you a very odd creature,' I said. 'But you would have fortune through your own exertions. However, I should point out that my fortune is there. I could make it go away, but I shall not.'

He gave an absent smile. 'I shall waive my right to it,' he said. 'That can be done. You shall have control of your fortune and your brother to advise you. Yes, that is the best way. Whatever befalls me, you, at least, shall be secure.'

I would not involve myself in such an argument. 'You must determine that with Hugh,' I said, knowing my brother would handle matters with delicacy. 'I take it you will not refuse me permission to make myself comfortable at Melrose Court?'

'Of course not! Heaven knows there is need, for I know it is no suitable home to offer a bride! How can you wish to exchange your home at Bennerley for Melrose Court?'

I thought of Bennerley and the happiness of my brother and his wife, a happiness that I had witnessed daily for the past few years. And though I rejoiced in it, and though I knew myself loved by both of them, there had yet been a loneliness in my own situation. That loneliness had sharpened to an unbearable ache during these last few months, since I had come to recognize my feelings for Sir Justin.

I made prosaic answer. 'Bennerley is my brother's home. I am welcome, but I can never be mistress. I have a fancy for my own establishment. Melrose Court is a fine house, needing only a little refurbishment. There can be no possible objection.'

'You could have better. Judith, have you considered how disadvantageous such a marriage must be? The stables take up my time, I cannot mix in society in the way you are used to. Excursions and visits must be short, parties are rare occasions, balls even more so. You will find us very dull.'

Here was a reason for his reticence which had not entered my head! I could only suppose such a reservation had been assisted by Amy, who made no secret of her own discontent.

I only said, 'I have mixed a great deal in

polite society and, I assure you, it has less to recommend it than you might suppose. I found most of it very dull.'

'Nevertheless, you will find life very different here. I thought you would marry a nobleman.'

'I would rather marry a noble man,' I said smiling, and I enjoyed seeing the colour rise in his cheeks. 'In any case, there is a title.'

'Oh, yes, indeed,' he nodded. 'I can easily comprehend how that must attract you, you, who have been known to refuse a viscount. Society must always consider an impoverished baronet a far more eligible choice of husband.'

'It is not ineligible,' I said, 'despite these scruples of yours. Well, sir? And have you finished arguing? For I am still awaiting your answer, you know.'

'Oh, my dear, can you be in any doubt?' He was flushed and smiling, and he dismounted and reached for my hand, drawing it to his lips. 'I can conceive of no greater happiness.'

'Then we are engaged?'

'So it would seem.' He laughed, excited and surprised. 'I can scarce believe this has happened! How have I deserved such a blessing?'

We rode on, taking no heed of time,

talking over the past.

He spoke of our first meeting and told me how he knew himself in danger that very first evening, even as I had, and of how forcefully he had felt all his disadvantages. Unlike myself, he had felt obliged to struggle against his feelings.

He told me how often he thought of me, and how he had been half excited, half afraid, when Hugh invited him to Bennerley. Unable to resist, he came, yet knew that a prolonged stay would not assist his struggle.

I was melting, dissolving, all my being committed to him, now. I no longer felt shame that I had been the one to speak out, but only wonder that I had so nearly denied myself, and him, this present happiness.

'Such restraint!' I mocked. 'Did it never occur to you that I might have feelings, too?'

'I had known you only three days when I discovered you had rejected a viscount. Later,' he added, 'I learnt of others who had been rejected too. Could I imagine myself succeeding?'

'How foolish you are,' I said fondly. 'You have witnessed how I am pursued and you understand the reason. Those who were not outright fortune hunters might be described as prudent.' Among these I counted Richard's half-hearted offers, although I made no particular mention of them. 'The viscount,' I admitted, 'had other notions. He wished an alliance of our families.'

'Is that why you refused him?'

'Certainly not. I understood the advantages of such a match. But he is such a rattle, Justin. He talks and talks and says nothing worth hearing. Even the prospect of becoming a countess could not reconcile me to such a husband.'

Arriving back at Melrose Court, I could have sworn there was distance between the ground and my feet. Never had I, until that day, believed 'walking on air' could be a real sensation.

We strolled towards the house, feeling self-conscious, trying to look as though nothing had occurred, and failing dismally.

Indoors, Helen was admiring the curls our maids had contrived for Blanche and Amy, but when she saw us, she squealed and flung herself forwards to hug me. 'Oh, Judith! I knew how it would be! Oh, I am so happy for you!' And she turned to my astonished betrothed, grasping his hand, shaking it and going on tiptoe to plant a kiss on his flushed cheek.

'Ahem!' Hugh had been watching this without much surprise. 'Well, my dear sister,

I would remind you that I am still your legal guardian and nothing can be done without my consent.' There was a smile at the back of his eyes and we both knew that consent would not be withheld. He turned to Justin. 'I take it you now wish to speak with me, sir?'

The gentlemen took themselves off, and Helen and I clung to each other and laughed and cried together, whilst Blanche and Amy regarded us in silent wonder.

Blanche grasped the implications, and said slowly, 'Do I understand this? You are going to marry our brother?'

'Yes, ma'am.' I dropped a curtsy. 'I hope you approve?'

Blanche looked a little dazed, as well she might at having a sister-in-law so precipitately thrust upon her. But she managed a smile and told me she thought her brother was indeed a fortunate man and added polite wishes for our happiness.

She was grappling with thoughts of the changes this would mean to all of them, and could not be blamed if manners took the place of sincerity.

Amy had been watching me open-mouthed. With her dawning realization, she began to gulp. Blanche spoke sharply to her, telling her to speak some word to the lady who was to become her sister.

Amy's shoulders gave one great heave and she said, strangely, 'So all, all has been for nothing!' And she began to laugh, helplessly, mirthlessly.

Watching her, I felt very uncomfortable indeed.

11

'I hope you appreciate the sacrifice I am making, Judith,' Hugh said; we had strolled into the garden, where no one was within hearing, 'for no man would consent to be tortured by such a mattress unless he loved his sister very much indeed.'

My brother had consented to remain at Melrose Court for one more day, but insisted I should go to Scarborough. At Helen's persuasion, however, he consented to shorten the length of our stay there and on returning we would again visit Melrose Court.

'When I am mistress here,' I said, 'you shall be furnished with a deep goose-feather mattress of the finest quality whenever you are pleased to visit. Sir Justin,' I added, 'has given me permission to make myself comfortable.'

There was a glimmer of appreciation in Hugh's eyes. 'I shall not be so presumptuous as to offer you any advice,' he said. 'For I see you have a clear understanding of the fundamentals. A comfortable mattress is, of all things, the most important.'

I blushed and changed the subject. 'Are

you pleased, sir? Shall you like to have Sir Justin for a brother?'

Hugh assured me he was perfectly satisfied. 'He is a little stiffnecked, to be sure, but I admire that in a man. I admire his enterprise, too. He has refused your fortune.'

'He has, but I thought you might persuade him.'

'Your fortune is advantageous,' said Hugh, 'as he has been at pains to point out. He can marry because you are safely provided. He desires your comfort, no profit for himself.'

'I understand that and indeed I honour him for it,' I said. 'But he has anxieties which I would spare him.' I knew he was paying interest on the money he had borrowed. I wished to clear the debt, and said so.

'Never think of it, Judith!' Hugh was vehement in his disagreement. 'A man can borrow and repay in accordance with a contract: that is business and understood. You shall not interfere; it will not serve to have him in debt to you.'

'By law and custom he would be within his rights to take all and do as he wished,' I said despairingly. 'So why should he be so nice about taking enough to clear his loan?'

Hugh laughed. 'You must learn to take account of a man's pride. Tread softly, my dear. Some concessions I may win when we discuss marriage settlements. His idea of your fortune is short of the truth, I fancy. Someone has deceived him.'

'Not I! Never have I mentioned its value.'

'Someone has, and misinformed him, by ignorance, or design.' Hugh sighed. 'He will not be easier when he knows the truth.'

Justin gave his head groom charge of the stables and awarded himself a holiday to spend the day with me. Rain threatened, but nothing could spoil our delight. We strolled away from the house, visited Pink Ribbon and made a great fuss of her.

We were to be married in late September: Justin asked where I wished to go for a honeymoon.

'I wish to be here,' I said, and he looked surprised. 'I do wish it so.' I felt too embarrassed to explain, and said awkwardly, 'Here, where we belong.'

I think he understood. I did not wish our first nights to be spent in a hotel, or a hired house, in a room which strangers had used before us and which we ourselves would soon be quitting. I wanted to be a bride in my husband's home, in the place which would become familiar and most dear, the place which held our future, where our history would be made.

His wish was that we should be alone. 'I

may contrive it,' he said. 'I shall beg a favour of my cousin Margaret: she will have the girls and their aunt to visit, after our wedding.'

He told me his cousin was a sensible woman in her late thirties, married to Colonel Allen, a Lincolnshire gentleman.

'I think you will like her,' he said. 'I have no doubt she will be here when you return from Scarborough, come to inspect you.'

He told me about her and seemed dismayed when I confessed that an earl, a viscount, and a general were among my own relations.

'I see Saxondale knew what he was about,' he said. 'I had no idea!'

'They will do you no harm,' I said. 'All my relations have an eye for beasts of quality. Yes,' I added thoughtfully. 'We shall invite them to visit Melrose Court, as soon as may be.'

Justin laughed, but I saw he was pleased by the notion of finding new customers. He knew the worth of his beasts.

I let my fancy rove: word of his enterprise would spread, Martin horses would be fashionable horses, the ton would flock to Melrose Court and my husband would become a wealthy man.

Leaving for Scarborough, Hugh said, with some asperity, that he hoped I was not going to behave like a watering-pot all through the holiday. I gave my thoughts another direction by reflecting upon the improvements needed at Melrose Court.

Here, I had much to occupy my mind. Hugh's contribution was another complaint about mattresses, but Helen had a sharper understanding.

'I hesitate to suggest another separation from your betrothed,' she teased me, 'but I think we must go to town, you and I, and visit the warehouses. In any case, you will need to order your bridal clothes.'

We talked of drapery and napery, of wallpaper, carpets and furniture. Hugh listened indignantly. 'Poor Justin,' he said. 'He will not know his own home when you are done.'

'Certainly, you will need more servants,' said Helen. 'And there, you must indeed tread carefully. However, I daresay Betty has the measure of the housekeeper.'

Already, my maid had proved valuable: she had told Justin's servants what I would expect, and that I would increase their number. They were reconciled to changes with the assurance that I would add comforts and improvements to their own quarters.

'There has been no mistress at Melrose Court for years,' she had told me. 'That

Miss Fox, the lady who is aunt to the gentleman's sisters, she has been companion and chaperon to the young ladies, but never had she any other duty.'

I had met Miss Fox, feeling it was proper to notice her upon my engagement to Justin: she was civil and agreeable and I felt I could deal with her, though she had struck me as a woman of poor intellect, and I cannot say I warmed to her.

As Helen predicted, Betty had taken the measure of the housekeeper. 'Mrs Payne has the running of things: she consults the master when she has to, but decides most things herself. And not from any idea of her own importance, but to spare him the trouble. Well, she has done her best without a lot of help, and will not be sorry to get more.'

'What is your opinion of the cook?' I asked.

I had observed the food was well prepared and I had not forgotten the rosemary-flavoured beef. Betty said, 'That one is well pleased. Give her a girl to fetch and carry for her, and have company enough to give her scope for her talents.'

Our holiday in Scarborough was disagreeable: we were unpleasantly crowded in a small lodging house, the weather had turned cold, the sea was rough and stormy. Hugh insisted our health would benefit by sea bathing, and we felt obliged to obey him, but we were thankful to clamber back into our bathing machines and return to the shore.

Two matters had been causing me concern.

The first was not one I could discuss with my relations, for I had promised Justin I would not speak of the way the fire had been started. Expecting him to open his mind now we were engaged, I had raised the question again. He had said only that he would deal with the culprit.

'Justin,' I said in dismay, 'have you not yet done so?'

'I have taken steps,' he assured me. 'I have reason for proceeding in this manner. Do not make yourself uneasy, my love. There will be no further mischief from that quarter.' Then he smiled. 'I would not have it spoil our time together.'

I was dissatisfied and could only assume Justin knew his business. Certainly, he would protect his horses from mischief.

Another disturbing matter was Amy's peculiar conduct upon learning of our engagement. She had, in time, gained command of herself; she had been quiet whilst she came to terms with the situation, coming at last to express pleasure in our news.

I felt this was merely a triumph of good manners over genuine feeling. Then I became aware that Amy was, indeed, truly delighted. I looked for signs of falsity in her, and saw none. And though I was pleased and relieved, I was puzzled, also.

Helen had witnessed all this. When I had the opportunity, I asked her opinion.

'You may depend upon it,' said Helen drily, 'it has something to do with the London season. No, Judith, I do not jest. She is far too occupied with that notion.'

'She can hardly be blamed for it,' I said, 'for she is very pretty, and I have reason to believe she has had the London season preached at her, constantly, by her aunt.'

I made Helen acquainted with what I had overheard and my own thoughts on the subject. 'Justin is her legal guardian and even if he could afford to send her to town he would not,' I said. 'He knows Amy would attract the wrong kind of attention.'

'She is, nevertheless, determined upon it,' said Helen. 'Perhaps your engagement upset some scheme of her own. And since she so quickly became reconciled, I presume she now entertains the hope that you will provide.'

'I cannot believe her to be so calculating!' I exclaimed. 'And she has much to learn before I will give her a season.'

'Then tell her so,' Helen advised. 'You may turn it to advantage, after all. Promise her she may have a season when you are satisfied she can conduct herself properly.'

I confess I had felt a little squeamish when speculating on how Amy might behave towards my visitors. Helen's proposal had great merit and could spare us many embarrassments.

When we returned to Melrose Court, Miss Fox had recovered from her fall and resumed her place in the company. Justin's relations, Colonel and Mrs Allen were there also, having made the journey from Lincolnshire to meet us.

Strangers together, we made the exertions of getting to know each other with inconsequential conversation about our holiday and the effect of bad weather upon the roads.

The gentlemen talked about horses, Helen discovered she and Mrs Allen had some mutual acquaintance, and I admired the embroidery Miss Fox was doing.

Blanche rescued me by talking about the house and promising to show me around: we could talk easily on this subject and

I expected Amy to join in, but she was quiet.

Upon turning her countenance towards me, I was startled and shocked to see in her eyes a look of deep and utter misery.

12

'Do not concern yourself with Amy's unhappiness,' said Margaret Allen. 'She deserves it, for she has behaved very ill and Justin is displeased with her. She will recover herself.'

Mrs Allen did not explain and I did not ask. Justin might be displeased with Amy, but he would not betray her misdemeanours.

Margaret Allen chose to accompany me to the paddock to see Pink Ribbon, and I knew she had some design. We had passed beyond the stables before she came to the point. Then she said, 'I hope you understand that marriage to my cousin will involve you with his family, also. It is not for the faint-hearted.'

I permitted myself a brief smile. The lady had obliged us by inviting Miss Fox and the girls to visit her in Lincolnshire after our wedding. Justin held her in esteem; I thought I could like her, but I was by no means certain how she liked me.

'What is your opinion of Miss Fox?' she asked.

I refrained from expressing my opinion. 'I

believe the girls are much attached to her.'

I think my reticence did not escape her. 'Yes, they are. It began very early in their lives, for she is a motherly woman, very comforting, very kind to children, with a fund of little songs and games. You saw how your nephew took to her.'

I had seen it, and remarked how like she was to Amy in that respect. Now, I saw another view: that experience had taught Amy how to please Christopher.

'Miss Fox,' continued Mrs Allen, 'has been constant companion to the girls and she was, for many years, the most important adult in their lives. Were she a sensible woman, that early attachment might have been a source of great good. But she is not. She knows how to comfort children and I cannot believe she has any evil intent. But she gave them no good advice and indeed, she has used her influence in a most improper way.'

'Amy and the London season?' I ventured.

'Ah! Yes, indeed.'

'Blanche does not seem to set any great store by a London season,' I observed. 'But they have reached an age when they must have some society, if not London society. They cannot remain confined at Melrose Court for ever. I must determine what can be done for them.'

We were strolling past the paddocks and I now changed the subject, speaking of horses, and my own filly-foal, Pink Ribbon.

'She is young, still, but moves well, I think she will be a very good horse indeed. But, of course, she has Blue John as her sire, and her dam is a lady of some stamina. And there she is! Is she not a beauty?'

I coaxed Pink Ribbon away from her dam, petted her, pointed out her best features and estimated that she would grow to sixteen hands.

'Some horses will shy at a moth,' I said. 'Justin's horses have better manners for he has a way of teaching them composure.'

'I thought you would persuade Justin to quit this venture,' said Mrs Allen. 'It is no fit occupation for a gentleman.'

'I can think of worse things he could be doing,' I said coldly. 'There are many who call themselves gentlemen, who occupy themselves only with idleness and dissipation. I am heartily sick of hearing his honest endeavour so condemned. He will not hear it from me. He is doing valuable work here, and deserves approbation and support.'

Her eyebrows rose. 'Do you tell me you approve?'

'Yes. I do. Justin has a feeling for horses and he is happy working with them. The disapprobation of society does not disturb me. He breeds beasts of quality which the world has need of. The world will learn to appreciate his worth.'

She was now regarding me in some amusement. 'Does Justin know you mean to change the world?'

'He knows my opinion.'

At breakfast, the others fell to discussing arrangements for our wedding: Blanche and Amy were quarrelling over their bridesmaids' gowns. 'Green may be your favourite colour, but it is considered unlucky at a wedding,' said Amy, settling it.

Justin and I were discussing another matter. He had seen an announcement in the *Morning Post*, concerning someone I knew.

'Can you guess who?'

I could not and teased him to tell.

'Your friend, Captain Hargreaves.'

'Richard? Oh!' I laughed. 'Then he has become engaged to Isobel Townshend! At last!'

Justin stared. 'Do you tell me you were expecting this?'

'I was, indeed. In fact,' I added smugly, 'I can claim to have played some small part in bringing it about. I cannot tell you how delighted I am. I must write to Isobel, immediately. Helen! Helen, here is some news!'

When Helen had heard the particulars, she said, 'Who is Isobel Townshend? Should I know her?'

'Oh! I think you have not met her. But she is a particular friend of Sophie's, you know, and certain I am that you will like her.' I went on to tell Helen what I knew of Isobel.

Justin said, 'Will they settle in Leicestershire?'

'I cannot say for certain. I hope so, for Helen's sake. Isobel will make a charming neighbour.'

I had time to write a long letter to Isobel, for the gentlemen had arranged for attorneys to visit Melrose Court to draw up marriage settlements.

They were closeted together a long time and emerged with Justin looking pale, the two attorneys somewhat bewildered, and Hugh with a gleam of humour in his eye.

'He has discovered, my dear sister, that your fortune is three times greater than he had supposed. He feels he has been abominably deceived, and so he has, but not, as I pointed out, by you. However, it has served. Nothing for himself, but he will allow you to settle a little money on his sisters. I persuaded him to look upon it as a gift, from you to them.'

'I see. Well, that is something, I suppose.'

'He has himself been setting aside an annual sum to settle upon them when they marry, and he will continue to do so. However, we have achieved one of your objects, for his mind has been relieved of some anxiety on their behalf.'

'Well, and if it has done so I am glad of it, but I do wish he would think of himself.'

'Does he have need, when you so desire his comfort?' asked Hugh. 'You will scarce believe how tactful I am become. I said nothing whatsoever about mattresses! I have, however, given him a notion of what is necessary for your comfort.'

I regarded him with suspicion. 'Hugh, what have you done?'

'I have told him you are no worse than most of your kind,' he said, 'but I did warn him he would find you extravagant and expensive. He found it very easy to believe.'

'I see. I beg you will not hesitate to malign me to my future husband whenever it suits your purpose.'

'My dear sister, you may depend upon it. I pointed out that you had been brought up to certain habits of expenditure. In view of your fortune, it would be unreasonable of him to expect you to practise economy.'

Hugh was enjoying himself at my expense, but he had persuaded Justin to let me take over the household expenditure. 'It is a backhanded way of assisting him, to be sure, but you will be taking a small burden from him.'

'Can you do no more?'

I had taken Hugh's word that I could do nothing to clear Justin's debt. 'It is better for both of you that he does it himself,' he told me. 'Come, Judith, you know he understands his business. He will succeed, you know.'

The details of our marriage settlement were complex: there was a great deal of morbid prose about what would happen in the eventuality of our deaths.

The next morning a neighbour visited Melrose Court, declaring she must be the first to wish us joy. Her name was Mrs Buxton, a young widow, who had been left in comfortable circumstances by her marriage.

I knew her kind: having received word of my presence, she meant to give herself consequence by being the first to report my appearance and demeanour around the neighbourhood.

This lady claimed great affection for Blanche and Amy and implied they were on the most imtimate terms imaginable, which had Amy looking confused and Blanche openly scornful. Towards Sir Justin she was familiar, telling him he was a sly, secretive creature to have kept so quiet about me.

Only a flicker of his eyelids betrayed emotion: the Allens were regarding the lady in some bewilderment. Helen and Hugh looked at each other, prepared to be entertained.

Mrs Buxton declared herself delighted by our engagement. If she did not declare her intention to patronize me, it was made clear by her manner.

'I shall insist upon your attending a little soirée at Buxton Lodge before too long,' she said archly. 'I shall introduce you to everyone in the neighbourhood.' She went on to speak of a lady who was considered a great musical proficient.

'Do you play at all, Miss Tremaine?'

'A little,' I said. I was persuaded she knew I did.

'Then you will be charmed by Charlotte Makepeace. Such a dear girl, and her performance on the pianoforte! Exquisite! I declare, never have I heard anyone to equal her!'

Helen enquired of the lady's own musical accomplishment. Mrs Buxton disclaimed any great talent, but assured us she was not devoid of taste.

'And we must not allow you to neglect your music, Miss Tremaine,' she said. 'I have often reproached Sir Justin for having no instrument here at Melrose Court. But you shall not suffer for it, no indeed! I am determined you shall make regular use of my own pianoforte. You must not hestitate to call at Buxton Lodge whenever you wish to practise. Indeed, I insist!' she added, when I would have spoken. 'Music is such a solace in times of trouble. I am persuaded you will be quite miserable without it.'

I could see Mrs Buxton did not understand her own implication and I frowned at my brother, who could barely keep his countenance.

'It is most obliging of you, madam, but I shall not disturb you,' I replied. 'My own instruments will be brought here.'

I know not what Mrs Buxton replied. I had caught sight of Justin's expression: his eyes had widened and held a look of wonder. The notion of our marriage supplying him with music had never crossed his mind.

' . . . Charlotte Makepeace!' finished Mrs Buxton triumphantly.

I had not heard a word she had said. Hugh came to my rescue and said smoothly, 'My dear sister, how pleasing it must be to know you are to come into such musical society!'

'Er — yes, indeed,' I said, trying not to let Mrs Buxton prejudice me against Miss Makepeace.

Margaret Allen seemed to have difficulty breathing. Helen, also, was suffering some distress. There were tears in her eyes and she was mangling her handkerchief.

'May I hope you will persuade Sir Justin to venture out more often than he does at present?' continued Mrs Buxton. 'For I fear he has a tendency towards seclusion you know. Lately, he has become quite the recluse! So many have remarked upon it.'

'Indeed?' With such a neighbour, I was entirely in sympathy with his tendency towards seclusion. 'You may depend upon it madam. I shall encourage Sir Justin to engage with whatever society is pleasing to him.'

If she remarked the irony, she gave no sign of it. She rattled on until it was time for her to be going.

Later, Blanche told me her visit had another motive. This was the lady who had entertained her own hopes of Justin.

'At present she is embarrassed by your engagement, for she made her intention of securing my brother very clear indeed,' said Blanche. 'Now, she wishes to show the world she has no ill-feeling. So everyone will learn she is quite enchanted with you. It will not be long, however, before she discovers you are by no means as pleasing as she first thought.'

'Dear Blanche, I am so relieved to hear it!' I said.

Blanche was explaining the house and showing me round, but I was less interested in domestic matters than her revelations.

'Amy wished Mrs Buxton to be our sister, that lady being sympathetic to her wish of a London season.' Blanche grimaced. 'We shall never know how long such sympathy would have continued in the event of the marriage.'

'Do you tell me she and Amy were allies?' I confess I was diverted. 'Poor Justin!'

For the first time, I saw Blanche grin. 'He told Amy that nothing, not even the prospect of giving her a London season, would induce him to marry Mrs Buxton.'

I laughed.

'Amy truly believes her destiny depends on a London season,' Blanche went on. 'It might be a good idea to let her go, for if she was obliged to return home with her ambition unfulfilled, she might settle into a more sensible frame of mind.'

I wondered how it was that Blanche had settled into a more sensible frame of mind. She knew Justin would never allow them to go to London with their aunt as chaperon. 'And whatever Amy might think, he would not let us go with Mrs Buxton, either.'

'No, indeed. She would completely do for you, at once.'

'Well, I am not so single-minded. I can do without a London season. But I would like to enlarge my circle of acquaintance.'

She entertained ambitions, though hers were more realistic. She now admitted, rather awkwardly, that she had looked forward to meeting my family. She had allowed herself to hope that she and Amy might soon be invited to Bennerley with their brother.

Our engagement had overtaken this idea, but I saw Blanche now had another design. She thought I would chaperon them in society, and this notion troubled me. I had no desire to leave my husband to go gallivanting with his sisters.

I would have to make some arrangement, for the girls did not share Justin's tendency for seclusion and, at their age, it would be wrong to deprive them of entertainments and society.

Three days had passed since we had returned from Scarborough and during that time others had made such claims on us that Justin and I had barely spent ten minutes alone together.

The next morning, Justin politely drew the fact to their attention. 'Tomorrow,' he reminded them, 'Judith must return to Leicestershire and we shall not see each other again until our wedding. So, with your permission, I intend to claim the society of my betrothed for myself, today.'

We watched a string of horses returning from exercise, wandered by the paddocks, stopped to fuss over Pink Ribbon, and strolled out into the countryside, through a wood which Justin said was famous for bluebells.

'Margaret,' he informed me, 'has given her seal of approval to our union. She says I have no idea what I am doing, but it will be interesting to watch me find out.'

'She approves of that?'

'So it would seem. She may be right. These last few weeks I have been so bemused, I can scarcely credit what is happening. Judith, do you realize that if we add up the days we have been in each other's company, they amount to less than a fortnight?'

'Does it signify?'

'My grandmother would have pointed it out, and told me it can hardly be sensible.'

'Some things are better than sensible,' I pronounced. 'This is one of them.'

We climbed a hillside which seemed steep

to me, but this was nothing, he assured me, to those in the heart of Derbyshire.

'I have it in mind,' he said, 'to take you through some of the famous parts of Derbyshire, very soon after we are married. I would like you to see Dovedale and Matlock and my own favourite place, which is Lathkill Dale. We may take a tour, put up at inns along the way. What say you?'

'It sounds delightful. Can you be spared from the stables?'

'October and November is the best time. There are locals wise in weather lore, who predict a fine, dry autumn. So, before the girls return from Lincolnshire to disturb our peace, you, my dear love, shall be acquainted with the beauties of Derbyshire.'

13

'I would remind you,' Margaret Allen spoke to Amy, 'this is your brother's special time, his wedding. It is not beyond your power to put a London season out of your mind for a few days.'

Bennerley was crowded with relations come to attend our wedding.

Margaret undertook the task of advising Blanche and Amy, succeeding so well that my uncle, the Earl of Ramsgate, had pronounced them to be pleasing, modest girls.

Justin was much as usual, reserved but pleasing. 'I confess, I was diverted by the way your uncle spoke of my business,' he said. 'Breeding horses is, to him, but another way of farming.'

'And so it is, when one comes to think of it.'

'So I am to be elevated from horse-trader to gentleman farmer by the use of semantics,' he observed.

'It will do no harm. Do not forget you have a title, sir.'

'And connections,' he added wickedly.

My friend Sophie was touring the continent

with her duke and could not attend our wedding, but she was represented by her parents. Mrs Burton had claimed kinship to my betrothed on account of her father being cousin to his grandmother.

I teased him about being third cousin to a duchess.

'I see you have been deceiving me,' he said. 'In view of this connection, I am a more eligible suitor than I supposed.'

'Yes, indeed. You are far too grand for me.'

'When you look at me like that, Judith, I am in grave danger of forgetting to be a gentleman.'

Other friends were absent from my wedding: Sir Matthew and Lady Hargreaves had gone into Essex for Richard's wedding to Isobel. I confess, I felt a pang of regret that Richard and I could not be witness at each other's nuptials.

For all this, there was a crowd at Bennerley. In the bustle of preparations, I began to suffer some disagreeable feelings. Wedding fright, I told myself, but reasoning did not change it.

Sometimes I would look at Justin and see, not the man I had yearned for, but a stranger, someone remote and unknowable. Sometimes I thought of Bennerley, safe Bennerley, where

I had been born and where I was known all around the neighbourhood, and I would quail at the distance of Melrose Court, where I must establish myself among strangers.

Seeking refuge in my own apartment, I took my prayer-book, reading through the marriage service, reflecting on the importance and solemnity of the vows I must take, weeping a little for what I would be leaving, trembling a little at the prospects before me.

The door opened to admit Helen. 'Here is a letter for you. I think it is from Mrs Armstrong.'

'Oh! At last! I wondered why I had not heard from her.'

The letter, from the lady who had once been my companion and chaperon, contained her sincere wishes for my happiness.

I had been rather hurt at not hearing from her before, for I had always considered that lady one of my most trusted friends, and I had written to tell her of my engagement some time ago, whilst we were at Scarborough.

The delay was explained: Mrs Armstrong had been much occupied in caring for an invalid sister. As a result, all her correspondence had been neglected during the past few weeks.

'You know, Helen, I mislike the sound of

this,' I said, looking up from the letter. 'Mrs Armstrong tells me her sister is suffering with the jaundice. I fear for the poor lady: her end cannot be long. Well, I shall pray for her.'

Conscientious as a brother and guardian, Hugh had engaged Mrs Armstrong to be my chaperon and companion. There had been times when I wondered if he had truly known what he was about when he had chosen that particular lady.

Hugh would not have objected to the way she taught me how to assess new acquaintance, or how to encourage some and repel others.

He might have smiled, had he heard her expressing some absurd opinion for the sake of teaching me to recognize error and gain experience in judgement and understanding. He would have smiled had he heard us giggling together when we had observed ambitious ladies attempting to captivate him. He would have looked askance, however, to learn she had no compunction about mentioning carnal desires: she had assured me that, whatever society might pretend, it was quite natural for a woman to have passions.

'They tell young ladies a gentleman's passions are stronger than a woman's,' she said. 'Do not believe it! Always, we put ourselves at risk of child-bearing, of extreme pain, and never can we be certain of survival. Our passions are strong indeed, strong enough to make us ignore the danger.'

It was because of her teachings that, observing Hugh's demeanour when he first introduced me to Helen, I knew my brother had fallen in love. I had been happy for him, then anxious, for clearly something was wrong between them.

'Is there nothing we can do?' I asked.

'Leave them to themselves,' advised Mrs Armstrong. 'You may depend upon it, they will come together in their own time.'

'I hate to see Hugh so unhappy.'

'Your brother is a kind and honourable man but just a little too used to having his own way. His present uncertainty will do no harm. He will value happiness the more for it.'

I had never known what had caused the trouble, but I had been as relieved and happy as Hugh himself when he wrote to tell me he was engaged.

A year after Hugh married, circumstances in Mrs Armstrong's family had obliged me to let her go. Hugh had brought me to Bennerley, with the intention of finding another companion. He had never done so, for Helen and I had learnt to love each other so well that I remained with them.

I sighed, recalled to the present when Helen chuckled, 'Why so sad, Judith? It is hardly a compliment to your bridegroom to be sighing so, when it is your wedding day, tomorrow.'

'I was thinking over the past and how very much I shall miss you and Hugh,' I said. 'You will write to me often, will you not? I quite depend upon you to tell me all your news.'

'We shall write and we shall visit,' promised Helen. 'Since we may now be assured of a comfortable mattress!'

Helen and I had made an excursion to town, had sallied forth to different warehouses and, as well as all the usual bolts of linen and calico and muslin and cambric, I had ordered pillows and mattresses of the finest goose down. I had also purchased other items to make myself comfortable at Melrose Court.

I had chosen wallpapers, and brocades in the fashionable floral stripe: I had sent to Aubusson for carpets: furniture, had I chosen, elegant Grecian sophas, chairs and window-seats and chiffoniers and tables. I had become bemused by a variety of chandeliers, candelabra and wall-sconces.

I had fittings for my bridal clothes,

restraining the impulses of my dressmaker, insisting on plain silk, allowing pearl buttons, refusing beads, embroidery and lace trimmings.

My wedding gift for Justin required some thought, but I determined at last upon a most handsome watch and chain, a hunter, the silver case engraved with a design of my own, with two Js, intertwined, set around a couple on horseback.

Justin's present for me was a pair of miniature portraits, painted on ivory, of the people I loved best, after himself. Hugh at his most benign, Helen at her most mischievous.

'How cleverly the artist has captured their expressions,' I exclaimed. 'They are so exactly like.'

'I thought it would please you to have their likenesses.'

When I was a little girl, the bell-ringers of Bennerley had promised me a full peal on the day of my wedding. They began in the early mists of morning one day in late September, and continued for three hours, calling out across the country of Leicestershire that Judith Tremaine was to take a husband.

My most vivid memory of that morning was the sound of bells. I awoke to the sound of bells, was hugged and kissed to the sound of bells, laughed and cried to the sound of bells, and was dressed to the sound of bells.

Time took on a new quality: I felt I was suspended in some far away place, whilst all around me figures drifted by in a changing pattern of colour. There was Helen, quietly elegant in coffee and cream, one of my aunts, resplendent in gold and black. Margaret Allen in lilac, a child in white, and ladies in pink, or peach or yellow, and my bridesmaids, Blanche and Amy, in misty blue gauze with white flowers around their bonnets.

The peal continued: someone fastened the buttons at my back, and when they had finished dressing me, Helen took my arm guiding me towards a looking-glass and I trembled, startled by the radiant creature in a gown of shimmering silk who stood in a pool of sunlight, dark eyes wide and staring.

A line of carriages stood in the courtyard, all of them polished, gleaming paint and brass and harness, and the horses, shining dark coats, plaited manes, hooves glossy with oil, all groomed to perfection, waiting to convey the company to church. I stood watching, as ladies adjusted their bonnets, picked up their gloves and left to take their places in the congregation.

I was left alone with Hugh. We stared at each other as the sound of bells echoed around the house. He came forward, took my hand and raised it to his lips, and suddenly we felt we were children again and lost all sense of decorum and, to the sound of bells we ran, laughing, my brother and I, hand in hand, down the grand staircase.

We recovered our dignity when we saw the servants gathered in the hall. Here the sound of bells was punctuated by a great sentimental sigh as I passed by, on my way to my wedding.

To the sound of bells I stepped into my carriage and was conveyed to the church to the sound of bells.

The bells grew louder as we approached the church and I saw they had called forth the villagers from round about, who now stood at the gates to watch. Some let forth 'oh's' and 'ah's' and some waved and cheered and shouted good wishes. I waved back, smiling though my eyes had grown misty.

Hugh handed me down from the carriage and Blanche and Amy came forward, fussing with my gown and handing me a little posy of garden flowers and herbs, myrtle and lavender and rosemary.

There was profound silence when the bells

were brought to rest: then the church clock chimed the hour of my wedding and I took Hugh's arm and entered that place, looking beyond the congregation to the man who waited at the altar.

There he was, looking pleased and embarrassed and very handsome indeed in his new blue coat and white stock. I met his eyes, and felt my heart swell in a great surge of joy.

We were wed, a brief ceremony, I felt, for an occasion which joined two people together in a holy, lifelong union.

When it was done, I took my husband's arm and we left the church and crossed a path which had been strewn with flowers, ducking and laughing as we were showered with rice and wheat. We stepped into our carriage to all the dear good wishes of our friends and another joyous, exultant ring of bells.

'Judith!' We had turned to each other as our carriage moved away and Justin reached for my hand. Now he said, almost in tones of surprise, 'You are my wife!'

I felt laughter gurgling in my throat. 'Yes, sir.'

'I — I can scarce believe it is true.' Shaking his head a little, he added, 'Never could I quite rid myself of the feeling that something would occur to prevent it.'

'Nothing can prevent, sir. We have been married for ten whole minutes.' Then I added, mock-plaintively, 'Ten whole minutes we have been wed, and you have not kissed me, yet.'

He smiled and looked at me without speaking. My heart thudded as his fingertips touched my cheek, and his lips, featherlight, brushed against my own, soft and tantalizing, before claiming my mouth in a kiss that was firm and sweet and lasted a long time.

We parted, each a little breathless and too full of emotion for speech. We returned to Bennerley, hands clasped, but in silence, scarce knowing what we were thinking.

A wedding breakfast had been set out in the long saloon and there we assembled and everyone shook Justin's hand and kissed me. Our health was drunk and for the first time I heard myself called Lady Martin. We toasted the bridesmaids and smiled at Amy and Blanche as they blushed. We ate rout-cakes, we called in the servants to drink punch.

We did not linger long, for we were to journey into Derbyshire that same day: only two hours after I had stepped into the church to be married, I stood with my bridegroom beside the new travelling carriage which had been Hugh's wedding gift.

We hugged and kissed all three of my sisters-in-law; I cuddled my nephew, and clung in brief sorrow to my brother at this moment of our parting.

'You will be happy, my dear,' he said gruffly. 'But oh! how we are going to miss you! Bennerley will never be the same.'

'We shall visit,' I sobbed. 'And you must visit us, as often as may be.'

So it was with mingled feelings of sorrow and joy that I took my seat in the carriage and I was sobbing still as we set off. Justin took my hand, and slipped an arm around me and held me against him. By and by, I was comforted.

To spare ourselves the necessity of resting the horses, we hired post-horses, stopping to change the teams along the way. On the journey we talked, snatched kisses when no one was looking and, as we drew closer to home, Justin pointed out the occasional landmark and I learnt a little about the county which was now my home.

Arriving at Melrose Court we were greeted by servants, and drank tea in the drawing-room. At this point, we began to feel a little awkward, a little self-conscious, and I stared at my left hand, aware of the implications of that bright gold band which now encircled my finger.

It was a relief when Justin suggested we should visit the stables and make certain that all was well with the horses.

We took lanterns and went out. The horses were quiet and all we heard were a few snorts as we passed.

When we had reached the furthest corner of the furthest paddock, Justin set his lantern down on the ground and took mine from me and set that down, also. Then he drew me towards him and in the darkness his eyes gleamed and his teeth gleamed as he tilted my chin and claimed my mouth with his own. He gathered me into his arms and I felt his heart thudding against mine and we kissed and kissed again and wanted never to stop.

We agreed, demurely, that we were both tired after such a long day and it would be sensible to retire early.

Betty was waiting for me when I entered our bedchamber, and I was undressed and washed and powdered and my hair brushed. I noticed that someone had been taking pains: the furniture and floors gleamed softly in the candlelight and a smell of beeswax mingled with the scent of lavender from the bowl on the dresser which Betty stirred with her hand before leaving me.

I had brought the Blue John with me. I

took it out, turning it in my hand as I had done so many times before, watching the play of candlelight on the silver surround, tracing my finger on the cool, polished stone.

The door opened to reveal Justin in his nightshirt and there was surprise in his eyes as he saw what I held out to him.

'I have brought your grandfather's luck home,' I said. 'This is where it belongs.'

He took it from me, wonderingly. 'How did you know?'

'Someone recognized it and told me about it. I knew I must one day return it to you.'

'Today it has brought me more than my share of luck,' he said softly. He placed it on the dresser and his candle beside it and turned back to me. 'How lovely you look with your hair let down.' He took my hair, bunching it in his hands, stooped to press a kiss on my forehead and, as I raised my hand to touch his cheek, my fingertips encountered smooth skin and I knew and was pleased that he had shaved before coming to me.

On the dresser, two candle flames burned, side by side, steadily into the night. He took my hands, raising me from my chair and led me towards the bed. He kissed me, murmured words of love, and I held him close, tracing the line of his jaw with my lips, letting my hands creep over his shoulders, spreading my palms across the strong muscles of his back. I felt a tremor run through him, and he stilled my sudden trembling with soft touches and soothing words.

'Be easy now, my love, my dearest one, be easy. All is well.'

Our breathing deepened, our caresses, shy at first, grew gradually bolder, more delightful, as we encouraged each other to greater intimacy. There was heat and moisture in me, a fierce ache as I drifted to the edge of abandonment.

'Now!' I gasped, and after a brief, awkward fumbling he pushed himself into me with one great thrust and I screamed with a sudden, sharp shock of pain as my maidenhead was lost.

He was still, waiting long enough for the hurt to pass, then he laughed and kissed me and I was moving, gasping, exulting in the rhythm of his body as we became husband and wife together.

14

I lost no time setting my own stamp on Melrose Court.

My maid had led me to believe I would deal easily with the housekeeper, and I discovered the woman anxious to please me.

How she could keep order amongst the servants was another matter. I said, 'I do not wish to be forever settling disputes in the servants' hall. That must be your responsibility.'

'Yes, My Lady. We have very little trouble of that nature. I assure you.'

'I am very happy to hear it. However, there will be changes. I intend to increase the number of staff, and I shall rely on you to keep everything in a regular train. Certain I am you will deal well with the footmen I brought with me. Wright and Gilmour have been in my brother's service. They know my ways, and should be valuable to you. Now, we need more housemaids.'

Mrs Payne spoke for two village girls. 'Good girls, My Lady, both coming up to twelve years old, and their mothers would be glad to have them close to the village.'

I gave her permission to engage them, advised her she might have more, then informed her how I intended the refurbishing of Melrose Court. 'The master and I will be away in mid-October,' I said, 'I wish the work done during our absence.'

I gave instructions on the matter, told her I wished my servants in livery and went on to make enquiries about sewing women, washerwomen and orders for produce, coal and candles. I ended by giving my approval to the dinner menu for the day.

She looked a little bemused when she left: I sat back and drew a deep breath, reasonably satisfied with Mrs Payne and even better satisfied with myself. I felt I had shown the right mixture of authority and affability: Mrs Payne would find me approachable, but she would not doubt that I was mistress.

Justin had gone out to inspect the stables whilst I had been closeted with the housekeeper, and he had not yet returned. The window from this room overlooked the gardens and I stood gazing out, vaguely considering the need to hire gardeners and speculating on the possibility of having hothouses built.

It was a subject which could not command my attention for long, on this, the day after my wedding. Somewhere a clock chimed nine: only twenty-four hours ago I had stepped into the church at Bennerley. I shed a few sentimental tears as I recalled the bells, the service and all the friends I had left.

There was a vague, pleasing ache in a certain part of my body, reminding me that I was now a married woman, and I chuckled with a secret amusement. For some had warned against disappointment if I did not, at first, find married life agreeable, and I had believed myself as well prepared for my wedding night as any virgin could be.

Pleasure, I had wished to give and hoped I might share, but nothing had taught me to expect so many spasms of delight, and never had I imagined there could be such an intense, culminating moment, when we had both convulsed in the grip of an all consuming turbulence of sensations, before collapsing together into a breathless and wondering embrace.

Justin had stirred eventually and raised his head and we looked at each other in a new way. Then he turned onto his back and pulled me with him so that my head was on his chest, and his arms tightened around me, and he rained kisses on me and murmured endearments. 'My love, my love, my dearest love.'

I, sobbing with the strength of my feelings, could only repeat his name, over and over.

'Do you recall what you said?' he had murmured. 'This is better than sensible.' He sighed. 'How right you were!'

I had fallen asleep in his arms and stirred at dawn, my mouth finding his instinctively, even before I was properly awake. We had been roused to another coupling, and this time it had been different, languorous and lazy, with more of tenderness than passion.

A fluttering inside reminded me where my thoughts were dwelling and I checked myself and blushed, even though I was alone. Then, with a sudden need to occupy myself, I put on my spencer and went out into the stable yard to find my husband.

He was there, talking to Jessop, his head groom, and he smiled when he saw me, a faint tinge of colour invading his cheeks and causing my own colour to rise again. But I smiled and walked towards him and he came forward to offer his arm, and dismissed Jessop with some instruction about a farrier.

'We have a filly with a tendency to peck a little to one side,' he said. 'Twice this month she has cast a shoe.'

'A nuisance,' I said, frowning. Such a flaw

would lessen the value of the beast. 'Can you correct her?'

'Were I able to ride her, I might, but she is young and she is not up to my weight. I must speak with Smartie.'

'Smartie?'

'Smartie Smith. Have I not mentioned him? Once he was a jockey, now he works for me. He is light enough to ride young horses, yet he is strong, with the skill to manage the most headstrong beast. I was fortunate indeed to procure his service.'

'Oh, I have heard of him.' Samuel Smith, popularly known as 'Smartie', had ridden Lord Marlpool's horses, winning several prestigious races, but he had fallen from favour when he had a valuable beast shot dead, without consulting His Lordship. The horse had broken a leg, the master was not available for consultation, and anyone with sense would have commended Smartie for his action: Marlpool had not.

Justin, I knew, would behave in an entirely different manner: with him, a man who failed to put a beast out of such misery would fall from favour. 'I fancy Smartie must feel himself fortunate to be here,' I said. 'Hugh has been heard to wonder what happened to him. Oh, Justin, I do love you!'

A remark which changed the conversation

entirely, in a most satisfactory way.

Over breakfast, he told me that every other thing in the stables was going forward in a regular way, and that he was not needed.

'It is mortifying,' he said, not looking at all mortified, 'to discover that Jessop is perfectly capable of keeping order without my presence and instruction. I now perceive myself as a useless creature, there only to be humoured by my men.'

'And I now perceive I must practise the wifely art of soothing a husband's wounded feelings. I shall begin directly by saying it is greatly to your credit that you have the vision and wisdom to employ those who are of trustworthy character who can be expected to use good sense.'

I spoke in a bantering way and Justin laughed, but what I said was true, and not just of the grooms. The household servants appeared willing, even eager, to accept the changes I intended.

That afternoon held a magical quality for me: Justin took me out in the gig to show me the countryside. The leaves were just beginning to take on their rich autumn colours, and hedges were wine-dark with berries. Patches of moss and lichen on the dry stone walls seemed to speak to me with a message of welcome: the air was fresh and cool with the scent of damp earth and the sunlight threw gilded ripples over all. It was a rich, dancing, laughing afternoon, in accordance with my mood.

There were trees overhanging the road and something fell into my lap, a green prickly thing, split open to show a glossy sheen of the fruit within. I laughed and showed it to Justin.

'Horse chestnut!' I said. 'A good omen, think not you?'

He smiled. 'I think there could be none better.'

He began to teach me of the villages within proximity, and the names seemed to conjour up the same magic: Clay Cross, Normanton and Wingerworth.

Presently, he went on to ask me about my horse, Jupiter, and what arrangements should be made about stabling for him.

'He does not care to be out in all weather,' I said. 'In summer he is happy in a paddock, but he likes his comforts, and prefers a stable in winter. But Justin, he is a gelding and of no use here. A pity, I grant you, but never would Hugh allow me to ride a stallion.'

'Indeed, I should hope not! Well, my dear, you will need him, because for all the horses I have here, there are times when none can be available. When mares come near to foaling we do not ride them. Your brother said he would send Jupiter.'

'Do you wish to keep him?' Jupiter was expensive in his upkeep, and though the offer caused me some pain, I made it. 'It would profit us to sell him and purchase another mare.'

'Profit is not the question, here. I know Jupiter is a favourite of yours. I wish you to keep him. You may harness him to the gig, also, should you have need. I have seen how well you drive.'

I was recalled to the day of our picnic and the quarrel between us as I drove home. His colour was heightened, and I guessed he was thinking of it, too.

'Yes, I flatter myself I drive rather well,' I said. 'Even in the worst of humours!'

'You had reason for ill humour, that day, as I recall. Never have I — I confess, I hardly knew myself! It was jealousy, of course. I had heard much about how fond you were of Hargreaves and I had observed your demeanour when conversing with him. You had a great deal to say to each other.'

'Well, now I can tell you what I could not reveal then: most of our conversation concerned Isobel Townshend.'

'Indeed? Then I cannot wonder at your displeasure.'

'Isobel is a dear girl and deserved better treatment than she had from Richard. Besides,' I added. 'I had another reason for displeasure that day, for he demanded my attention when I entertained hopes of spending time with a different gentleman.'

'Am I permitted to know who?'

'If you cannot guess, sir, I shall think you a simpleton.'

'Oh, Judith!'

Fortunately there were no one in sight, for here my husband lost all sense of decorum, and stopped the gig, seizing me in his arms and kissing me in a rough, unmannerly way, which crushed the breath from my body and delighted me excessively.

When he let me go, I chuckled and tidied myself and teased him but left him in no doubt of my sentiments. And indeed, I was greatly moved by this shedding of his customary restraint.

I felt the compliment of it all the more because I knew he had been hurt, and I knew also that those who have been so hurt do not easily demonstrate their feelings. Something important had happened, and though I did not perfectly comprehend it, I understood that I had broken through one of his reservations.

That night he was bold enough to suggest

the removal of our night attire and I giggled and made him promise not to tell. I knelt before him, trembling a little as he made me naked, and felt a deep tremor run through me when I saw the look in his eyes. Then he pulled off his nightshirt and I stared at him, fascinated by the swell of his muscles, the golden glints in the hair on his chest and the darker hair around his genitals.

'How beautiful you are!' I reached for him and our coupling was instant and over very quickly, but we held each other for a long time afterwards, kissing and talking until we were roused again, coupled again, and fell asleep with our bodies entwined.

'Today is Sunday,' Justin murmured one morning. 'I know our neighbours are impatient to determine how pretty you are, how well we are suited, what a handsome couple we make. Wear your most stylish bonnet, madam. We go to church to be looked at.'

I chuckled. 'Is that the reason for going to church? Pardon me! I thought it was for divinc worship.'

He appeared to give the matter some consideration. 'That also,' he agreed at last.

'And you, sir? Why do you go? Is it' — I rubbed my finger against his morning stubble — 'is it to repent your sins?'

'No, madam. I go to give thanks — for yours!'

We were looked at, as much as was seemly. Upon leaving, there were smiles and bows from strangers, who went on their way whilst I exchanged civilities with a couple named Kirk, particular friends of Justin's, whom he made a point of introducing. Later, he asked my opinion of them, and I was pleased I could say I looked forward to knowing them better.

He went on, 'You understand how I cannot always be going into society. I prefer to have a few close friends with whom I can be easy, rather than a wide circle of acquaintance.'

'I confess, I am inclined to share your sentiments,' I said, 'but only by making acquaintance can we begin to make friends.'

He laughed. 'True, O wise one!'

'Here in Derbyshire,' I went on, 'I have as yet, no friends other than yourself. Who is the dark-haired young lady who wore green? I thought she looked a pleasing, sensible girl. She was with an older gentleman.'

'Colonel Makepeace and his daughter, Charlotte,' Justin informed me. 'I believe you have heard them mentioned?'

'The lady who performs so exquisitely on the pianoforte?'

'I believe she performs well. I have dealings with the colonel from time to time but, as I have said, I do not often venture into society. I have not been privileged to hear her.'

'What of Blanche and Amy? Do they know her?'

I judged her of an age to be intimate with the girls, but Justin thought they had only a lukewarm friendship.

There had been another family at church who, even allowing for natural curiosity, had seemed a little too pointed in their interest. Neither had they struck me as friendly: I thought they had been looking to find fault.

I asked about them. 'Who are the elderly couple with two daughters?'

'The Cartwrights.'

The brevity of his tone and the stiffening of his posture told me I was not mistaken. 'What have you against them?'

'Nothing at all.' But his smile was strained as he added, 'Truly, I have no quarrel with them. But there is something I should tell you, for if I do not, others will, and I would not have you distressed by what is past and matters not at all.'

He went on to tell me the Cartwrights had another daughter, Arabella, who had married and gone to live in Somerset. 'I was engaged to that lady, when it was believed I had expectations of my own. When the truth emerged, after my father's death, I was obliged to release her from our engagement.'

I experienced a peculiar hollow feeling inside, and could say no more than: 'I see.'

'Judith, you have never been poor, so it may be difficult for you to understand, but she had no money of her own and how could I insist she made so imprudent a marriage?'

'You could not.' All kinds of horrid thoughts ran through my mind. Most of the time, I could forget I had proposed to him, but I was uneasy to discover that somewhere in the world was another lady, to whom he had proposed.

His voice took on a gentle tone. 'Judith, you know I love you. I tell you this, for you are certain to hear of it and there are some who pretend to be wiser than they are. You may believe,' he went on, 'I can most fervently rejoice and give thanks for circumstances preventing that marriage, for I would not have happiness to equal that which you have brought me.'

I smiled at him and disguised my uneasiness. And because he had much to say on the subject of his love for me, and embraced me at the first opportunity, I soon felt better.

Reflecting on it later, I understood the wisdom of his mentioning the matter and laughed at my own jealousy. For it would be remarkable indeed, had he not reached the age of eight-and-twenty without liking some lady.

He was married to me now, and he was happy. He said so, but more telling was the light in his eyes and the laughter which frequently crept into his voice.

It was a happiness which I would take pains to preserve. Arabella what's-her-name mattered not at all.

15

'Justin, please wait! I must rest for a moment.'

Since the path was narrow, and overhung with brambles here and there, Justin had taken the lead, holding back the growth for me. Now I stood in the middle of a wilderness, horribly aware of the weakness and frailty of womankind.

'What is wrong, Judith, are you ill?'

'I am uncomfortable. I told you, my bleeding time has come. I have some pain, but it will pass.'

Justin, having sisters, had required no explanation of my condition. I had, I confess, been relieved when the bleeding came for though I hoped to bear children I was by no means eager to begin at once.

Clearly, though, this was to be one of the bad times. 'I am sorry,' I said. 'I should not have undertaken this excursion, but truly, I thought all would be well, for I am not one who suffers, as a rule. There have been but few occasions when — ' I broke off, gasping a little, and felt my face drain of colour as I was seized by cramps. 'Oh dear!'

He came to me, holding me, supporting me until the worst had passed. 'We cannot stay here,' he said. 'Can you go on?'

'I have a vinaigrette of hartshorn in my reticule. Can you find it?'

He did so and held the sharp salts under my nose, reviving me for the time being. 'How are you feeling, now?'

'Better, though I confess I wish nothing so much as to curl up in bed! Do we have far to go?'

'Some distance, I fear, but the path becomes easier and I will help you.'

I had been eager to see this place, for Justin had expressed a liking for it. It was a long walk, impossible to go on horseback, but I had not shrunk from the prospect. We had left the carriage in a place called Monyash and descended a rock-strewn path into a dale which was lonely and sombre, even when the growth was decked in autumnal colours. The only sound was the harsh cry of kestrels wheeling in the sky. Yet this wilderness spoke to me with a rough friendliness.

We had come upon the river, the Lathkill, before pain took me and since we had come so far, Justin said, it was senseless to turn back, for walking on was easier and our carriage was to meet us at the other end of the dale.

We went on when the pains relented, with Justin assisting me to walk. We stopped when the cramps seized me again and he held and supported me and when, in the end, a respite would not come, he lifted me and carried me. despite my protests.

Thankfully, I was at last settled in the carriage, and Justin wrapped me in his greatcoat and regarded me in some concern. 'Does this happen every time?'

'No, indeed. I can perfectly recall the last time because it was Christmas. Not last Christmas, either, but the one before. So you see, it is by no means a regular occurrence and I had no thought but that all would be well. I am sorry, sir, to bring our excursion to such a poor ending.'

'That does not signify. Is there something you can take for your relief? Some laudanum, perhaps, if I can procure some?'

'No, certainly not. Laudanum is an opium drug and can induce dependency. I never take it.' Mrs Armstrong had been most strenuous in advising me thus. 'I will weather this pain, sir, for I know I will be better tomorrow. But if you do not object, I believe I will forego dinner and go directly to bed.'

We were staying at an inn in Bakewell and arriving there I discovered Justin had determined upon a remedy. 'Brandy in hot water,' he ordered. 'It can do no harm and may bring relief.'

It did, though I found the loving concern most comforting. Worn out by exertion and pain, I fell asleep soon after climbing into bed, waking briefly in the night to discover my husband was close, his body curled snugly around my own.

As I had predicted, I had no pain the next morning, though I felt weak and was not sorry to be going home. We had been away for ten days, wonderful days, travelling the county, moving first southwards to Derby, turning west to Ashbourne, returning northwards and eastwards, taking in Matlock and Bakewell.

The important part had been having my husband to myself. We exchanged views, expressed opinions and laughed together, strengthening a bond of friendship as well as love.

I had arranged that the refurbishing at Melrose Court should take place whilst we were away. I had made Justin sensible of all my intentions, a little warily in case his pride should revolt against so many changes being made at his wife's expense. Had he voiced the least objection, I would have taken heed. But he did not, neither did his expression betray any displeasure. His was a generosity which understood that, to be comfortable, I wished for the house to be pleasing, also.

'I know very well, my dear,' he said, 'that you would soon wish for a return to the elegance of Bennerley, were I to forbid changes. Make whatever dispositions you choose.'

I had no wish to imitate Bennerley: I looked for elegance but here there was also the need for practicality. I hoped to combine lightness and warmth, to combine pride of place with comfort and ease. Much advice had I sought, and spent many hours planning. Now, I was impatient to see the result.

Returning home, we inspected the alterations. For the hall I had chosen wallpaper with a yellow background and a chain pattern of brown leaves; with new wall sconces and polishing on the wainscot and staircase; the effect was most pleasing.

In the drawing-room, the hideous fireplace had vanished and in its place stood a plain marble affair in the Rumford style with a gleaming mahogany fender. The walls were papered with an ivy-leaf design and a fine carpet from Aubusson had been laid. Sofas faced each other on either side of the fireplace, chairs and little tables were placed at convenient intervals and my pianoforte stood at the far end of the room.

I waited impatiently for Justin's reaction: when, at last, we came to the great dining-room, he drew in a deep breath and laughed. 'How very fine we are become!'

Here, I had determined on formality, with the design of offering impressive hospitality to any who might become useful in procuring customers for our horses. I had the walls papered in the fashionable floral stripe, and gold brocade hangings at the windows, handsome mahogany furniture, with fine china, glass and silverware displayed to advantage.

'For formal occasions only,' I assured him. 'We will be more comfortable dining in the breakfast-room, I think, when we have no company. Well! The application of my notions has been even more successful than I anticipated.'

The following day, Justin sent his head groom, Jessop, with a string of horses to be sold at Tattersalls.

'Do you not take them yourself?' I asked.

'I have done so in previous years,' he smiled at me. 'This year, my affairs are circumstanced otherwise.'

In the absence of Jessop he was obliged to spend more time around the stables and supervise the horses at exercise. I rode out with him when I could, but there were other matters to engage my attention, not least the visits of our neighbours.

Mr and Mrs Kirk, as Justin's particular friends, had taken the lead and there had been visits from others, also. I took a liking to the quiet, courteous Colonel Makepeace, and his daughter proved to be a pleasing, sensible sort of girl.

I was less pleased with the Cartwrights; their daughters impressed me as being sly and secretive: neither of them were pretty and they behaved in a way which would have been excusable only had they been ten years younger. They whispered to each other, giggling, and it was clear their remarks were of a disparaging nature.

I was thankful Justin had warned me, for they were quick to let me know an attachment had once existed between my husband and their own Arabella. They watched me, hoping they had discomposed me, and upon discovering I was not dismayed, they went on to imply, without being bold enough to speak openly, that only my fortune could have persuaded Justin to marry me.

'My dear Lady Martin,' said Mrs Kirk. 'I would not raise this subject had not the Cartwrights been so ill-bred as to mention it, but I beg you will allow me to acquaint you with the truth. Arabella was pretty, but much like her sisters in other respects, and amiable only when it suited her purpose. Never was your husband more fortunate than when she jilted him, and though one cannot, in general, approve of Sir Robert's extravagance, he did his son a great service by bringing about the end of that affair.'

Mrs Buxton had called and although Blanche had promised me she would soon grow colder, she showed no signs of so doing. She had gone into raptures upon seeing the alterations I had made in the drawing-room, declared that my taste was quite the equal of her own, and begged that she might venture to suggest a few, a very few, trifling rearrangements of my furniture.

'You seem to be all the fashion, Judith,' said Justin, for invitations were arriving all the time. Mrs Kirk had taken the lead, arranging a dinner party in my honour.

There was a week when we did not dine at home once, and Justin confessed himself rather tired of company and wished our neighbours would take account of our natural desire to be alone together. 'Although we cannot, with any civility, refuse these invitations,' he said. 'And soon we must begin to return them.'

'I thought of arranging a dinner party,' I said. 'Though it would be better, I think, to wait until Blanche and Amy return home.'

This plan was thrown into disarray when an express arrived for Justin. It came from Lincolnshire and contained news of a distressing nature, for Margaret Allen was obliged to inform us that the girl's aunt, Miss Fox, had suffered a seizure and, was now partly paralysed and quite unable to leave her bed.

'*The girls,*' she wrote, '*have been very much affected by this turn of events. They are desirous of your permission to remain here with their aunt, for the lady cannot possibly undertake the journey home. Indeed, I must add my own entreaties to theirs, for they have taken on much of the burden of caring for her and I believe their aunt finds in their presence a comfort which should not be denied.*'

'No, indeed,' I said when Justin read it to me. 'We must allow them to remain. Do you think we should go there, ourselves? They may wish for some of their belongings. We could take them with us.'

'Perhaps we should,' agreed Justin. He tapped the folded letter against his hand. 'I am concerned, Judith. I have imposed upon my cousin more than I knew. Margaret does not say so, but I see it is the case. A seizure of that description — I fear Miss Fox cannot recover.'

I was very still. 'You believe this is the beginning of a decline and signals her eventual demise?'

'I hope I may be mistaken. But whatever the case, I have placed a great burden upon Margaret. Miss Fox may remain bedridden for many months.'

I shared his concern, for although Margaret Allen was not a lady who would shrink from the task, it seemed unjust that it should have been so thrust upon her.

'Then write express to your cousin, sir, that she may expect us, for certainly we must go and see for ourselves how matters stand. Then we can consult together and determine what is best to be done.'

My thoughts were with Miss Fox. Distressing indeed, to be taken ill so far from home, and separated from her friends.

I looked to take with us some familiar objects which would comfort her and chose a patchwork quilt which she had worked herself, a few china ornaments and a herb pillow.

Mrs Payne thought the girls would read aloud to their aunt: upon observing their taste in literature, I added a few romances of my own which I thought would entertain them.

'There is a portrait,' suggested Mrs Payne, 'which is precious to Miss Fox. Her sister, the former Lady Martin.'

She showed it to me, a head and shoulders portrait of Blanche and Amy's mother. Her hair was powdered and dressed elaborately high in the fashion of her time and she wore silks and pearls. But I could detect little expression in her blue eyes, and there was something mechanical about the curve of the lips which gave an impression of emptiness.

Justin told me it was painted by a local artist, who had captured her features but nothing of her character. 'Not,' he added, 'that my stepmama was a strong character. However, she was kind. Miss Fox will be pleased to have the portrait.'

We were shocked, upon arriving in Lincolnshire, to witness the pallor and fatigue in Blanche and Amy.

'Justin, I am so glad you are come!' exclaimed Margaret. 'You must exert your authority at once, and demand these girls have a care for themselves. They refuse to leave their aunt's side, even though they know she receives every attention.'

Justin nodded slowly. His expression was carefully impassive which taught me he had read the truth. Miss Fox, propped against many pillows, was already shrunken. Her countenance was twisted, and her speech, coming only through the left side of her mouth, was laboured and difficult to comprehend. She was, however, quite sensible. Death would not claim her at once, but it had set its mark on her.

To Blanche and Amy he said, 'You do your aunt no service by exhausting yourselves. You must keep strong if you are to assist her recovery.'

He insisted they took a turn around the garden and I sat by the bedside, telling Miss Fox of all the kind messages our neighbours had sent. The servants carried in those things we had brought with us and happy indeed had been the thought which prompted us to bring the portrait.

The girls would have been miserable had we forbidden them to return to their aunt, but we allowed them only one hour in the sickroom, then sent them to bed. When Miss Fox herself was sleeping, we left a maid with her and went downstairs, to discuss the situation.

'No one is at fault, sir,' said Margaret, after Justin had expressed regret for imposing the care of Miss Fox upon her. 'Your sisters have done far more for the lady than I.

Indeed, my concern has been that they should have care of themselves. They insist they are young and strong, and so they are, but the shock has taken its toll. Neither girl will speak of it, but I believe they understand what the outcome will be.'

We were silent. At length, Colonel Allen roused himself. 'You may rest assured, sir, that every attention is given to her comfort. We called in the doctor immediately, an excellent man, full of sound common sense. He said to let her rest and keep her warm and comfortable and she would do very well. And so we have done, and the girls have devised some hand signals for simple requests, to spare the poor lady the labour of speech.'

'Ah, that was a good thought!' I exclaimed.

'Indeed it was, and it has proved beneficial. She can answer us yes or no, and tell us if she is uncomfortable or tired or thirsty, and such things as that. Amy thought of the scheme. Never have I understood how she can sometimes be so wise and yet so foolish at other times. Well, Justin, I know your sisters have given you little cause for pride in them, but certainly you can be proud of their conduct in this emergency.'

'I am pleased to hear it. I hope they remain serviceable, for I fear there is little assistance

I can offer. I shall do what I can, of course, but we are disadvantaged by distance.'

'It occurs to me, sir,' I said, 'that we could assist your cousin by leaving my maid here.' I turned to Margaret. 'Betty is a sensible woman and willing to be useful.'

'Oh, my dear, I could not ask that of you!' she exclaimed, but I could see she was tempted and needed only a little pressing to accept the offer, and Justin was pleased we could lend some practical help.

So it was arranged, and if Betty herself was less than enthusiastic, she was at least resigned. 'If you must make do with a housemaid for yourself, you might as well have the best of them. Tell Mrs Payne you want Hannah.'

We could stay only a few days, but whilst we were there we had a small pianoforte carried upstairs and I entertained the invalid with country airs and jigs. Such was her pleasure that I felt quite contrite to be going home.

'Do not distress yourself, Judith,' said Margaret. 'My neighbour will spare an occasional hour to play for Miss Fox.'

'It would be a kindness,' I said.

Not until we were journeying home did it occur to me that Miss Fox might have other relations, besides Blanche and Amy, who should be informed of her present infirmity, but Justin, when I asked him, told me she had none.

'Well,' he amended, 'there may be cousins in Sunderland, but never did she have contact with them. Her parents have died, of course, and my stepmama was her only sister.'

'Sunderland?'

'That is where she lived until her sister married my father. Then, since Papa was so often away, she came to keep Stepmama company and when she died, Miss Fox stayed with the girls.'

'And she kept no friends from her former life?' I knew Miss Fox was regarded with some affection by our servants and many of the village people, and was thought to be a good, kind lady, if sometimes a little foolish. 'How strange that is!'

'I had the impression she was never happy there.'

'I see. Well. I suppose that must account for her always being so rapturous about the London season! It must have been the highlight of an otherwise dull and uneventful life. And, of course, her sister met your father.'

That would have been considered a splendid match. I nodded, recalling all Amy's expectations of making a 'good' marriage, and could easily comprehend how she had come by her notions.

We were now into November and darkness came early and it was dark when we reached home after two days of travelling. Mrs Payne told us Jessop had returned also and Justin sent for him to report news concerning the stables. Some news was good, for we had made profitable transactions at Tattersalls, and some news was bad: at home, one of our mares had slipped her foal.

'It happens,' said Justin. 'What have you there, Judith?'

'A letter. I recognize the hand. It comes from my friend Sophie.' When he raised his brows, I reminded him, 'That illustrious cousin of yours, sir, previously Sophia Burton, now the Duchess of Flamborough.'

Justin ordered extra candles to be brought in and I settled myself to read in comfort. What I read had me on my feet, instantly. 'Heavens! They are travelling northwards and mean to pay us a visit. They expect to arrive here, very soon. In fact, sir, we may expect them tomorrow.'

16

They came in splendour, our illustrious guests, their chariot emblazoned with the Flamborough crest, and their servants very fine indeed in green and gold livery.

We went outside to greet them and as soon as the carriage steps were let down a small red-haired creature descended, resplendent in dark-blue velvet and a hat trimmed with satin and feathers. She was followed by a gentleman who had donned his hat, for no purpose other than doffing it as he made his bow to me.

'Your servant, ma'am. Will you do us the honour of introducing us to your husband?'

I did so, and Sophie twinkled her eyes at Justin. 'I have known Judith for many years, so it is no surprise to learn she had the good sense to marry into my family. We are related, sir, as I understand?'

Justin's reserve melted as he saw Sophie's friendliness. 'I believe we are, though I have but recently been made aware of it. The connection between us is a distant one, I fear.'

There was no shortage of conversation or

laughter as Sophie and I exchanged our news and if the gentlemen had less to say than we did, they were at least diverted by our prattling.

I heard they had been in Leicestershire and had taken the opportunity to visit Richard and Isobel. Richard had resigned his commission in the militia and was now living in a modest house, not three miles from Bennerley.

'Oh, did you see Hugh and Helen?' I demanded eagerly.

'We did, and they are both well and sent their love.'

She had more to say of Richard and Isobel. 'I believe,' she said slowly, 'it is not wise for them to live close to Richard's parents. Lady Hargreaves is still lamenting the failure of her own scheme to marry Richard to you, Judith.'

'Oh really!' I exclaimed. 'I have no patience with Lady Hargreaves. Why can she not accept the situation?'

'Had Isobel fortune to match yours, she might. She was against their marriage and gave way only because Sir Matthew prevailed upon her. When she heard news of your engagement to Sir Justin she became quite absurd, insisting that you, Judith, were marrying another expressly to set Richard free.'

'Heavens!' I exclaimed. 'How noble and self-sacrificing I am, to be sure!'

'Indeed, you are, ma'am,' said the duke. 'We have heard all about it!'

I laughed, but I was troubled by this news of my friends. Having accidentally come between them once, I had no wish to become a source of vexation now.

We talked of other matters and our husbands contributed more to the conversation. When the duke expressed an interest in the stables, we took them out of doors to show them round.

I watched the two men in satisfaction, seeing advantage for Justin in this visit. The duke was impressed with his knowledge and enterprise and since he had to purchase his horses from somewhere, I thought he should favour our stables with his custom.

In such a promising case, I wished to avoid giving offence so later I advised Sophie of Justin's aversion to card games. 'Should your husband wish for cards this evening . . . '

'Henry has no great enthusiasm for cards,' Sophie assured me. 'He plays, of course, but other matters interest him more. My Henry,' she said proudly, 'has a wider vision than most.'

As a result of this conversation, I made certain of occupying that evening in a manner which I knew would be pleasing to the gentleman.

'I understand,' I said, 'you have an interest in astronomy, sir?'

The duke admitted it and mentioned his plans to build an observatory with a greater telescope than any yet achieved.

He had the means and the leisure to pursue such an interest but he had to be encouraged to elaborate on the subject. I did so, and if my design was to be of benefit to my husband, I make no apology for it.

For the duke, the complicated mathematics of astronomy was second nature, but he was patient with our struggles to follow him. He spoke of constellations, of individual stars and of distances so vast they exceeded comprehension. He drew a diagram of the solar system and explained it. Such was his enthusiasm that we ourselves became entranced.

Had anyone observed the four cloaked figures with lanterns climbing a wooded hillside in the cold darkness of that November night they must have thought we were about some nefarious business. Had they known it was for the purpose of inspecting the heavens, they must have thought we were mad.

We reached the summit and stood upon an outcrop of millstone grit, taking turns with the duke's telescope. The scent of pine was all around us, wind soughed through the trees sounding like waves breaking on the shore. Above us, stars shone recklessly, like diamonds scattered on a cloth of black velvet.

'Stars,' I murmured, bemused by all the information I had received. 'There are thousands upon thousands of them. And so far away. Why so many? What is their purpose?'

No one answered. We had no answers, only a suspicion that understanding would be lost in the infinity of question.

Wondering and silent and remote we stood, whilst the darkness wrapped around us, isolating us from our regular lives with the spellbinding quality of a dream. Scudding clouds blotted out the moon, wind poked icy fingers into our cheeks and Sophie began to shiver. We turned away from the heavens and began our descent to the house.

Raindrops stung like nettles as we scurried indoors, laughing now, finding the warmth and comfort of our drawing-room had been enhanced by our expedition out of doors.

I arranged a dinner party whilst our guests were with us and one evening we attended a ball arranged by Colonel Makepeace for his daughter, Charlotte. Delightful as these occasions were, we four were agreed that the most memorable experience was the mystery we shared, in the darkness, on the hill.

Sophie passed on to me a letter from Helen, who reminded me they were soon to pay their annual visit to the Wysalls. Sarah meant to invite Justin and myself, also, and Helen hoped we would accept as she and Hugh longed to see us again.

When the invitation arrived, Justin saw my speculative look and asked the reason.

'I know not whether I have the courage to tell you.'

He groaned. 'Does society make yet more demands on us? Are we never to be left in peace?'

'Why, sir! Did you not like Sophie and her duke?'

He caught me, held me tight against him and kissed me until I was breathless. 'I liked them very much indeed, as you well know. But best of all, I like having you to myself.'

Who could be proof against such flattery? It was later, much later, that I told him of the invitation.

He fastened my buttons, for poor Hannah would be scandalized to be called on to dress her mistress for a second time that morning. Now he held a mirror so I could view my back through a mirror behind me. 'I believe I have it right?'

'Indeed you do and should you require a position as a lady's maid I know just the situation that would suit you.'

He laughed. 'Do you wish to accept this invitation?'

'I confess, I would like to see Hugh and Helen. And it is not so very far away, after all. Can you contrive some time away from the stables?'

Justin thought four days was the longest possible time he could be away, but Hugh and Helen were to be there for several weeks and he would allow me to stay with them, if I so wished.

'I daresay your brother will escort you home.'

'Certainly he would, should I desire it, but I would prefer to return home with you.'

Justin looked serious. 'I fear, Judith, there will come a time when you will wish yourself less beset by circumstance. I cannot move in society in the way that I ought, and there is little entertainment for you here.'

I begged him not to make himself uneasy on that account. 'Never have I considered parties and balls to be the main business of my life. I wish this visit only because I long to see Hugh and Helen.'

I wrote to Sarah and to Helen, and then set about writing a long letter to Margaret Allen and the girls. I received replies, which I read aloud to Justin.

The girls were hopeful, for their aunt was showing signs of improvement. They mentioned the books I had taken for them. Miss Fox had been delighted by *Evelina* which they had read aloud to her. Amy had now begun a second perusal of the novel.

I laughed. 'I knew that book would interest Amy,' I said. 'It is about a young lady having her London season.'

'Oh, Judith, do you encourage her?'

Margaret had written to say Miss Fox was comfortable and there was no reason to suppose her in any immediate danger.

'I think we may visit the Wysalls with a clear conscience,' observed Justin. 'What of your other letter, Judith?'

'It is from Mrs Armstrong.'

She had written to advise me of her new direction. Her sister had died and she was now staying with friends as she looked about her for a situation. Her letter was short enough to make me suspect she was exhausted, and I fretted, for there was nothing I could do to help her.

'I do wish she was not so far away,' I said.

'Surely her friends will not allow her to take up a new situation too soon?'

'If she is distressed for money, she may do so, regardless.'

The stables were busy in an orderly way. Justin spent some time with the horses, but he was also much occupied indoors, writing letters of business and dealing with his accounts.

All was in good order and we felt we could be easy in our minds as we set off to visit the Wysalls.

At Brinsley Park, after we had exchanged our news, I asked Helen what she knew of mischief caused by Lady Hargreaves.

Helen confessed she knew nothing. 'Lady Hargreaves has made no insinuations to us and none of our neighbours has mentioned any such nonsense. Perhaps Sophie was mistaken?'

'She was not. Helen, could you discover what is occurring? Whatever nonsense Lady Hargreaves is proposing, I cannot believe Isobel imagines I am hankering after Richard for Sophie thought of a scheme to dispel any suspicion of that nature.'

Sophie had hit upon a notion which would appear innocent of any design. 'When I write to Isobel,' she said, 'I shall tell her of our visit here. I shall go on to describe how touching it is to see our forceful, rational Judith so besottedly in love! I believe I shall be quite witty on the subject!'

Helen laughed when I told her. 'Such a letter will dispel any suspicion that you wished for Richard,' she said, 'but it will not serve if she believes Richard is hankering after you.'

'Oh dear! I had not thought of that! In such a case, even Richard may have difficulty in convincing her.'

Helen promised to investigate. 'Should I uncover mischief, you may depend upon it, I shall exert myself to restore good sense.'

Mr Wysall had arranged for the gentlemen to join a shooting party the next day, and I was pleased, for Justin would enjoy good sport and good company. I had no objection to being left alone with the ladies for I was easier with these familiar friends than I could yet be with my new neighbours.

Helen surprised me by saying, 'You know, Judith, should Mrs Armstrong require a situation, you would do well to engage her yourself, for the time is coming when someone must replace Miss Fox as companion for the girls.'

I stared at her. 'Could I do that, I wonder?'

'I think you should. For even if Miss Fox

recuperates, her health will not allow her to go about in society, and the girls must be chaperoned. I would advise against taking on the burden yourself. Can you think of anyone better than Mrs Armstrong?'

I liked the scheme and when we retired for the night, I put it to Justin. 'The girls are of an age when they should mix in society and Mrs Armstrong will teach them a great deal.'

'She may try, but will they take heed of her?' Justin sighed. 'Knowing my sisters, I have to say I think it most unlikely.'

'Well now, I have a scheme which will persuade Amy, I think.' I went on to outline the notion of securing good conduct by holding out the promise of a London season.

'I do not care to make promises such as that,' he said. 'And certainly I will not consent to my sisters gadding about in London with a lady of whom I know nothing.'

'You know that Hugh had no qualms about engaging her for me,' I pointed out. 'And when you are become acquainted with her, I am persuaded you will see no objection. Besides, I was not suggesting we should promise absolutely — what I propose is more in the nature of a bargain.'

He was silent, thinking it over. 'It might

answer,' he admitted. 'But bargains have to be kept and I am by no means certain I can meet the expense of giving them a London season.'

'Oh, but I had intended — '

'To pay for it yourself? No, Judith! That which you have done for your own comfort I can accept, but I, not you, am responsible for my sisters.'

'But Justin, it is as much for myself to encourage them to learn from Mrs Armstrong. They will benefit and so will I, for I do not wish to be forever settling their disputes! A season is a small price to pay for harmony in our daily lives.'

I thought I had handled the matter with delicacy, but Justin saw my design. 'All this comes within the province of making yourself comfortable?' he asked and he laughed when I nodded. 'It will not do, Judith! We will promise a London season only when I see my way to meeting the expense.'

I agreed, meekly, as a wife should when her husband lays down the law, though I meant, later, to wheedle him into letting me have my way.

'Meanwhile,' he went on, 'I will agree that we must engage a chaperon for them. Will your friend accept the situation?'

'I cannot say for certain, but I think it most likely.'

He nodded. 'As for a season, I might have enough set aside by next year. That is, if all goes well, but I deal in horses, so how can I predict? Shall you wish to go to town with them?'

'I have many reasons for wishing to engage Mrs Armstrong,' I said, 'and one of them is precisely that I may not be obliged to do any such thing. I have not married you, sir, so that I may go gallivanting with your sisters!'

This remark changed the conversation and there was a very pleasing interlude whilst I explained, to our mutual satisfaction, exactly why I *had* married him.

17

Early in February, five days after learning that Miss Fox had taken a turn for the worse, we received an express telling us her life had ended. We were obliged to beg another indulgence from the Allens in the matter of escorting Miss Fox and the girls home, for we could not go into Lincolnshire.

Justin felt he was neglecting his duty, but our beasts did not take account of such matters and he was needed in the stables. Two foals, born prematurely, now required special care. Eight brood-mares had arrived, heavy with foal, from owners who wished them mated with Blue John and more were expected. We were growing ever more busy.

Colonel Allen had the lady coffined, hired a hearse, and a post-chaise for Margaret and the girls. The three ladies arrived earlier than expected, for Margaret had determined to travel as expeditiously as possible.

'The colonel is following the hearse,' she said, 'but I felt it best to get the girls home. They are very distressed.'

They were clearly fatigued, as pale as wraiths, and both of them had lost weight.

We took them indoors, settled them by the fire and comforted them with tea and toast.

'I confess I did not expect such an outpouring of grief,' said Margaret, when we spoke privately. 'They have been quite helpless these last three days. It cannot be good for them.'

'They have lost the lady who has been a mother to them,' said Justin soberly. 'We should not forbid them to grieve.'

'No, but they do need respite,' said Margaret. 'Do what you can to distract them, Justin.'

Justin surprised me by proving himself adept at providing distractions. First, he suggested they should look around the house to admire the alterations. Over the next two days he gave them a duty of caring for foals, encouraged them to write letters and to assist me when visitors came to condole.

'Judith needs you,' he said. 'For she scarce knew your aunt.'

'No distractions today,' he said on the third morning. 'Let them weep if they so wish. It is her funeral day, after all.'

Blanche and Amy conducted themselves with solemn dignity all through the proceedings and their tears did not surface until the mourners departed the funeral repast. Then, they collapsed into great heaving paroxysms of grief. I held them and gave them brandy and dabbed at their temples with lavender water and when at last their tears were exhausted we sent them to bed.

'I think we have seen the worst of it,' said Justin, when I exclaimed. 'Now they may begin to recover.'

He turned to Colonel Allen. 'Now, sir, I do not forget you have been put to some expense over all this. You must give me an account of it, that I may reimburse you.'

The matter was dealt with, but this exchange brought to my mind a matter to which no one had yet given any thought. 'Justin,' I said, 'what of Miss Fox's affairs? Did she leave any money?'

They all turned to stare at me. 'None that I know of,' said Justin. 'What gave you that idea, Judith?'

'I did not suppose she had fortune,' I said slowly, 'but I did think — Sir, did you give her an allowance?'

'I did not,' he said, looking rather shaken. 'You are right, I should have done so. I should have thought of it, but I confess I did not! Heavens! How remiss I have been!'

'Nonsense!' I said quickly. 'If she was distressed for money, then surely the girls would have told you so! No, she had some little fund of her own, she must have, for I know she had a subscription with a circulating library, and we may presume she purchased her own items and apparel.'

Four of us examined what was known of her expenditure which led us to estimate an income of forty pounds a year. Colonel Allen suggested such an income would most likely come from a capital of £1,000 invested in the four-per-cents.

Justin said he would look into the matter. 'Blanche and Amy are her closest kin,' he said. 'If there is a legacy, they have the right of it, and it is what she would have wished.'

The next day, we were at breakfast when a footman announced that a Mr Wiseman had called and was begging the favour of a few words with Sir Justin on a matter of business.

Justin looked so astonished that I enquired the identity of Mr Wiseman. 'I believe he is a local attorney, My Lady.'

'He is!' said Amy. 'Oh Judith, may we have him in? I have never met him, you know, but I have heard so much about him!'

'He is not my attorney,' said Justin. 'Never have I had dealings with him! I cannot imagine what brings him here.'

'Well, we lose nothing by civility,' I said. I made another place at table. 'Ask Mr

Wiseman to join us, Gilmour.'

He was a strange, misshapen man, with one shoulder raised and twisted, and he had the look of a simpleton, though we quickly discovered he was no such thing.

He apologized for troubling us so soon after our sad bereavement. He himself felt the loss, he felt it most keenly. Miss Fox had been as much a friend as a client.

This immediately threw light on his reason for calling, but when I looked at Justin he seemed wholly dazed and bewildered. So, as I offered cocoa, and pressed hot rolls and butter and pound cake upon our visitor, I spoke for my husband. 'I take it you have something to say about Miss Fox's affairs?'

'I have indeed, My Lady, indeed I have. Miss Fox was so obliging as to trust me in the matter of her Last Will and Testament, Sir Justin. My dear Lady Martin, you are too kind! Well, perhaps just a very thin slice. Upon my soul, this is most agreeable.'

'Do you tell me Miss Fox made a will?' demanded Justin. 'I confess, I had not thought her so businesslike.'

Mr Wiseman laughed softly. 'Indeed, she was not. But she was an amiable lady, with many friends. An honest man gave her good advice, and insisted on bringing her to me.

The lady made her wishes quite clear and definite.'

'Indeed? Well, I am very happy to hear it. I confess, I had anticipated some difficulty in settling — '

He was interrupted by Amy, who had been staring at our visitor in astonishment. 'Are you,' she demanded, 'the one they call Mr Worldly Wiseman?'

Mr Wiseman somehow contrived a very gallant bow in Amy's direction even whilst seated at table. 'I have heard that soubriquet has been applied to myself, madam, and I hope you will pardon me for saying it is one I do not despise. For even in this blessed land of ours, where the law is designed to uphold the morality of our Christian religion, worldly wisdom is very necessary for a man such as myself, who undertakes to arrange affairs for others. Yes, indeed.'

Amy regarded Mr Wiseman with even greater astonishment as he talked. Now, her face cleared and she favoured him with a most brilliant smile. 'Oh, how droll you are!' she said. She looked at the rest of us. 'I like him!' she announced. 'Do not you?'

'My dear lady!' Mr Wiseman was now all confusion. 'Quite charming of you, madam, indeed it is. I beg you will forgive me if I seem a little flustered. I am not at all accustomed to finding myself a favourite with the ladies!'

'Well, now I know you were a friend to Aunt Agnes, I am quite determined to preserve the acquaintance,' said Amy.

Justin still looked dazed when he took Mr Wiseman into the library to learn the terms of the will. And when he sought me out, an hour later, I learnt the reason for his confusion.

'I knew at once,' he said, 'that Mr Wiseman would not come here in person over so small a fortune as one thousand pounds. Judith, I cannot tell you how I felt! You understand her sister had ten thousand pounds when she married my father? We know what happened to that,' he added, wryly. 'And never did Miss Fox seem at all well-to-do! Only when Mr Wiseman appeared, did I suspect she had fortune equal to her sister.'

It was my turn to feel dazed. 'And did she?'

'Rather more in the end, for she had very few expenses. Her income has accumulated to increase her capital. She left almost thirteen thousand pounds.'

'Well, this is a day of wonders, indeed!'

I was rejoicing for the girls but also for his sake: this legacy would spare him the obligation of setting aside his own money for them, and relieve his mind of much anxiety.

There were bequests: friends had been remembered, and so had our servants and a generous sum was to go to a foundling hospital. But what pleased me best was that Justin had not been left out. She had left him £1,000.

Mr Worldly Wiseman had advised his client well. The residue was left to Blanche and Amy, but any extravagances would be checked, for their inheritance was to be administered by trustees and for that purpose she had appointed sensible men, our own friends, Mr Kirk and Colonel Makepeace.

When we told Blanche and Amy of their fortunes, they were very much astonished, and still too grieved for their aunt to rejoice.

I did not share that grief and when I had recovered from the surprise, other thoughts intruded. For I felt Miss Fox should have told Justin there would be an inheritance for the girls, and spared him all those years of anxiety on their behalf.

'And there is another matter,' I said, upon expressing my indignation over this. 'For she lived here, and knew of your difficulties, yet never did she contribute one farthing to the household expenses! Were she poor I could excuse her, but now I find it very hard to forgive!'

'She owed me nothing,' he said, 'and she was not paid for her services as a companion to the girls, as you pointed out, yesterday!'

'In my opinion, she was no suitable companion. To be forever preaching the London season, as though it were the Holy Writ! The girls will do better with Mrs Armstrong.'

It remained to make the girls acquainted with our plans for their future, and when Justin spoke of Mrs Armstrong, he said, 'This lady was one-time companion to Judith, which is excellent recommendation, I think. She will teach you how to conduct yourselves and chaperon you at assemblies and parties.'

Blanche began to look animated, but Amy was clearly dissatisfied. 'Local amusements? Is that all? Our aunt wished for us a London season, and now there is no reason why we should not have one, for we can afford it, easily.'

'Dear as your aunt was to you, she was not the best person to advise you on that subject. Learn from Mrs Armstrong, pay heed to her. When I have seen how you can conduct yourselves with propriety, then I may consent to your having a season.'

'Oh, Justin! Truly? Is it a promise?'

'No, it is not,' I said. 'It is a bargain, and you must keep your side of it. And I hope you will be kind to Mrs Armstrong,' I added, to soften the lecture. 'For she has recently lost someone very dear to her, just as you have.'

Mrs Armstrong came and began by giving the girls an opportunity to observe her, chatting with me, and recollecting diverting episodes from the time she had been my own companion. She could not have done better. The girls were entertained and so was Justin. It was clear they were taken with her.

Within a week, 'Mrs Armstrong says' was a phrase frequently heard in our house. 'Mrs Armstrong says elegance and grace are just as important as beauty,' confided Amy. 'Which is something our aunt never mentioned, but I think she is right. We are to practise good posture until it becomes a habit.'

She discovered they needed practice in dancing and began to coach them. But her foremost concern, she told me, was to help them through their grief, which still occupied them.

For myself, I was happy, though it pained me to see Justin looking so tired sometimes. Our stables grew ever more busy: mares were foaling and some of them needed help, and when they came into season they had to be put to the stallions.

We had disappointments. There was a mare with whom Blue John refused to mate, two foals were stillborn, and one was born deformed and had to be destroyed. Nevertheless, there were more strong, sturdy foals in our stable every day.

We could not go into society, but I often invited Justin's particular friends, the Kirks, to dine with us. I discovered Mrs Armstrong had had some previous acquaintance with Colonel Makepeace, and invited him and his daughter Charlotte, also.

Everything settled into a regular train and now I was looking forward to having visitors, for Hugh and Helen and the Wysalls were to spend three weeks with us over Easter.

When they came, Helen gave me news. 'You were right, Judith,' she said. 'Richard and Isobel would be happy but for their exasperation over nonsense coming from Lady Hargreaves. We have heard that Isobel was a scheming little hussy who had captivated Richard by her designing arts, and you, Judith, have been in turns, noble and self-sacrificing for Richard's sake, or foolishly taken in by a penniless fortune-hunter.'

'Heavens! Is there no limit to her inventiveness?'

'I have laughed at her and told our neighbours I look forward to hearing her next piece of nonsense. But Isobel, I fear, takes it a little too seriously, so I prevailed upon Hugh to have a quiet word with Sir Matthew. He has hired a house in town and taken Lady Hargreaves away, and when they return, Isobel and Richard go to spend the summer at Flamborough.'

'Ah, well done, Sophie!' I exclaimed. 'Given long separations, Lady Hargreaves may forget her discontent.'

'They will have respite, at all events,' said Helen. 'And that can do no harm at all.'

This visit occurred when it was time for our yearlings to be broken, and the gentlemen were pleased to assist. Both Hugh and Mr Wysall were skilled; Justin could trust them not to ruin a horse's mouth, and their assistance gave him respite from always being so busy.

'I confess, I had not fully appreciated how demanding such an enterprise must be,' said Hugh on the day before they left. He looked at me. 'I need not ask if you are happy,' he said. 'I can see that you are.'

'I am fortunate in being of some use here.'

'Hmm. How do you deal with your sisters-in-law?'

Hugh's opinion had been formed on his first impression, when the girls had been at their worst. Now, I spoke with some warmth, making much of how they had cared for their aunt.

'Miss Fox,' I went on, 'was not a sensible woman and the advice she gave them was not to be trusted. Blanche suspected it, but we cannot blame Amy for listening to nonsense which was so flattering to her vanity! Well, she is intelligent, they both are, and they are naturally kind hearted. With Mrs Armstrong helping them I believe they will turn out well.'

He nodded. 'I have observed improvement,' he admitted. 'No doubt they were obliged to grow up when their aunt was taken ill. I have told Justin we expect to see you at Bennerley in the summer. You may bring the girls, too, if you wish.'

I was pleased: our visit would occur at just the right time, when we could put off our mourning.

Our guests stayed for three weeks. A month later, Justin was less busy: we had all our foals, the yearlings were doing well, and at times he could leave Jessop in command.

I began thinking how agreeable it would be for the two of us to have a few days to ourselves, and with this in mind, I formed a scheme which I believed would be pleasing to everyone. Since Blanche and Amy would like to have some new clothes for Bennerley, I asked Mrs Armstrong to take them on a visit to Nottingham to go shopping and visit a dressmaker.

My two young sisters-in-law became quite intoxicated by my offer, especially when I said they might each have a special gown for Helen's ball.

Both girls were thankful they would put off dark mourning clothes with the approach of summer, and all might have been well had not Amy chosen to express this in the most thoughtless way imaginable.

'Oh!' she exclaimed. 'I am so glad that Aunt Agnes died during the winter!'

'How can you say such a thing?' Blanche demanded in a swift and spiteful fury. 'Are you utterly devoid of proper feelings? Have you no idea how wicked you are?'

'I only meant . . . '

'You are evil. Do you know that? Evil! You care for nothing and no one! All you care about is primping and preening and thinking how beautiful you look. Well, handsome is as handsome does, and you have nothing to be so proud of!'

'That is not fair!'

'Fair?' Blanche repeated the word with the

utmost contempt. 'When did you ever care about being fair? All you have ever cared about is your precious London season.'

'Now, Blanche,' I protested.

'Do not defend her,' she snapped. 'Our aunt cared more for her than anyone else, and now she says she is glad she died!'

'I did not mean — '

'She is so much in love with herself, she cares nothing for anyone else! She may think I have forgotten the way she tried to blackmail Justin, but I have not. Do you know, she thought she could get a London season by setting fire to the stables?'

'By *what?*'

'Be quiet!' cried Amy. 'Justin said Judith was not to know.'

'Dressing up in men's clothing and sneaking out like a thief in the night. You could have set the house alight; you could have murdered all of us. Did you think of that? Would you have cared? No, of course not. Why should you? You are the Grand Amy, why should you care about we lesser mortals?'

'Dear heaven!' I exclaimed. 'Amy, was that you? How could you do such a thing? Had you no thought for the horses?'

'All the horses were in the paddocks,' protested Amy tearfully. 'I knew that. I had no wish to hurt, you cannot think I would!' She turned on Blanche. 'Why do you speak of it? Justin promised Judith would not be told.'

'Oh, I can believe that!' I said angrily. 'He would never betray you, even though you ruined him! Is that what you were about? Were you trying to ruin him? After all his care for you, all his anxieties, is that how you repay him? And what on earth did you think to gain by it?'

'A London season, of course,' said Blanche scornfully. 'What else would she think to gain by it?'

I sat down, pressing my hands to my temples, unable to find any grain of sense in these shocking revelations.

Mrs Armstrong was present during this scene, at first taken aback, later making attempts to intervene: now she began a careful questioning, and though the explanations were garbled and incoherent, we discovered reasoning, of a kind.

It was no coincidence that the episode had occurred when we Tremaines first paid a visit to Melrose Court: it was, strangely, a consequence of our visit.

Justin had told his sisters of his visit to Bennerley, his pleasure in our society, the schemes for his entertainment. Blanche was impressed and, unsuspicious of my interest in her brother, she had formed a modest ambition: she hoped the two girls might be included in any future invitations.

When Amy displayed herself in her inappropriate finery and prattled about her London season, Blanche had been ready to sink, and felt that after such an exhibition, they had not the smallest hope. In her bitterness, she accused Amy of spoiling everything.

Amy herself suspected she had gone too far, but Blanche's fury hardened her: she asserted that it did not signify, for whatever Blanche might think, a London season was assured.

She supported herself in this because she knew of a wealthy widow who was desirous of becoming Lady Martin. When Justin married Mrs Buxton, all her fine ambitions would be fulfilled.

Justin had come upon their quarrel and made his contribution by stating that nothing, not even the prospect of giving Amy her London season, would induce him to marry Mrs Buxton.

'You would marry her were it to save your precious stables!'

Justin had shrugged, considering this unworthy of an answer.

Somehow, Amy had convinced herself she was right: she had brooded over her imagined injuries and had formed the scheme of damaging the stables, expecting the cost of repairs to force her brother into a marriage of convenience.

'Of all the selfish — ' I had listened to the recital in growing indignation, appalled at the extent of her wilfulness: now I was angrier even than Blanche. 'Have you no thought for anyone,' I cried, 'that you could make such an attempt? You would force your brother into a distasteful marriage, so that you might spend a few months gallivanting in town? Shame upon you, you wicked girl!'

'I do not see how a marriage to Mrs Buxton should be distasteful,' muttered Amy. 'She is far prettier than you!'

'Oh, how foolish you are!' said Blanche. 'You know Justin does not like her, and he would not marry her.'

'Well, it does not signify now, for we have our own money and Justin has said we may have a London season, and we go to Bennerley, too!' said Amy triumphantly.

'Your brother made no promise of a season!' I snapped. 'He made a bargain, and that was at my persuasion when I knew nothing of this. Had I known how wicked you are, I would not have teased him so.

You have a great deal to learn, my girl, a very great deal, before I exert myself again on your behalf!'

I hardened my heart against the crumpling of her features and the tears in her eyes. As I left, she turned on Blanche, crying this was her fault. 'You have made Judith hate me, now!'

By the time I told Justin what had occurred, my anger had died and I felt a little contrite for upbraiding her so severely over a matter that he had dealt with at the time.

'Amy will recover,' he said reassuringly. 'She always does. Do not make yourself uneasy, Judith.'

He was unconcerned, and it was easy to comfort myself with the reflection that Justin knew his sisters better than I did and that squabbles in this family were frequent and of little consequence.

So I was utterly shocked when, the next morning, Mrs Armstrong discovered Amy's bed had not been slept in and Amy herself was nowhere to be found.

18

'Certainly, she has determined to run away,' said Justin. 'And she has gone on foot, for none of our horses is missing. Silly girl! What foolish scheme is in her mind this time, I wonder?'

'Would she have sought refuge with a friend?'

'No friend would support her folly. No, I imagine she has gone towards Chesterfield, intending to ride the stagecoaches to London.'

'That sounds like Amy,' I agreed. 'We should look for her, for who knows what might have befallen her, if she went out on foot during the night!'

Justin took Blue John, I followed in the gig and it was fortunate that Jupiter was a good-tempered horse, for in my anxiety and self-reproach I could scarce concentrate on driving, and gave many wrong signals.

Now, I felt all the force of Amy's distress: though I could never approve of fire-raising, I knew she had been found out not long after it occurred, had suffered anger and reproaches, and possibly been punished. Small wonder she had been shocked to find herself in trouble for the same thing, all over again.

I was occupied with these painful reflections when a shout caused me to look up: Justin had reappeared, with a companion.

'My dear Lady Martin!' Mr Wiseman, mounted on a sturdy cob, drew alongside the gig and flourished his hat. 'Allow me to set your mind at rest: your sister is safe and at present resting in my own humble abode under the auspices of my dear wife. She is perfectly sound, only a little tired and cold and dirty.'

'Mr Wiseman, you are a saint!' I sighed with relief. 'How did you come upon her?'

Amy had presented herself at Mr Wiseman's office when he opened at eight o'clock. 'I understand she was desirous of leaving home, My Lady, on account of some trifling quarrel, but I persuaded her it was not wise. No, indeed. Quarrels occur sometimes, even in my own family and no one could be more fortunate than myself in my dear ones. However, she was most distressed. I beg you will not be angry with her.'

Knowing she could not go far without money, Amy had recollected her inheritance. She had made no attempt to approach her trustees, knowing they would not consent to such a scheme. Instead, she had formed the plan of prevailing upon Mr Wiseman to act on her behalf. She thought he would lend her money for her immediate needs and make an arrangement for her to draw funds when she had determined a new situation.

Mr Worldly Wiseman would do no such thing. 'I took the liberty of talking to Miss Amy, for she was obliging enough to trust me with her trouble. I have explained that your anger was natural, and I am sure you will forgive her, in time.'

'Heavens! Has she told you everything?'

Mr Wiseman looked bashful. 'I have methods of extracting truth from those less naturally truthful than your sister.'

I laughed. 'Oh, Mr Worldly Wiseman, I believe you!'

'I believe she has learnt a lesson, for I have explained that arson is a serious crime, very serious indeed. And she is regretting her foolishness, for she spent a most uncomfortable night. May I beg you will not be too severe upon her?'

When we came to the town, Mr Wiseman led the way through a market square, clearing dogs and geese and small children out of the way. At last, we were in a pleasing thoroughfare outside a tall, red-brick house. There, we were shown into a parlour, where we found Amy looking wretched and woebegone. Her face was scratched, her hair awry and her garments dishevelled.

Justin eyed her with disfavour. 'Amy, have you any idea how disreputable you look?'

'Well, I have torn my gown,' said Amy. 'And it was dirty behind the laurel bushes, you know.'

Justin's face was a picture. 'I suppose,' he enquired, 'I may be permitted to know what laurel bushes have to do with anything? When you are quite ready to explain, of course?'

'I arrived too early,' said Amy.

Never before having been obliged to walk a distance of five miles, it seemed to Amy a vast undertaking. She had set off at midnight, thinking to arrive by eight o'clock, and had been disconcerted to find herself in town by two o'clock, with six hours to wait before Mr Wiseman opened his office.

To evade the Watch, she needed somewhere to hide: she had crept into a thicket of laurel bushes and there, cold and dirty, she had spent the night.

'Were you not afraid?' I asked curiously. 'Alone in the dark?'

'Of course not,' said Amy. 'There is a circle of light around me.' As I blinked, she added, 'It is quite invisible, but it is there, always, to protect me in the dark.

Aunt Agnes told me about it when I was very small.'

I stared at Amy in some awe. 'I — er — I see.'

Justin remembered that others at Melrose Court were waiting anxiously for news and when we had taken leave of the Wisemans' he rode on ahead, leaving me to reprimand Amy for her escapade.

'Well, Blanche has become so horrid,' said Amy miserably. 'She just wishes to spoil everything! She knows I am not really glad our aunt died, but I hate wearing these dreary mourning clothes, and I cannot feel it is wrong, for Aunt Agnes herself did not like them, and I love her just as much in my heart whatever I am wearing. I know I spoke in a clumsy way,' she admitted, 'but Blanche knew what I meant. Yet she had to seize upon it and take to herself a holier-than-thou posture, as though she is the only one who cares. Well, she is a hypocrite, and so I told her, for when our aunt lived she was not always so caring: often, she was downright unpleasant. And she should not have mentioned that fire: Justin said it was to be forgotten and she did it to make you hate me. Mrs Armstrong says she has never seen you so angry and now we had better not expect an excursion to Nottingham or any new clothes.'

Amy was sobbing, and ended her speech with a great wail of grief, all her disappointment muddled with distress over her sister's malice and my own anger.

'I was angry,' I said. 'It pains me to know how hard things have been for your brother. Your papa squandered his substance and yours, and left him with debts, and the responsibility of providing for you. He set aside funds and denied his own comfort so you girls might have a home and a marriage portion.'

'But I told him I would not need a marriage portion, only a London season! For I expect to make a good marriage, you know.'

'Many ladies have such schemes,' I told her. 'And most of them are disappointed! Your brother wished you to have substance. He might have been easier had he known your aunt would leave you comfortably provided, but he did not! *He* still has debts and too much work. It would be helpful if you would remember that, instead of teasing him with your ill humour.'

Amy shifted uncomfortably. 'I have noticed how tired he is, sometimes,' she said. 'And I can comprehend how silly I was to think he would marry Mrs Buxton.' After these admissions, her grievances rose again. 'But none of this would have happened had not Blanche determined to be so beastly!'

'You set the fire,' I reminded her sharply. 'Our talk of allowing you a season had nothing to do with that, but your sister may have felt you were having all your own way, in spite of your nonsense and your pranks! For those who behave well, there is nothing so galling as to see mischief rewarded!'

This last remark seemed to strike Amy more forcibly than any other. 'Do you suppose that is why Blanche . . . ?' Her voice trailed off, but she was clearly giving thought to the matter.

I said no more but I was heartened by her evident wish to understand her sister. How it was achieved I know not, but in the days that followed, the girls came to an awkward truce, which would, I hoped, lead them to closer harmony.

In the interest of promoting harmony, Mrs Armstrong advised I should allow the proposed shopping expedition to Nottingham, after all. 'The shared pleasure can only bring benefits.'

I confess, my agreement had more to do with my wish for time alone with Justin than any desire of pleasing the girls.

I had my reward, for before they went, Justin said wonderingly, 'She came to me, Amy did, and said there was something particular she wanted to say to me. When I asked what was on her mind, she blurted out that never before had she realized how thoughtless and wicked and selfish she had been, in setting the fire — and — and other things, but now she did and she wanted to tell me she was sorry, for all of it.'

I confess, I was moved. 'Well, then,' I said, 'I hope you were so obliging as to forgive her. I begin to expect great things of Amy, for she is quick to learn and willing, also. But I beg you will not forget you have another sister, sir, who did not set fire to the stables and indeed lent her own exertions to the effort of putting it out.'

'No, indeed. Though I confess Amy does demand attention more than Blanche.'

'Well, sir, for the next week, both sisters will be away, and you may direct all your attention towards your wife.'

'How agreeable that will be,' he said complacently.

It was indeed most agreeable.

Already committed to Bennerley, we were obliged to refuse an invitation from the Flamboroughs. When I wrote to Sophie, I proffered an invitation of my own for the autumn.

Sophie was disappointed by our refusal and held out little hope of visiting Melrose Court, as travelling made her quite ill in her present condition. Her infant was due in January and she had much to say about the discomfort of her condition.

I myself was in no such condition. This did not trouble me: I hoped to present my husband with a son, but I was pleased to enjoy the first months of my marriage without the symptoms of child-bearing.

Before going to Bennerley, we had an unexpected visitor in the form of my uncle Ramsgate. He stayed a sennight, during which time he inspected our yearlings and ordered and paid for four of our greys for his own carriage.

After that, we had letters from other gentlemen who had heard about our horses, either from Flamborough, or Wysall, or Tremaine, or Ramsgate, and all of them expressed an interest in calling to see for themselves.

In jest, I said we should let it be known we held our sales in October: a moment later, I saw advantage in the idea of sending out invitations, offering hospitality to prospective customers.

'You appear to have given the matter some considerable thought,' said Justin, for I had discussed the practicalities with Mrs Payne before presenting the idea. 'But it will be taxing for you, Judith, and for our servants, too.'

'Mrs Armstrong will assist me, and I shall hire extra help, and the gentlemen will bring their own servants,' I said. 'And we must open up those rooms soon, if the house is not to deteriorate, so we might as well put them to some profitable use. I doubt any of the gentlemen will stay long, for in October they will have sporting engagements.'

So it was decided upon, and I made arrangements to have all the work done whilst we were at Bennerley. There, we spent five wonderful weeks, my only disappointment being that I saw nothing of Richard and Isobel, for they had gone to visit with Sophie and her duke.

When we dined at Hargreaves Hall, I was dismayed to discover Lady Hargreaves had the idea that I was not well. Nothing could have been further from the truth, but she would have it.

'I fear the Derbyshire air does not agree with you, my dear,' she said sympathetically. 'Such cold winds blowing down from the Pennines, I declare you look quite thin and pinched. I have heard,' she went on, 'that Derbyshire cows do not produce such a fine quality of milk as our Leicestershire herds. And how long do you stay, my dear? Only five weeks? Well, we must do the best we can. Do take a little of this calves foot jelly! It is really quite excellent and is sure to do you good!'

I protested that I was in perfect health, that the wind from the Pennines gave a quality of freshness to the air which I found most invigorating, that we had excellent pastures, excellent herds, and milk which could equal any in the country.

Lady Hargreaves said I was very brave. Later, I heard she was anxious about me. 'Poor Judith! She seems to have quite lost her appetite. I fear for her, indeed I do.'

When I discovered Justin was studying my imaginary ailments, I was most indignant. 'You have been listening to Lady Hargreaves!' I accused him. 'Do not let that woman succeed in her mischief!'

'What is she about, Judith?'

I shrugged. 'She is disgruntled because I did not marry Richard. I declare, Lady Hargreaves herself is the most telling argument against her own proposal!'

The girls were heeding the advice of Mrs Armstrong and were lively, but not boisterous. If Amy was too frank towards some, she was too appealing in her innocence to give offence.

On the day of Helen's ball, both girls confessed themselves nervous, this being the first ball they had ever attended.

Mrs Armstrong assured them they would not lack partners, and admired them when they appeared in their ball gowns.

They did indeed present a pleasing appearance. Blanche had chosen olive green, with a pattern of gold leaves embroidered around the bodice. She tied her hair with a ribbon of the same green and wore a gold cross at her throat. Amy wore dark-blue satin, with a skirt that fell in rich folds to the ground.

I danced with gentlemen of my acquaintance and more often with my husband, which occasioned some witty reproof from certain rattles.

'I declare you are grown quite rustic, madam. Do you not know that marital attachment is most unfashionable in this day and age?'

Blanche and Amy received their share of notice. 'He called me Fair Persephone,' giggled Blanche the next morning, 'and told me my hair reminded him of moonlight! I declare, I did not know how to look.'

Amy expressed disapprobation of Mr Butterworth. 'His collar points were so high he could not turn his head.'

'Do you judge a man by the way he dresses?' challenged Mrs Armstrong and Amy said, 'Some things may be deduced.'

'How they have improved!' said Helen, privately to me. 'Do you mean to send them to London this winter, Judith?'

When consulted, Mrs Armstrong advised against. 'They are not always at ease, for they have mixed little in society. For this winter, I recommend you hold a ball and they may attend the local assemblies: such experience will be valuable.'

Home from Bennerley, we were surprised one evening by the sound of a visitor arriving on horseback and we were astonished when a footman announced Mr Hargreaves.

'Richard! This is a surprise indeed! What brings you here so unexpectedly? I understood you were with the Flamboroughs.'

Richard stared at me. 'Heavens, Judith, I expected to find you on your deathbed!' he exclaimed.

'Oh dear!' I said, instantly comprehending. 'Do you tell me your mama has been alarming you with that nonsense?'

'She wrote to me,' he said. 'I know she has been behaving foolishly, but I could not help being uneasy at her description of your suffering!' He turned to Justin. 'Your pardon, sir, for this intrusion. I see my anxiety was ill-founded.'

Justin bowed and said that any friend of mine was welcome at any time. 'I am pleased you are now satisfied, sir, that my wife continues in good health.'

Belated civilities took place. Richard was introduced to Blanche and Amy, and told Mrs Armstrong what a pleasure it was to see her again. I ordered refreshments and commanded him to sit by me and give me all the latest news of Isobel and Sophie.

I watched him, interested to see the effect of his marriage. His petulance was removed, replaced by a new responsibility, and he had an air of gravity that was not unbecoming.

He was speaking of his mother. 'She is vexed because you have bestowed your fortune elsewhere,' he said. 'Now she wishes to believe you are unhappy and had done better to marry me. Even Papa seems unable to reason with her.' His eyes were troubled. 'I shall tell her we mean to move far away from Leicestershire if she persists with her nonsense.'

Richard would not stay for more than one night, for my friends thought me unwell and were anxious for news. 'I can reach them faster than sending an express,' he said. Towards Justin, he directed a rueful look. 'We meet but briefly, sir, but I hope to improve my acquaintance with you, very soon.'

Wishing to observe for myself how Richard and Isobel were dealing with each other, I pressed Richard to bring Isobel for a visit after leaving the Flamboroughs.

They came in October, when we had many other visitors, for I had put into action my scheme of offering hospitality to gentlemen who expressed interest in our horses.

My plan worked very well: most of our horses were sold, more profitably than they would have been at Tattersalls, and I had the added satisfaction of knowing that our visitors would recommend us to others of their acquaintance.

My design of profiting my husband by offering hospitality had another benefit which I had not foreseen: with Mrs Armstrong to help them, Blanche and Amy observed the strangers, grew sharper and more accurate in their judgments, and gained practice in making polite conversation.

As hostess, I divided my time between our visitors, apologizing to Richard and Isobel for offering less attention than I felt was due to such particular friends.

'Do not make yourself uneasy,' said Isobel. 'I confess, I find it quite educational to watch you. Your knowledge of horses is impressive, but what strikes me is the delicate way you have of persuading the gentlemen to retire for the night, when they would be up and drinking and talking into the small hours. I declare, they do not know they are being managed!'

I laughed. I was happier now about my friends, for I saw they had both benefited from the marriage. Isobel had always been serious, and she had gained from Richard's liveliness.

My mind was relieved of all anxiety: I was persuaded they understood each other too well for Lady Hargreaves to succeed with her mischief.

Richard and Isobel outstayed our other visitors and did not leave until after I held the ball I had promised the girls, at the beginning of November. This was a great success, but my own enjoyment, and Isobel's, was undone by the distressing news, received that day, that Sophie had miscarried.

'You seem fretful, Judith,' observed Justin, after Richard and Isobel had taken their leave. 'Could you not persuade your friends to remain longer?'

'What? Oh no; Richard has business which

cannot be delayed. No, but I confess I am distressed for Sophie. She was an only child, you know, and she felt it. Always, she said she meant to have many children. After such a reverse, I fear she may give way to melancholy.'

'Indeed? Well then, I propose we leave the girls with Mrs Armstrong and visit your friend.'

'Oh, Justin, may we? Oh, how good you are!'

'I cannot help but feel she will recover the more quickly with you to help her.'

We found Sophie attended by Mrs Burton and the dowager, both of them uneasy because Sophie was too much given to weeping. 'Do you try if you can to give her thoughts a more cheerful turn, Judith,' said the dowager, and Mrs Burton said, 'If anyone can do it, Judith, you can.'

Justin proved himself wiser. 'Let her weep away her grief,' he said. 'She will be better for it, in the end.'

Sophie did weep and I wept with her, and then she slept and wept again when she woke and continued in this fashion for several days until one day she dried her eyes and laughed a little shakily and apologized for being such a watering-pot.

'The doctor has told my husband there is

no reason why we should not have many fine children,' she said, 'but I confess I am disappointed! I had so wished for this child!'

Thankfully, her spirits were improving by the time we were obliged to leave. Both the dowager and Mrs Burton thought our visit had been of benefit.

Our lives continued, agreeable, busy and orderly all throughout the next year.

During the winter there were more visiting broodmares so we were even more occupied with the stables than we had been the previous year, but Justin could now afford to engage more help.

Blanche and Amy squabbled less frequently and became friendly with Charlotte Makepeace. Mrs Armstrong chaperoned all three girls at the local assemblies, we held parties for them and they were invited out at least twice every week.

Hugh and Helen visited in the spring again: again we visited Bennerley in the summer and whilst we were in Leicestershire, Isobel gave birth to a girl. I confess, I was diverted to see Richard dandling his daughter. Even more pleasing was that Lady Hargreaves, now that she had a granddaughter to occupy her, dropped all her former nonsense.

So we were happy, with little to disrupt

until the following September, when something occurred which I should have foreseen but which, I confess, took me completely by surprise.

Justin and I had been out, and returned home to discover Blanche and Amy waiting for us, hopping with excitement.

'Justin! Judith! Can you guess what has happened? Wonderful news! No, we shall not tell you, Mrs Armstrong must do that. Oh come, hurry, do! We cannot wait to see your astonishment!'

We looked at each other in some perplexity dismounted, and followed the giggling girls indoors. There, we were astonished to see Mrs Armstrong blushing. She had, that day, accepted an offer of marriage from Colonel Makepeace.

I was pleased she would be our neighbour, for I was greatly attached to her, and I was thankful also that her influence would continue with the girls. They could visit her at any time: she promised me she would continue to chaperon them, along with Charlotte, whenever there were balls or parties.

And so she would, within our own neighbourhood.

Only later did I realize this turn of events had left the girls with no one to chaperon their London season.

I would have to take them myself. Against all my own inclinations, I would now be obliged to leave my husband and go gallivanting off to town with his sisters.

19

'I hope to find the girls a companion to equal Mrs Makepeace,' I said. 'I shall look about me for such a lady and when I know they are in good hands, I shall return home. We may be easy, for Sophie and the duke will stand as their friends.'

It was ironic that the season should occur at the time of year when our stables were busiest. There was no question of Justin coming with us. 'Were I better circumstanced,' he said, 'I could do my duty as a husband and a brother — '

'Never think you do not!' I exclaimed.

We would have the protection of manservants on the journey and the duke had promised Justin to lend his own countenance and protection whilst we were in town.

'Sophie plans to give a ball in February,' I told him, 'and she insists I remain in town for that. But if I can contrive a suitable companion for the girls, I shall return directly.'

Sophie was in town because the duke wished her near the best physicians. Having conceived again, she had none of her previous discomfort, which encouraged her to hope for a safe delivery.

Last July, Isobel had given birth to her daughter. Helen, when we met at the Wysalls, had detected in herself the early signs of pregnancy and her child was due next July.

I remained barren and now I was beginning to worry about it: I wished for Justin to have a son.

I thought he wished it himself, though he was too generous to reproach me in any way. 'We cannot order these matters, Judith. I must say it is for the best, at present, for you will enjoy your amusements in town better for being carefree.'

'I do not go for my own amusement, as you well know.'

'Whatever your reasons for going, madam, you have my permission to derive from it as much enjoyment as possible, and why not? Heaven knows you have had little enough in the way of fashionable entertainment this last two years.'

'Have I complained?'

'Not once.' He kissed me. 'You deserve some diversions. Enjoy them. Be extravagant. The girls will teach you how.'

I told the girls we would visit shops and dressmakers when we had observed the latest fashions. 'You may depend upon it, within a very few days we will be as fine as any other lady.'

'May I have some slippers decorated with sapphires?' asked Amy demurely.

'No, you may not!' spluttered Justin.

Amy gave a little crow of laughter, pleased with herself for getting her brother to rise to her bait.

Justin subsided with a rueful grin. 'Surely you know that such vulgar ostentation does not become a young lady?'

Such funning was becoming a regular occurrence between Justin and his sisters and after the trials he had had with them my heart rejoiced to see it.

We waited for a spell of good weather for travelling, and it came in January. Justin instructed us to behave ourselves and enjoy ourselves and he laughed when Blanche said, 'Which?'

'Well, try not to break too many hearts.'

'Oh, Justin, we will miss you!' said Amy impulsively. She hugged him, and said, 'You will take care of yourself, will you not?'

'Yes, indeed.' He stood with one arm around Amy and reached for Blanche with the other, hugged them both, then, releasing them, he came to me, took my hands and raised each in turn to his lips. We looked at each other and neither of us spoke. Words were unnecessary.

I had taken a house in a fashionable quarter of town and we arrived without mishap, after travelling for three days.

'Promise me,' I said conspiratorially, after we ladies had spent a week enriching dressmakers and milliners, 'that you will not disclose to your brother how much money I have spent. Do you like this waistcoat? I am going to purchase it for him.'

Several of my former acquaintance were in town and I was able to procure many introductions and invitations for the girls. Before long, we were much engaged with parties, attending balls and routs and masquerades, joining excursions, riding in the park, and going to art galleries and exhibitions and to the theatre.

We saw Sophie several times and I was delighted to see how well she looked. 'Judith, dear, never have I felt better,' she assured me. 'My poor Henry is anxious, of course, and so I am being very obedient and resting, but I am determined I shall dance at my ball! How fortunate are these high-waisted fashions for ladies in my condition! I shall be utterly disguised. Why are you looking at me like that, Judith?'

'Oh, I beg your pardon. Something is

causing me to have heartburn. I have experienced that complaint several times, since arriving in town.'

'It is the water, I expect,' said Sophie. 'I have noticed an alteration in the taste of tea, even though it is prepared in exactly the same way: it can only be a difference in the water! These two ladies are your sisters? Such pretty girls, I declare they will become all the rage.'

'I am seeking a suitable companion for them,' I said. 'Do you know of any sensible woman who would suit, Sophie?'

She did not, but promised to make enquiries.

I had tried an agency and asked other friends for recommendations, and I had interviewed several ladies: none of them impressed me and I would not leave the girls with an unsuitable companion. So I had no good news to impart on that score when I wrote to Justin.

One day, we were surprised to be visited by Richard, who had been obliged to come into town on a matter of business. Having called to pay his respects to Sophie, he had learnt of our own presence.

'Surely you knew of it before?' I said. 'I told Isobel I was bringing the girls this winter.'

'It may have been mentioned, but I had forgotten,' he said. 'I have much to occupy my mind, for I am a papa now, you know!'

It was the day before Sophie's ball and Richard had been invited: now he offered to escort myself and the girls.

Sophie's ball was to be a truly grand occasion, and Blanche and Amy were looking forward to it with a degree of excitement. Long had they deliberated about what they should wear, and how they should have their hair dressed.

In order to be fresh for the evening, we rested during the day. I sent Betty to assist Hannah in dressing the girls and, when I went along to their room, I found Amy looking very pretty indeed in coral pink, and Blanche cool and elegant in her favourite green.

I admired them and was myself admired in my oyster-coloured silk and since Blanche was very animated it was several minutes before I noticed Amy was quiet and her smile rather strained.

'Is something wrong, Amy?'

'I have a headache,' she said. 'It is very slight, Judith, I am sure it will pass.'

Her brow was cool when I touched it, and she had no other symptoms. She attributed her distress to smoke in the atmosphere of London. 'I have noticed once or twice that it has brought about headaches,' she admitted. 'I am not used to it.'

I thought Amy had determined the most likely cause. 'You have not mentioned it before.'

'Always, it passes. Please, Judith, do not fuss. I shall not have my London season spoilt by trifling headaches.'

I produced a vinaigrette of hartshorn and waved it under her nose and she declared she felt better. She would not hear of missing the ball and I thought it unnecessary. I said only that we should leave early if her discomfort persisted.

We went downstairs when Richard arrived, preening under his compliments as we waited for our carriage to be brought round.

When we arrived at the duke's town house the girls were gasping in admiration. Indeed, it was very grand, with Corinthian columns, marbled floors, great chandeliers, gilded furniture and a most magnificent double staircase. Our cloaks were taken by liveried footmen, we were ushered towards the ballroom, to be greeted in person by the duke and duchess. We spent the next half-hour greeting our acquaintance and, despite my protests I was there to chaperon the girls, I found myself engaged for several of the dances.

By the time the duke led Sophie onto the floor to open the dancing, both of my charges had their cards nearly full. I inspected the names and found all of them unexceptional gentlemen. I felt I could be easy and enjoy the evening.

I did not neglect my duties as chaperon, but since the girls showed every appearance of enjoying themselves in a perfectly proper manner, I felt no compunction in dancing myself, when requested.

'Your pardon, sir.' A young man interrupted my dance with Colonel Kent. 'Madam, I fear your sister has been taken ill.'

'Oh dear!' I spoke to the colonel. 'I must beg to be excused, sir.'

The colonel offered assistance: we followed the young man to an anteroom, where Amy lay on a sofa and Blanche hovered uncertainly.

'Amy's headache is worse, much worse,' she said worriedly, as I approached. 'It seemed to come upon her very suddenly.'

Amy opened glazed eyes when I spoke to her. 'Judith? Is that you? My head is very ill, please help me.'

'Yes, of course, dear, we will have you home to bed in no time at all.'

'Might I suggest we procure some laudanum, madam?'

'I do not — ' I stopped as Amy groaned and when I saw tears trickling down her cheeks I decided that for once it was a good idea. 'Yes, please, if you would be so good.'

The colonel left with a footman. Blanche went to find Richard and I held the weeping Amy in my arms. 'Hush, dear, you will be better soon, I have some hartshorn. There! Is that better?'

Richard came and sent for our carriage to be brought to the door, then went to make our apologies to Sophie and the duke. They returned with him, concerned, and by this time Amy was shaking and sobbing and begging us to help her.

We held her between us, and never was I more thankful than when the colonel returned with laudanum. Blanche shook a few drops into a glass of wine and knelt before her persuading her to drink it, and we were relieved to see it taking effect within a very few minutes.

'Sophie, dear, I am so sorry, but I do feel we should leave. Richard, would you be so good as to make our excuses? There are several gentlemen who expect us to dance . . . '

'I am coming with you, Judith.'

'What? Oh no, I do not expect — '

'Nevertheless.' He took our dance cards and gave them to Sophie, who said she would attend to our excuses. She kissed Amy and said she hoped she would be better by morning, someone said our carriage was ready, someone held our cloaks for us, and between us, Richard and I supported Amy to the carriage.

The effect of the laudanum did not last as long as it should. We had barely set off before Amy was groaning again. It seemed the pain increased in intensity, for after another five minutes she was screaming and throwing herself around and it was all Blanche and I could do to hold her still.

'Stop this, Amy,' said Blanche. 'It does no good; you will simply make yourself worse, and you will bring the Watch down upon us.'

The screaming stopped and I thought Amy had taken heed of her sister: then I noticed that her breath was coming in strange little gasps and when she went rigid in my arms, I began to be very frightened indeed.

'I think,' said Richard quietly, 'as soon as you are home Judith, I shall take your carriage to fetch a physician to her. This is no ordinary headache.'

'She is having convulsions!' I said desperately, as Amy began to shake with queer little spasms. Her heels were drumming on the floor of the carriage and Blanche gave an exclamation of disgust. 'Ugh! She has wet herself!'

'Never mind. Just help me to hold her. Amy! Amy dear, can you hear me? Dear God, have mercy! What is to do, here?'

The convulsions stopped only when Amy passed into a merciful swoon. Our carriage pulled up outside our door, Richard jumped down and set our doorbell jangling and he and our butler between them brought out a chair, lifted the unconscious Amy into it and carried her upstairs.

'There is not an instant to lose!' said Richard, as soon as we had her in her room. 'I shall bring a physician directly.'

I held the hartshorn under her nose as the maids undressed her and got her to bed, and when she was propped up against the pillows, I told Hannah to continue with it and made an attempt to get some brandy into her. She did not swallow, and it simply ran out of her mouth.

I turned my attention to Blanche who was utterly shocked and dismayed and very fearful for her sister. I made her take some brandy, took some myself, then approached the bedside and leaned over to listen to Amy's heartbeat. There was something irregular about it which worried me excessively and, in spite of Hannah continuing with the hartshorn and Betty attempting to revive her with burnt feathers, she showed no signs of coming out of her swoon.

I pulled up a chair and sat beside her, taking her hand, chafing it, impatient for Richard's return with the doctor.

'Is she going to die, Judith?' asked Blanche in trembling tones. 'Is Amy going to die?'

I swallowed. 'I think not,' I said. 'She is young, she is strong, she should pull through. We must wait and hear what the doctor has to say.'

At last Richard returned with a fussy, self-important little man who did not impress me. He took out a watch and felt her pulse and said 'Hah!' and went on to propose that her collapse had been caused by too much excitement.

Blanche disagreed. 'I have known ladies swoon with excitement,' she told the doctor, 'but even though my sister wished a London season above every other thing, she is not of a disposition to make herself ill with excitement.'

I agreed with Blanche. 'I fear you are

mistaken, sir. This is something more serious, and requires immediate remedies.'

It was clear the doctor thought we were fussing unnecessarily. We were female and, in his opinion, it was only to be expected we should suffer the vapours. His suggestion that cupping might be of benefit was made to humour us, but I agreed to it because I would try anything.

It was done, and though it had no visible effect, the doctor told us he fully expected her to be recovered by morning.

His manners vexed me. I knew that Amy was ill, very ill indeed, and I could place no reliance on what he had to say.

'Well, sir,' I said. 'I mean no disrespect, but our sister is very dear to us and we must exert ourselves to the full. I believe we must seek a second opinion.'

In this, I was supported by Richard, who obliged the doctor to give directions as to where he might find another physician: so he bowed and said he perfectly understood, but thought Doctor Harrison would merely confirm his own opinion.

We women waited, watching Amy, weeping, praying, attempting now and again to revive her with hartshorn, and we kissed her and held her hand, telling her she was beautiful that we loved her, that we wanted her to g better, hoping her spirit could hear us, even if her ears did not.

Amy's breath was rattling in her throat by the time Richard returned with a second physician. This gentleman was of a very different stamp. He checked her pulse and peered into her eyes, looked grave and asked us a great many questions. We told him everything that had happened.

'Has she complained of these headaches previously?'

'No,' I said. 'She has not complained. I learnt of previous headaches only this evening and I now suspect she has concealed the severity of them. Did you know anything of them, Blanche?'

'I did not. I do not believe they were so very severe, for never did I see her with hartshorn or vinegar or any other thing she might use to get relief.' She looked at the doctor. 'Why do you not do something for her?'

The doctor avoided her gaze. 'Did she suffer an accident?' he asked. 'A bang on the head, perhaps?'

'I know of none.'

'Hmm. Well, let me see.' The doctor turned to Amy, feeling around her head with his fingertips. 'There is a swelling.'

He guided my fingers to it, a small bump,

no bigger than a walnut and when we had so arranged her hair to inspect it, we saw the skin was not broken.

'She has bumped herself recently, madam, and I suspect she thought it too trifling an occurrence to mention.'

'It would seem to be very slight,' I said. 'Could such a thing cause this collapse?'

'Such cases are rare indeed,' he told me. 'I have known only one other like it. I believe a bleeding was started inside her head: the merest trickle would give her the headaches she has been experiencing, but now, I fear, it has become more severe.'

Terror gripped me: I clutched at my middle with one hand and clung to the bedpost with the other. 'You are saying,' I had to force my words through a tight throat, 'you are saying that the bleeding has entered into her brain?'

The doctor looked relieved at my grasp of the situation. 'Either that, my lady, or it has set up an inflammation. I cannot be certain which it is.'

'Well, and what can we do about it?' demanded Blanche. His silence was the only answer and she raised herself from her chair in alarm. 'No! You cannot let her die! You cannot! You must do something anything, you must! Surely,' she demand distractedly, 'surely there is something that can be tried?'

'I am sorry, madam, very sorry indeed, to have no better news to give you. We doctors know too little about these matters,' he admitted. 'There is no treatment for what ails your sister. Prayer may be the answer.' he added kindly. 'Miracles do sometimes occur.'

He went on, in a fatherly tone, speaking to Blanche, soothing her, but I scarce heard him. I sat down, staring at the still figure in the bed, unable to comprehend how such a thing could be happening. Amy! Dear, volatile Amy, so young, so eager, so full of animation, how could she be taken from us with so little warning?

The doctor went away and Betty sent Hannah to fetch some tea for us whilst she helped Blanche and myself out of our ballroom finery and brought our dressing-gowns. When we had drunk our tea and I had sent the maids away, we settled ourselves down to watch over Amy.

Blanche said, 'How could two doctors have such very different opinions?'

'Should I know? It is my belief the doctors know less than they pretend. I would like to believe the first doctor, but I cannot. I do not feel that Amy's excitement was intense enough to make her ill, not like this.'

'Do you believe the other? Must we give up hope?'

'Not while she breathes,' I said. 'They may both be wrong, and she is strong: she may recover.'

We fell into a silence which was broken only by the occasional fall of coals in the grate. My mind was beginning to work in an odd way, raising memories, distracting me from the present horror. I remembered the time we had found her in the Wiseman household after her foolish attempt to run away. I felt a lump in my throat as I recalled the bold and generous way she had become reconciled to her brother and her sister, the caring heart beneath a sometimes frivolous exterior.

I thought of a time, not very long ago, when she had offended an ardent young admirer by giving him some practical advice on how to improve his complexion.

'I declare, he scarce has room on his face for all his spots,' she had told me. 'I thought he would be pleased to learn of a remedy for how, with such an affliction, can he hope to attach any lady?'

I smiled as I recalled this and other scenes. A gasp from Blanche recalled me to the present, and I saw there was blood trickling from Amy's nose. I applied my handkerchief to it and after a while it stopped. I sat down again, taking her hand, and fell into silent prayer.

Hours passed and I cannot now say whether they went slowly or swiftly. As though from a long distance away, I saw Blanche get up, bending over Amy, pressing her own forehead against her sister's as though in some silent communion.

I stood also, and with one hand holding Amy's, I stretched the other across the bed to take Blanche's hand and we stood there, we two, holding hands across the bed, each of us grasping one of Amy's hands as though we could pull her back from the abyss.

There was nothing, no gasp, no sigh, to mark the actual moment of Amy's passing, and indeed neither of us could say exactly when it occurred. Only when we became aware of a change in her features did it dawn upon us that she was lost.

Blanche shuddered and covered her face with her hands and let out a great howling wail of grief, and I ran to her, held her in my arms and together we stood, rocking, weeping, clinging to each other, anguished beyond bearing and as yet, scarce believing.

Coldness seemed to crawl into me, a serpent of coldness, twisting itself around my heart, mauling me from within. And as I looked once more at the lifeless figure on the bed, I thought for the first time of one who, as yet, knew nothing of this, and I jerked into a new horror of realization.

'Dear heaven above!' I whispered. 'How am I to break this news to Justin?'

20

Richard proved himself a true friend. He had been waiting downstairs, ready to give any assistance he could, and he was there all through the following days to lend his presence and support. With a mind dazed and shocked, I was like a helpless child, and he told me what I must do, and how to do it, and took all other matters to himself.

Somehow, he had procured sleeping draughts: Blanche was advised to take one and retire. She protested she would not sleep, but she did, after an hour of trembling and weeping.

I found myself talking, repeating myself again and again, as though under some compulsion: 'What am I to tell Justin? Oh, I cannot bear it! Oh. Richard, how am I to tell him? He is alone! All alone, at Melrose Court and thinking no evil! How can I deliver such a blow?'

'You must write to him now, Judith, and send your letter express, for he must have the news as soon as may be.'

'A letter! Such news, and no one to

comfort him. He — he is expecting a letter, a happy letter! I was to describe the ball. Oh, Sophie! Oh Amy! Oh, Richard, how can I tell him? He is all alone, no one is there with him.'

'Perhaps you should write to your brother,' said Richard, 'and persuade him to ride into Derbyshire to lend support and assistance. You know how fast Hugh can travel when he sets his mind to it. Your husband will not be alone for long.'

'Oh! Oh, yes! Yes! My brother will not fail me at this most grievous time. Bless you, Richard, for thinking of it.'

'Come, Judith. I know it is painful, but you must write. Tell him how it occurred, what you did and what the doctor said.'

I shuddered, braced myself, and took up the pen Richard placed before me, struggled for words, and made at last a painful, delicate beginning, preparing him for bad news, before setting down a plain account. It took a long time.

'Read it, Richard. I scarce know if I have written sense.'

'It is well, but you should tell him I am here to help you. No, wait! I will write it, there is room on the page. Do you mean to take her home for burial? I believe you should. There! I have told him we will, and he must arrange her funeral.'

Her funeral! How could we be talking about Amy's funeral, Amy, who only twelve hours ago had been dressed for a ball!

'Now you must write to Hugh.'

'What are you doing?'

'Writing to Isobel. She expects me home, but I am persuaded she would wish me with you in this emergency. I shall escort you into Derbyshire.'

The letters finished, Richard put my seal upon them and called a servant to take them to the express office.

'Now you must follow Blanche's example. Take a sleeping draught, Judith, and retire.'

I had not the strength to argue. The draught was chalky and unpleasant to taste and gave me heartburn, adding to my misery. Eventually, I fell into an uneasy dream-infested sleep.

I woke with a sour taste in my throat. Sophie was beside me and held a basin as I vomited. Then we clung to each other and wept together, and when we had talked over what had happened I asked after Blanche.

'She is awake and very distressed, of course. I left her writing to inform some cousins, Colonel and Mrs Allen.'

'Oh yes, of course. I had no thought of informing them.'

'All has been so sudden, one cannot wonder at it. Richard says I am to take you both into the park for fresh air and exercise. It is a fine day. My carriage will be ready as soon as you are dressed.'

'I cannot go out of doors! I have no mourning clothes.'

'You have some dark colours which will serve.' Sophie rang for my maid. 'I shall wait with Blanche until you are dressed.'

'Always,' said Blanche as she stared out of the carriage, 'always, Amy wished for a London season. She was persuaded her destiny depended upon it. Well, she was right, though not in the way she imagined! Do you suppose it was meant?'

'Can we know? She was foolish sometimes, but she did not deserve to die! She had no intimation of her own death.'

'Do you see that old woman?' She pointed. 'Ugly old crone and eighty if she is a day! Why should she live when Amy . . . ?'

'Blanche, dear Blanche, do not torment yourself with such thoughts. We have lost a dear sister and we must accept it, and mourn her passing, but we shall not tease ourselves over questions we cannot answer.'

'Must you be so insufferably sensible?' snapped Blanche.

'Life is too short for brooding introspection,

as we have only too recently been reminded,' I said coldly.

Blanche burst into tears, I followed suit and we hugged and comforted each other and I gulped as I thought of my letter being rushed across the country to my unsuspecting husband.

In the park it was cold, but we could not exert ourselves to walk briskly. Sophie told me Richard was dealing with undertakers. 'And your mourning clothes should be ready by tomorrow,' she said. 'I sent instructions to your dressmaker and let it be known it was a matter of some urgency. The woman has your measurements, of course.'

They had taken it upon themselves to cancel our engagements and the duke was dealing with our visitors.

With such good friends, practical matters were out of my hands and I was grateful, for I was still distracted and could not think properly. I was haunted by a vision of Justin, smiling as he opened my letter, the smile fading and paling into shock as he took in the dreadful news. I prayed my brother would reach him without delay.

None of us had appetite for dinner, but Richard insisted we must eat. Without tasting anything, we consumed but little.

'May I sleep in your bed, Judith?' asked

Blanche, 'for I cannot face being alone in the dark, not tonight.'

I agreed and found it comforting to have her beside me: when the sickness came upon me again she was there to help.

'I am not ill,' I assured her. 'It is merely the distress. Always, it affects me in this way.'

She poured some brandy and water for me and I sipped gratefully, and settled back to sleep.

Our mourning gowns had been delivered, and we wore them the next day, though I discovered my own hastily prepared garment was tight across the breasts, causing me some discomfort.

Richard joined us at breakfast. 'We may begin our journey northwards later today,' he said. He went on to outline the arrangements he had made, but though I was grateful to him, I scarce heard the details.

'I expect Justin has received my letter by now,' I said.

'I expect he has, and Hugh will not be long in reaching him. Judith, you have done the best you can and no one could do better. Now do not fret. I have sent instruction to your maids to begin packing. By noon we will be ready to set off.'

After a long, miserable journey we at last

arrived home on Saturday afternoon. Hugh was there and he told me he had reached Justin ahead of my letter, and had been obliged to break the news himself.

'How could that happen?' I asked.

'Justin's letter had further to travel, of course, so I was the first to receive the news. It so happened Valiant was saddled and full of oats, and I was dressed for riding, so as soon as I had made Helen acquainted with the situation, I set off. And when Valiant was tired, I was near the Singletons, so instead of hiring a fresh mount I borrowed Jack's best hunter, and further on I exchanged him for a horse belonging to Charles Wysall, so I had deuced fast horses all the way. I beat the courier by half an hour, and Judith, though I detested having to deliver such a blow, it was well that it happened so. He has taken it very hard.'

'I know.'

Something seemed to have frozen inside Justin: he had been perfectly civil, and said everything that was proper. He had thanked Richard for all his assistance; he had told me he was sorry such a burden had fallen upon me; he had assured me he was quite certain I had done everything possible for Amy and that no blame could be attached to any person. Yet he had stiffened and put me aside when I moved to embrace him and there was something mechanical in his words and behaviour that made me feel very uneasy indeed.

'Has he talked to you, Hugh? To me, he will say nothing. I do not know him in this humour.'

'Well, he reproached me for riding into Derbyshire instead of making all speed in the other direction. He said I should have gone to London to assist you, but I told him Richard was there to help you. And he said he should have been there.'

'And that is all?'

'I believe he feels it, and I cannot help but sympathize.' Hugh sighed. 'We know his circumstances and no one could have foreseen such a tragedy.'

'He says he does not blame me, but I fear there is doubt in his mind. Should I have forbidden her to go to the ball?'

'Oh, come, Judith! No man of sense would say so, and Justin is no fool. He has suffered a heavy blow and I perfectly comprehend his feelings, for I would feel the same should anything — God forbid! — happen to you. He needs time: he will not recover easily, but he will come to it, eventually.'

'I could help him better had it not sapped my own strength,' I admitted. 'It seems to have knocked me down and I feel so tired. I loved Amy, you know. She was so brave and sweet and funny, I would have sacrificed my own life to save her.'

Hugh and Richard left after the funeral: I would have given much for my brother's continuing support, but Helen was carrying his child and she had the greater claim.

Colonel and Margaret Allen stayed a day longer. At first, I was unwilling to admit my unease to Margaret: later reflection taught me that her life-long acquaintance with Justin might be of some assistance, so at last I spoke of my fears.

Margaret shook her head, aware of some alteration in Justin which she, too, attributed to the shock of Amy's death. 'He became more attached to her these last few years than he had been previously, so for him there is an irony that she should die, after they were so reconciled.'

This made sense: I could understand how it made Amy's death harder to bear. I took comfort in Hugh's assurance that Justin would recover, but I was hurt by the way he distanced himself.

The stables were at their busiest, and I knew he was needed there, but in previous years he had snatched time to be with me, talking of business or discussing our correspondence or even gossiping about our neighbours. Anxieties would be shared and there would be smiles and banter and hugs and kisses, also.

All this was gone. At breakfast he retreated behind a newspaper; after dinner, he disappeared to the library to deal with business. All remarks of mine received polite replies but none encouraged conversation. When I opened up the pianoforte, hoping that music would reach him, he remained indifferent. Watching my husband become a stranger, I was bewildered and helpless, but found no means of dealing with it.

I might have done better had I been feeling well, but I was not, though my complaints were trifling enough, and I made no mention of them. Amy was dead; how then, could I make a fuss about minor disorders? So when I was plagued with heartburn I dosed myself with rhubarb powder and when I was sick I took a little brandy in water. I had to exert myself to eat, but I consumed enough to avoid attracting attention.

When the Kirks and the Makepeaces came to dine with us, Justin exerted himself to be agreeable. I allowed myself to hope that having company had done the trick. My hopes were dashed, because he reverted to coldness the instant they left. It seemed he felt they were worth the trouble and I was not.

During the day, he was occupied around the stables, and often during the night, when mares were foaling. One night I had fallen asleep before he came to bed and woke to a sound of uncontrollable shivering.

'I am s-s-sorry,' he said. 'I d-d-did not mean to wake you.'

'It is of no consequence. What time is it? Heavens, what have you been doing?'

'B-b-breech b-b-birth. F-freezing!'

The fire in our room had turned to ashes, and the air was chilled. I moved across the bed, wincing as the linen struck cold. 'You must lie here, where I have made the sheets warm.'

He was very cold indeed, shuddering, and I nestled around him to give him warmth. He refused to put his feet on me but I insisted. 'You must get warm, Justin, or you will be ill.'

I reached my feet towards his: they were like two frozen lumps of clay, and I had the strange sensation that he was actually drawing heat from me.

At last his shivering stopped and he sighed and fell asleep. I followed suit and we slept with our bodies curled together. It was the closest we had been since I returned from London.

In the morning he made an attempt to thank me and since he was uneasy, I changed the subject, asking which mare had been in difficulties and how she was faring, and what of her foal?

He answered me, talking easily now and I felt my spirits rising. I persuaded myself we could come through our trouble, that we could talk again, become easier together, and the time would come when we could reach each other.

I was encouraged at breakfast when the newspaper was left folded against his plate. He pulled out a chair for me, as he always did, and touched my shoulder with a restrained smile.

In such circumstances it was difficult to think of an easy topic for conversation, and my difficulty was increased with the discomfort of being plagued by heartburn.

I might have mentioned my heartburn then, but Blanche had something on her mind. 'Judith, I had the strangest dream,' she said. 'You and I were in a place we did not know and Amy was there also. There was a young man with her and you told her she should not encourage him because he was dead. Then she said she was dead, too, and it was so because they must be together. Is that not strange?'

'Very strange indeed,' I agreed. Privately, I thought her dreaming mind had invented this comfort, but I did not say so.

Justin put down his knife. 'The Bible tells us there is no giving and taking in marriage in heaven,' he reminded her.

'It does not say there is no love,' retorted Blanche. Then: 'She called him Augustus.' Neither of us had anything to say and she shrugged. 'Well, it was only a dream, after all,' she said. 'But I thought you would like to know.'

'A heaven-sent dream, I am sure,' I said, willing her to take her own comfort from it. 'For who knows, it may be true.'

Justin's expression was closed and I could see he was not yet ready to discuss Amy's death. Blanche's dream had no comfort for him, rather the reverse: he had withdrawn again, just as I had hoped for an easing of the situation between us.

Blanche spent much of her time with the Makepeaces and I made no objection. No one could help Blanche better than Mrs Makepeace and Charlotte was a sympathetic and agreeable companion, also.

Easter brought no visit from Hugh and Helen or the Wysalls, for Hugh wished

Helen close to her own doctor and the Wysalls arranged to visit at Bennerley.

We received visits from our neighbours, but most of the time I was left to my own occupations. This was advantageous, for not wishing any to-do, I could conceal my sickness. I knew my discomfort was caused only by the shock of Amy's death and the strain of trying to reach Justin.

I was too occupied with my troubles to take account when our neighbours informed me of another death, for the name meant nothing to me. Mr Parsons was not one of our neighbours and I could not imagine why so many people took such an interest.

The interest, I soon discovered, was because the widowed Mrs Parsons was a lady known in our neighbourhood. I was told that, inconsolable in her grief, the widow was to return, on a visit to her own family. As I was told, some looked at me in a way I did not understand. Comprehension came only when I realized the widow was none other than the lady who had once been engaged to Justin.

Arabella Cartwright!

And I knew, though I cannot say how I knew, that upon her return, the fair Arabella meant to seek consolation for her loss in the arms of my husband.

21

'They say she is returning home,' I said.

Only two of us were at table that evening, for Blanche was dining with the Makepeaces. I waited until the servants had left the room before I spoke.

'Who is returning home?'

'Arabella what's-her-name, do you tell me you have not heard? It has been the talk of the neighbourhood this last few days.'

There had been interest, I might almost call it anticipation, in the way I was looked at by those neighbours who had previous acquaintance with the widow.

'I heard her husband had died,' he admitted coolly. 'Nothing of her return, though it does not astonish me. It is natural she should wish the support of her family at such a time.'

'No doubt she will find comfort in renewing all her old acquaintances, also,' I said.

His expression closed. 'Perhaps.'

I wished to know how he felt about it, but he was good at concealing his feelings, when he chose. I had no means of knowing what he was thinking. For myself, I could not help feeling a little reassurance would have been acceptable.

I first saw Mrs Parsons in company with her relations, at church. I could not observe her during service, for their pew was behind our own, but on going in we had been obliged to pass them, and acknowledge them. Arabella had seated herself next to the aisle, and perhaps it was unkind of me to suspect she had done so deliberately, intending that all should see her.

I did not allow my gaze to linger, but I remarked her very carefully with one passing glance: she was slender, and her widows weeds gave her a becoming air of fragility. Her skin was fair, her hair raven dark, and a huge pair of green eyes looked soulfully at my husband. It was enough to revive my suspicions.

Heartburn plagued me through service. Afterwards, I braced myself for the introductions which would take place outside.

Justin's colour rose as he introduced the woman he had married to the woman he had proposed to. Her eyes were cold as she looked at me, but I kept my countenance, made the proper remarks, offering condolences on the loss of her husband.

Her replies were brief and she turned her

attention to Justin. After expressing regrets about Amy, she went on to speak of the stables. 'I am told you become prosperous, and I am not surprised. Always, you were skilled with horses. How pleased and proud your grandfather would have been.'

Then her eyes widened. 'Heavens! Is this Blanche? How you have grown up!'

'It has been seven years, madam,' said Blanche coolly. 'One must expect to grow up between the ages of twelve and nineteen.' Then she added obscurely, 'Or not at all.'

Mrs Parsons gave an affected little laugh. 'Oh, dear me, yes, of course. So many changes! And dear Charlotte, too! I declare you are both become quite elegant young ladies.'

As Colonel Makepeace introduced her to his wife, I watched the reactions of both my husband and Mrs Makepeace.

Justin was watching Arabella, his expression impassive, his sentiments concealed. Mrs Makepeace paid polite attention to the lady and only those who knew her well would detect her scornful amusement at the patronizing manner of the newcomer.

I knew I would gain nothing by expressing disapprobation to Justin. On the way home, I spoke mildly: Mrs Parsons had an elegant appearance, I said. I risked a shaft at him by suggesting she would not long remain a widow and remarked she must discover many changes in the neighbourhood.

'I admired her when I was a child,' said Blanche, 'but either my perception has changed, or she has, for I cannot say I was at all taken with her, today. I think Mrs Makepeace did not like her, either. Do you think she has changed, Justin?'

'Very little, I think.'

Beyond that, he would not be drawn, and Blanche went on, 'I wonder what Amy would have thought of her?'

This brought up in me a surge of grief and longing for Amy with her clear, pointed remarks. Tears welled in my eyes, and Blanche exclaimed, and thrust a handkerchief towards me.

'Oh dear! I am sorry. I do so miss her, you know.'

'We all do,' said Justin curtly.

I said nothing. That he was grieving, I did not doubt, but he had refused all comfort and neither had he offered any. I felt twice bereaved: I had lost a sister and a husband also.

The next day I was thankful to find myself free of heartburn and sickness. I felt a renewed vigour and addressed myself to the task of recovering my husband with more energy. I had Pink Ribbon saddled and asked if he could spare time to ride out.

Once, he would have found time; now he made excuses. Blanche suggested a visit to Mrs Makepeace, and Justin looked relieved when I agreed.

Charlotte took Blanche away shortly after our arrival, and I have no doubt it was done purposely, to leave me alone with Mrs Makepeace. So far, the gossips had been given nothing to wag their tongues over, but little escaped that lady: she understood me and knew I was unhappy.

'Justin is grieving over Amy's death,' I said, for I had no intention of voicing other fears. I did not care to discuss my husband, even with a trusted friend such as Mrs Makepeace. 'He is not one who overcomes such feelings with ease, and he is most unwilling to discuss it. I know not how to help him.'

'Perhaps you should try giving him some Pol Thompson,' she suggested and I smiled.

Mrs Makepeace had been excessively diverted to learn this local term for verbal abuse. 'I rather fancy my husband has too often been the recipient of Pol Thompson, without deserving it,' I said. 'It would not jolt him out of his present frame of mind. He is more likely to withdraw even further.'

She sighed. 'You know your husband best,' she conceded.

I shook my head. 'Once, I did: now I am at a loss. I could wish I had been not so tired, but Amy's death sapped my own strength. Well, I am feeling better today so I may prevail. But I do fear I have overlooked something of vital importance.'

'I wish I could help, but I am persuaded any meddling on my part would make matters worse.' She hesitated. 'Judith, what do you know of the widow, Mrs Parsons?'

'I know what the gossips have told you,' I said. 'She was once engaged to Justin — and jilted him when she discovered his expectations had been squandered. It was a long time ago.'

'It was, and now he is married to you and she cannot hope for anything,' said Mrs Makepeace. 'But I have met her kind before, Judith, and I must advise you to beware. She is one who does not easily relinquish. She would prefer — after all these years, she would still prefer to believe Sir Justin is languishing after her. She resents your marriage and if she can make trouble, she will delight in so doing.'

I said nothing. At times, I thought my suspicions were based on my fears, but now Mrs Makepeace had given her opinion, I could no longer chide myself. I was not mistaken.

I sighed. Arabella could not make trouble unless Justin allowed it, and if he did allow it I had no power to prevent it.

Upon returning to Melrose Court, I was told Justin had gone to Chesterfield on some business matter. He did not mention seeing Arabella whilst he was there and I heard of it later, when we were troubled with a morning visit from Mrs Buxton.

'A chance encounter, my dear Lady Martin, I am persuaded it could not be otherwise.' she said, hoping to convince me it had been an assignation. 'But Dr Gillott did remark how they seemed to have a lot to say to each other.'

I merely expressed concern that Mrs Buxton had occasion to consult the doctor.

For a few days I remained free of sickness and heartburn but I became ill again on Friday and cursed inwardly when Arabella Parsons chose that day to pay a morning visit.

She came with her relations, the Cartwrights, and I remarked a certain narrowing of her eyes as she looked about her. I think she was disconcerted to see how thoroughly I had put my own stamp on Melrose Court.

It was the only satisfaction I had that

day. Arabella had spent her early years in the neighbourhood and when Justin joined us in the morning-room she engaged him in conversation about former times, reminiscing over long ago events, reminding him of his grandparents and things they would say.

She had drawn him into realms where I could not follow. I knew his grandparents had influenced his boyhood, and he had spoken of them from time to time, but Arabella had known them and I had not. With all the designing arts at her command, with fluttering eyelids and wistful smiles, she was now making use of this advantage to exclude me from the conversation.

Perhaps I would not have resented the lightening of his countenance, his smile, or the ready way he responded to her, had he not become so distant with me.

A few months ago I had felt so secure in his love that I would have laughed at the impertinence of a newly widowed woman having any expectation of receiving his attentions.

Now, everything was changed: I was by no means secure. I was married to him, and I hoped I could expect his loyalty, but as I watched him I could not help recalling that I had been the one who had wished this marriage and proposed it myself.

They left after half an hour and I, feeling nausea rise in my throat, had to excuse myself quickly. When I returned to the drawing-room, Justin had gone outside again.

Between us, matters remained the same, with Justin remaining polite, courteous, but always distant, and I exerting myself to reach him.

I talked to him: I enquired about our horses and expressed optimism about the profits he would make this year. I spoke of our acquaintance, not forgetting to include careful mention of Mrs Parsons. I told him of the letters I received from Helen and Sophie and Isobel. I expressed opinions and ventured to enquire of his. I tried to appear easy, but all the time I was waiting, watching for a softening of his manner, a sign that I might move to bridge the gulf between us.

We were obliged to return Arabella's visit. To my relief, Blanche said she would accompany us. There may have been quiet conspiring, for when we paid that visit, the Makepeaces and the Kirks paid their duty visits at the same time.

The room was crowded. 'Dear Mama!' Arabella smirked. 'I declare, we seem to be all the fashion today!'

She was given no opportunity, that day, to monopolize my husband, or to dominate the conversation. There was talk, determined talk, of the weather, and the crops and schemes which had been proposed for the approaching summer.

Justin said little, speaking only to Colonel Makepeace about poulticing a mare. He looked at Arabella, but his expression gave no clue to his thoughts. His gaze travelled over the rest of the company and once he looked at me, but he glanced away quickly when I met his eyes.

If Arabella could not speak to Justin, she could signal with her eyes, and I could interpret her looks. I saw her mother's fond smiles and was roused to anger as I saw knowing smirks on the faces of her sisters.

'I thought I disliked her,' said Blanche on the way home, 'and now I am certain of it. Did you hear her Judith?' She raised her voice in imitation. ' '*Once my affections are placed, nothing has the power to change them*'. This, when we all know her affections are placed according to her ambition! I wonder she can dare to speak so!'

'She has certainly been unlucky in losing your good opinion,' answered Justin, 'yet I think she will not greatly suffer for it, when so many are disposed to admire her.'

Blanche flushed and I was angry on her behalf. Clearly, Justin felt the number of visitors was an indication of Arabella's popularity.

On Sunday, after church, Justin invited the Kirks and the Makepeaces to dine at Melrose Court. This was by no means unusual, but on this occasion he invited the Cartwrights, also. Following some malicious impulse, I invited Mrs Buxton.

Fortunately for him, he had the wisdom to refrain from reproaching me, for had he done so he might have found himself, after all, the recipient of some Pol Thompson.

They came on the Tuesday: on Wednesday morning, Mrs Makepeace returned to talk over the evening, and she was laughing. 'Oh Judith,' she said, 'such an inspired idea to invite Mrs Buxton! I confess, I wondered what you were about.'

'Do not credit me with foresight I did not possess, madam,' I said, 'for I had given no thought to what I was about.'

Mrs Buxton had come determined to shine, or as Mrs Makepeace shrewdly observed, determined to outshine Arabella.

At table, she had no scruples about speaking of the events surrounding dear Amy's death. Her design was to mention her acquaintance with the dear Duke and Duchess of Flamborough, and she contrived it by saying how dreadfully they must feel to have had their ball blighted by such a singular occurrence.

Having scraped an introduction, that lady chose to mention her acquaintance with the Flamboroughs on every conceivable occasion. Wishing to boast of it to Arabella, she enquired of me how they did and expressed approbation of the duchess.

'Such a sweet lady, how beautiful, how stylish! And her hair, such a delightful auburn! In general, you know, I do not admire redheads, but in her case one has to concede a point.'

Her conversation when we ladies had withdrawn from table, ran along similar lines. She talked to me, enquiring after the Tremaines with an appearance of intimacy. She conveyed she knew my uncle, the Earl of Ramsgate. She made much of me, of my skill as a horse-woman and my musical accomplishment. I could neither approve nor like Mrs Buxton, but I confess to an indecent feeling of triumph, for Arabella could only listen to her in silent indignation.

I believe Mrs Buxton's position was calculated to establish herself and to set down Arabella, rather than any design of assisting me, and I said so to Mrs Makepeace.

'Calculated, certainly,' she replied. 'Do not underestimate Mrs Buxton, Judith. She may have been discomposed by your marriage to Sir Justin, but she has had time to get over that and she believes her own advantage lies in being on terms with you. With your connections, you have greater consequence in polite society than the widowed Mrs Parsons.'

I said nothing. I had enjoyed a pleasing social triumph, but it was of no assistance in the matter of recovering my husband.

Last night, in my anxiety, I could not ignore anything that passed between Justin and Arabella: my ears had stretched and what I heard was wholly upsetting.

He had been standing some little distance from my chair, talking to Charlotte Makepeace and when Blanche claimed that lady's attention, Arabella had sauntered over to him.

'Justin, I do so pity you,' she murmured. 'However came you to marry such a drab little creature, so lacking in animation?'

'Surely, my dear Arabella, my reasons for marrying should not require any explanation?'

She had laughed, roguishly. 'No indeed! I have been hearing all about her fine friends and connections. No doubt they have been most advantageous to you.'

'How well you understand these matters, madam.'

She laughed again. 'Well, it is not to be wondered at, for I know she brought with her some fortune, also.' She allowed her voice to soften to sympathy. 'My dear, I do fear you are learning, even as I did, that material advantage is not a good motive for marrying.' She sighed, and made a hint of distress thicken her voice. 'How often have I wished I had not allowed myself to be guided by notions of prudence in my own marriage. But then, dear Mama and Papa were so very pressing.'

'You were young: no doubt they had your interests at heart.'

I did not hear what he said next for Mrs Kirk came to speak to me. But I thought he was disposed to excuse her desertion and accept that her parents had persuaded her to act against her inclinations. No doubt he accepted also, in her expressed regrets, the implication that she cared for him.

I recalled how sturdily he had once defended her decision to cry off from her engagement. I suspected that in Justin's eyes, Arabella could do no wrong.

I was recalled to the present when Mrs Makepeace asked if I thought Justin would allow Blanche to accompany her family on a touring holiday that summer. I thought he would, and she spent the rest of her visit discussing the scheme.

When she left, I fell to brooding. Last night, Justin had mentioned he would be riding into Chesterfield today on a matter of business. Arabella had heard and I had no doubt she herself meant to visit the town.

I was tortured by my own imaginings: Justin was often riding into Chesterfield, making business his excuse. He had left two hours ago. I was persuaded he was, even at that moment, smiling at Arabella as she fluttered her lashes at him.

Upon his return Justin said Mr Wiseman had sent his compliments: no encounter with Arabella was mentioned. Yet I was persuaded she had determined to meet him.

Once, Justin had paid his addresses to her. I had received no such compliment. Now, I tortured myself with the suspicion he had taken me only because I had made myself available when he thought the woman he truly loved was lost.

My thoughts were poisoned. I recalled how quickly he had spoken of love after I declared myself, and now I suspected that love as being very convenient. By taking me, he had a wife who loved him, and who had a fortune which, even though he refused to avail himself of it, would certainly have been placed at his disposal in any situation of need.

Arabella was right in observing my fortune and connections were advantageous to him. My relations and friends had purchased horses, and also recommended his beasts to their acquaintance.

I had taken upon myself the refurbishing of Melrose Court, at no little expense, disguising my designs under the pretence of 'making myself comfortable', but really seeking to make him comfortable. This had also made it possible to offer impressive hospitality to prospective customers, which had done him good service.

More service had I done him, in the matter of his sisters, for I had secured a companion who knew how to reconcile them to each other, and to him. They had come to affection and respect, and if this made Amy's death hard to bear, it was not my fault she had died.

He had been very sensible of all the advantages of marrying me, and I felt I had done well by him: I had schemed to profit him and I had schemed to please him, and thought only of his comfort.

Yet I, too, needed comfort and was being denied. I needed assurance and was being denied. I needed his love and was being denied.

He had not even noticed I was not quite well. It had never crossed his mind! It was true I had taken pains to conceal it, yet I think that had either he or Blanche been out of sorts, I would have noticed.

I began to feel myself very ill-used. In anger and resentment I ceased all my attempts to recover my husband.

22

Weeks passed. I made no complaints, neither did I make any further attempt to recover my husband. If he observed my retreat, he made no exertions of his own to mend matters.

My resentment died, my anger died and I grew listless and apathetic. I felt that all was lost, but I could not yet bring myself to consider any arrangement for the future.

My bouts of sickness came less frequently and eventually stopped, though I was still plagued by heartburn. Since exertion made it worse, I took little exercise As a result I experienced a dull ache in my back, which further disinclined me to exertion and I began to gain weight.

We saw Arabella at church and in company and often she came to Melrose Court to pay a morning visit. Always she behaved as though she was on intimate terms with my husband.

'I cannot tell you how delightful it is to be home again! So many of my old friends, still here, just the same. Dear Blanche, I declare your brother has not changed at all!'

Justin was more reserved. He was agreeable

to Arabella, but so he was to others of our acquaintance. I suspected he was captivated, but he did not behave in a way to declare it openly.

Every Wednesday, Justin had business in Chesterfield. No word reached me that he met Arabella; our friends remained silent.

Blanche must have observed the distance between Justin and myself, but she said nothing. No doubt Mrs Makepeace had advised her to leave us to ourselves.

Blanche joined the Makepeaces on a touring holiday that summer. I was pleased for her, for she would escape the uneasy atmosphere between Justin and myself and have good friends for company.

They went in June and I then determined what I must do. Hugh had written, asking me to go to Bennerley to assist Helen in her confinement. Her child was due in July, but she was grown large and thought she might deliver early.

I told Justin, with no hope or expectation that he would offer to accompany me. He only said, 'When do you return?'

'I think I shall not,' I said calmly.

He looked at me then, without expression. 'I see.'

'I told you once, sir, that I would have no reluctant husband. As I recall, you were not in the least reluctant at the time, and although that has changed, I have not. What I said, I will hold to. I shall trouble you no longer.'

Justin frowned. 'You cannot — I do not feel it advisable for you to remain in Leicestershire. Judith — he is married, and a father! Your own happiness cannot be served by seeing him.'

'I have never begrudged my brother his happiness, as you well know, and I shall not do so, even now.'

I forced down a sob, determined I would not be a watering-pot. I own I had some dread of being at Bennerley, for I knew that seeing Helen and Hugh together would be the most painful reminder of what was lost.

'He wishes me for Helen, for her lying-in. When she is recovered, I shall determine my future.'

We were at breakfast. Justin seemed intent upon drawing patterns on the tablecloth with the handle of his knife. I could not determine his expression: his head was tilted and he appeared to be listening to some voice from far away.

He put down the knife. 'Do you wilfully misunderstand me, madam? Do you think to blind me to your preference? Simpleton have I been, but once undeceived, you will not persuade me against it. I have seen where your affections lie.'

He paused, clearly struggling with himself, whilst I gazed at him in speechless incomprehension.

'For your own sake,' he said, his voice softer now, 'I advise you against remaining in Leicestershire. I am sorry to pain you, but you must know if you see him often you will be miserable.'

Heartburn was plaguing me and my thoughts were upon Helen and Hugh. I was utterly confused. 'I see no misery in having affection for my brother, and certainly you have no right to complain of it. Upon my soul, I never heard of such a thing!'

I was perturbed, but there was a set look on his countenance which I had seen before, and this brought to my mind a shock of recall. 'Oh!' I gasped, struggling with my realization. 'Now I understand. Yet again, you accuse me of wishing for Richard.'

'Do you deny it, madam?'

'I do not.' I was outwardly calm, but anger was boiling inside me, prompting me to malice. 'Certainly, I do not. You said I shall not persuade you against, therefore I shall not make the attempt. I thank you for your trust in me! I do not ask how you have come to this determination, for I have heard enough absurdities this past half-hour, and I have not the patience to hear more. I beg you will excuse me, sir!'

I left the room, too angry to believe he had any serious doubts of my affection. He was the one grown cold, not I! After all my patience, my exertions, my hopes of recovering our happiness, he could not fail to see how I was pained. This nonsense was because he wished it! He longed for Arabella, he was tired of me and thought only to excuse his own inconstancy.

'Judith . . . '

He followed me from the room, but now I was halfway upstairs. 'You may spare yourself any further trouble on my account,' I said coldly. 'I leave for Bennerley directly.'

'You used to be wiser,' he said, catching up with me.

'Indeed?' I paused as I reached the top of the stairs. 'And when was that, pray? When I was desirous of your comfort, always, and exerting myself to please you? I can easily comprehend how you must think so! I hold the opposite opinion, that I am come to wisdom late, for these last few months it has been most painfully clear to me that I have been wasting my time. Be so good as to order the carriage, sir.'

He stepped in front of me, barring my

way. His countenance was flushed and he struggled for speech.

'These reproaches I might consider deserved had you not concealed from me that Hargreaves was with you in London!' he said at last. 'Never did you mention any expectation of seeing him, no word of his presence did you write to me! And that I should learn of it from your brother in such abominable circumstances! I do not take kindly to such concealment, madam, for there can be only one explanation! Small wonder you found no agreeable companion for my sister! Never had you any intention of doing so, for you had found a most agreeable companion for yourself, had you not?'

'Richard — Richard has been a good friend, a very good friend indeed, and fortunate it was that he happened to be in town, for he was there to lend all his support and assistance when I was in dire need of it. How dare you slander him so, when he did so much! And me! To accuse me of misconduct is bad enough! To be accused of cavorting over Amy's deathbed is the most pernicious . . . and this is your opinion of me!'

'Madam, you — '

'Oh, do not speak to me!' I was sobbing with rage and disgust. 'I have not the patience to hear more! All this is to excuse your rejection of me! I could laugh at myself, I could indeed, for believing it was Amy's death you had taken so hard! Hugh told me I should have patience, and so I had, waiting and watching for a sign that I might reach you and comfort you and be comforted myself! And all in vain! You had no grief for Amy, none at all! In truth, I believe Richard felt more and he scarce knew her!'

I worked my way round him and marched away. I was halfway across the gallery when he caught my arm and swung me round.

'Do not now pretend to sympathy for my loss!' Justin had paled to an alarming degree and his voice came in a forced whisper. 'I will not speak to you of my grief for very quickly it was clear your own grief was for loss of your London pursuits, which Amy's death so inconveniently curtailed!'

His fingers were cutting into me, but I scarce felt his grip. I stared at him, appalled. 'How can you speak such calumny?'

'Oh, come now! Your expressions betray you, even as you make these protestations! Ever since your return from town you have looked all your disdain — of me — of this neighbourhood. I have remarked all your discontent at being separated from the amusements and elegance of fashionable society! You should have exerted yourself to secure Hargreaves, madam, before he became attached to another.'

'Had I wished for him, I could have had him,' I said coldly.

Justin's hand fell from my arm and I rubbed against the aching imprint of his grip. I was sobbing now with all the injustice of his accusations. Small wonder if I had looked my unhappiness, when he had been so cold to me! After nearly three years of being married to him, of loving him so, I could not believe he truly thought I wished for Richard.

'I could have had him,' I repeated. 'And no need to lower myself in my own esteem by proposing the match myself, for twice he proposed to me!'

Neither of Richard's proposals had been at all flattering to my vanity, but that was something I did not impart.

'You are surprised, sir, that a man could wish for such a drab little creature, so lacking in animation?'

'You must know — '

'I see what you are about! Willing as you were to take me, you now resent me, since *she* was widowed and returned with all her arts and allurements to draw you back to her.'

'If you mean Arabella — '

'After all, how could such a drab creature hope to compete with the fair beauty? So beguiling, so wistful, but not too innocent to understand the forces of financial prudence! Such an interesting discussion you had with her on the subject!'

'Never did I encourage — '

'I should have left then, for it was clear I had nothing to hope for. Now I am done, I shall leave for Bennerley. Be so good as to stand aside. I shall waste my time no longer.'

'Judith — '

'I wonder you still seek to detain me: you have made your opinion of me quite plain. It could not be plainer! There is nothing more to be said.'

Sobbing, I whirled away from him, reached my dressing-room, closed the door and locked it, fighting for breath. I was seized with such a fit of trembling that I could not support myself and fell to my knees and lay down upon the floor. Despair clutched at my sides and tears fell hot and silent, as all my thoughts twisted and taunted and jeered.

I know not how long I remained alone with my grief for I passed through a time when my mind was blank. When I regained my senses I laboured to get to my feet, rang for my maid, and gave orders to pack.

Never had I felt so tired, so bemused. I could do nothing myself, all was left to Betty. It was the greatest trouble to walk to my carriage, for I felt such weakness.

At first, I found relief in sleeping, huddled in a corner of the carriage. I woke when we stopped to change horses. Travelling on, I tried to think, but my mind was so muddled I achieved nothing sensible.

The light remained long at that time of year and I could have reached Bennerley before nightfall, but travelling made me feel queasy so I took Betty's advice, putting up at an inn. I retired early, slept heavily and awoke with a dull feeling of resignation and a resolve to pull myself together.

I spoke to Betty. 'I know you are sensible of discord between myself and the master,' I said. 'I wish you to remain silent on the subject: I would have no word of it reach my brother from his servants, as it undoubtedly will, should you gossip.'

'As you wish, My Lady.'

She sounded hurt, for she had been my maid a long time and deserved better than curt orders. 'I do not wish to add to my brother's anxieties,' I explained. 'When Mrs Tremaine is safely delivered and recovering, I shall make him acquainted with my situation. Meanwhile, I shall keep my own counsel and

I may reach some decision before I need to trouble him.'

'High time you did,' said Betty. 'Lord knows, it has been going on long enough.'

I arrived at Bennerley with a smile which wavered in the loving embraces of my relations, so different from the cold atmosphere at Melrose Court. I blinked back tears, told them Justin sent his love, spoke of 'business' to explain why I was alone, and managed to laugh. 'He is like all gentlemen,' I said, 'and prefers to keep out of the way when there is women's work to be done! Helen, dear, how are you?'

She spoke feelingly about the energy of her unborn infant. 'I declare, he thinks my womb is his ballroom,' she complained. 'At this present he is dancing the boulanger. Come, Christopher, you have not seen Aunt Judith for many months, but surely you have not forgotten?'

I embraced my nephew, talked to him and we all sat down to a late breakfast. At table they talked of Bennerley and enquired of Melrose Court and when my eyes filled with tears, I said, by way of explanation, that we were all missing Amy.

Helen teased me about 'my friend, Mrs Buxton', and I told them of the new widow. I got some relief by delivering slighting remarks about Arabella, and I was quite witty as I described the two widows at my dinner party.

I am a lady who prefers to be open in all my dealings and I do not care for disguise of any sort. But here, I could not escape the necessity and I felt some astonishment at the ease with which I could deceive. I confess, I was glad of it: I could not be happy, I could at least give the appearance of it.

So I was dismayed when Hugh brought his fist down on the table. 'If looks could kill!' he exclaimed angrily. 'My dear sister, if I have offended you, speak plainly what is on your mind instead of regarding me with such an expression of silent disgust. I declare it is enough to freeze my blood!'

'Sir?' I was all astonishment. 'You mistake me, sir,' I said as the truth dawned on me. 'Indeed, I mean no disrespect. It is merely that I am a little distressed with heartburn.'

'Oh!' Hugh's lips parted and he blinked at me as his anger cooled. 'Oh! Is that all?'

'Heartburn, Judith?' enquired Helen. 'Never before have I heard you complain of such. Are you — Oh! Oh! Rascal!'

The child in her womb had kicked, upsetting the cup and saucer she was holding against herself. We laughed and mopped up and in this trifling commotion my complaint was forgotten.

When Helen was taking rest and Hugh dealing with business of his own, I wandered into the gardens and seated myself upon a bench within the hermitage.

Justin's words came back to me.

'*Your expressions betray you madam! Ever since your return from town you have looked all your disdain — of me — of this neighbourhood. I have remarked all your discontent at being separated from the amusements and elegance of fashionable society* . . . '

I knew not whether to laugh or weep! Plagued with heartburn I had, quite unconsciously, been pulling faces, which was quite enough to cause uneasiness in my husband, as it had with Hugh.

As a boy, pained by his father's absences, Justin could scarce have avoided the reflection: 'Papa would prefer to be in town rather than with me.'

It was a wound that had never quite healed because for years he had been confronted by Amy who made no secret of her longing for all the amusements and elegance of fashionable society.

In my grimaces he had found that same interpretation: 'Judith would prefer to be in town rather than with me.'

I recalled his unease on that account when I proposed.

'*You are so accustomed to living in the style of elegance, so accustomed to fashionable society . . .*'

I now recalled how often he had sought my assurances that I was content with him at Melrose Court.

'*I fear there will come a time when you will wish yourself less beset by circumstance. I cannot move in society in the way that I ought and there is little entertainment for you here.*'

Often, Justin had taken the trouble to arrange excursions, often he had proposed visits from my friends, and when we made our own visits, he said I might, if I wished, prolong my stay. Once, he had enquired if I would like to join Hugh and Helen on a holiday, although it was impossible for him to be with us.

To misinterpret my grimaces, to suspect a longing for diversions was excusable: but my resentment revived when I remembered he had accused me of misconduct, and with Richard!

'*You had found a most agreeable companion for yourself, had you not . . . ?*'

He knew I did not wish for Richard, of course he did, none better! He had seen how concerned I was to remove all such uneasiness from Isobel's mind, and he had all the evidence of our daily lives together to show him where my affection lay.

He wished to believe me attached to Richard! I saw all the truth of it! He sought to excuse his preference for Arabella.

' . . . *and to learn of it from your brother in such abominable circumstances . . .* '

'Oh!' At the time these words were uttered I had been too indignant to take proper notice. Justin's withdrawal had begun when we returned from London, some weeks before the news about Arabella had reached Derbyshire. Whatever he now felt, his first suspicions had nothing to do with her. I swallowed and tried to set aside my misery as I struggled to read his mind.

'*Never did you mention any expectation of seeing him . . . no word of his presence did you write . . .*'

Of course not! I had no expectation of seeing Richard and he had been but a few days in town.

'*I do not take kindly to such concealment . . .*'

Again, I was aggrieved and indignant. Justin had no cause to suspect me of concealment!

' . . . *to learn of it . . . in such abominable circumstances . . .* '

Abominable circumstances, indeed. He could be excused for being not quite rational at such a time. And I, sick and weary from the journey home, must have been pulling faces, even as I stepped from the carriage. Heartburn!

'*I have seen where your affections lie . . .*'

Justin had always been a little stiff in his manner towards Richard, perhaps not properly understanding our friendship. With all her schemes and ambition, Richard's mother had forced me to be very frank with him: we understood each other, but I knew some were confused by Lady Hargreaves. I had seen Isobel must be brought to a proper understanding, but never had I imagined Justin might feel some uneasiness.

Well, indeed, how should it? To him, I had made myself clear. I had proposed the marriage! My indignation surfaced again. I had gone so far as to propose to him, so how could he be in doubt of my affections?

My back ached, my head ached and I returned to the house in confusion. Was it due to our misunderstandings that Justin's affection for Arabella had revived? Was it possible that, with misunderstandings out of the way, he might yet renounce her and look for contentment with me?

He was married to me: separation was

possible, but I did not wish the scandal of a divorce, and I could not feel that he would either. Could I seek a reconciliation on those terms?

I could not. Once I had lowered myself in my own esteem to propose to him. I had married him, loved him, concerned myself with his comfort and thought of no other. I had been a true and faithful wife.

I could not flatter myself that he would seek a reconciliation. Always, I had been the one who had done the most, who cared the most.

Indoors it was darker and cooler than outside and a breeze drifted through an open window, cooling my flushed cheeks. For some reason, this brought about a change of feeling: an image of Amy rose in my mind, and I imagined her voice.

'Do put off these dreary mourning clothes, Judith, you know I do not like them.'

'Oh, Amy, I do so love you!' I said aloud.

I abandoned reflection and walked upstairs as though in a dream, no thought of anything except changing my drab mourning gown for something more pleasing to wear.

My dreamlike state continued; fresh and cool in sprigged muslin, I regarded myself in the looking-glass in surprise, as though

I was looking at someone I did not know and, for a reason I did not know, I recalled something Sophie had said.

'*How fortunate are these high-waisted fashions for ladies in my condition! I shall be utterly disguised.*'

I gasped as I felt a fluttering movement inside me: I raised my head, attentive now, and once again I felt it.

Scarce believing my suspicion, I began to calculate: lately, there had been no intimacy between myself and Justin. If I had conceived, it must have happened before going to London.

Five months! And again I felt the quickening in my womb.

At last, I understood all the symptoms which I had so long been attributing to other causes. There could be no doubt about it. For five months, without knowing it, I had been with child.

23

I was very calm. I knew I could use the child to draw Justin back to me, but I determined I would not. He would learn of this only when I had resolved my position.

I recalled the coldness of the last few months, I recalled all his bitter accusations, and my anger was fuelled now, by a new idea. It occurred to me that Justin might attribute my condition to my supposed attachment to Richard.

Any such doubt in his mind could easily be removed, for Blanche, when she returned from her holiday, would support my word concerning the very short time Richard had been in town. But I then determined I would not accept my husband, should he need any corroboration of my word.

For our child's sake, I resigned myself to making the first approach. For my own sake, I resolved on maintaining dignity. I would ask if he wished to discuss a reconciliation. The rest would depend upon how he responded to this first overture, and how far he would go to content me. Should he fail me, he would not later draw me back to him when he learnt of his child.

We had no company at Bennerley that evening, so after dinner I excused myself to my relations and sat down to write to him.

As I wrote, I was careful to recommend that he should give his own serious consideration to the matter. We would be reunited only if I could be satisfied that he truly wished it, and I would expect him to set aside his fancy for Arabella and abide by me, giving me his loyalty and his trust.

I was choosing my words with difficulty and so intent was I upon expressing all in a firm, dignified way that I did not hear the door open. When a hand came down upon my shoulder I started, upset the inkwell, and watched in dismay as my whole endeavour was ruined in pool of spilt ink.

'Oh, Helen! Look what you have made me do.'

'Such a long letter, too!' There was something faintly mocking in Helen's tone. 'For you have not seen him since yesterday, and consider all the exciting things we have been doing! How much you must have to tell him!'

I tried to mop up with my handkerchief. 'It is wholly ruined! I shall have to write it again, all over!'

'I may spare you the labour. Whatever is

so interesting, you may tell him now, for he is here.'

'What?'

Certainly there was a mocking twist to her lips. 'I said, he is here. Your husband arrived but minutes ago, madam, and now begs you will grant him permission to speak with you. He seems to feel,' she added, 'that you may prefer not to see him.'

'Justin is here?' I could scarce take it in. After all the coldness of the past few months, I could not believe he would come for me.

'He is, and astonished to find himself welcomed so cordially after the abominable way he has behaved to you.' She slanted a quizzical glance at me. 'Not,' she added, 'that he was so obliging as to make me acquainted with the particulars. He seemed to believe I must know.'

She had taken up an attitude, making it perfectly clear she was sensible of discord. I felt myself blushing over my deception. 'Oh, well, I did disguise from you that we had quarrelled, for I did not wish you distressed on my account.'

'Now you are writing to patch over your quarrel, and he has come here to patch over your quarrel, and I expect he means to be noble and take all the blame and you mean to fall upon him and weep and say it was all your fault.' She clasped her hands in an exaggerated posture. 'I do think it is so romantic!'

'Helen, please, do not mock.'

She relented when she saw my unhappiness. 'I confess, I do find the quarrels of other people far more diverting than my own,' she said. 'Well, do you wish to see him?'

'What? Oh goodness, and such a fright as I look, my fingers covered with ink and my gown spotted too! Helen, dear, do you entertain him whilst I — '

Helen let out a peal of laughter. 'Judith, this is your husband, who knows the best and worst of you! I think he will not be dismayed by a few splashes of ink. Come now, do! Compose yourself and I shall send him in to you directly.'

I swallowed hard as I tried to still the thudding of my heart. And between amazement and joy that he had come to me and apprehension as to his motive, my mind was in turmoil. I could not remember, even, what I had been writing this last hour. I could not imagine what I should say to him.

I was unwilling to advertise that I was with child. I seated myself and arranged my gown the better to disguise it. And then there was no time left for reflection or agitation, for he was in the room, and we were staring at each other.

He bowed, a deep formal bow and his first words startled me utterly. 'I have come to be your suitor, madam.'

I felt my jaw drop. Words came to me, equally absurd: 'Sir, I have to inform you that I am a married woman.'

'I know your husband for a poor creature, madam. Indeed, I do. A jealous, suspicious brute. Even though he loves you to distraction, it does not excuse him. He is not worthy of you. You know he is not. How should you care for him?'

There was a wry twist to his mouth, but his eyes were very serious, searching my face. I remembered to keep my countenance even though heartburn troubled me. 'Do you love me, Justin? I had thought your attachment to Arabella — '

'Pshw!' The sound he made and the swift gesture of his hand dismissed Arabella in an instant. 'My dear, you have persuaded yourself into suspicion, just as I did over Hargreaves. How should I wish for a cold, vain creature such as she, after knowing all your warmth and kindness, hmm? A blind fool have I been, yet not so blind nor so foolish as to wish for her.'

'Once you wished for her,' I said sulkily.

'You proposed to her!'

'I confess I did, and shortly thereafter I learnt how I had been taken in.' He saw my surprise and spoke with some awkwardness. 'I did not wish to speak bluntly, but I see I must, for I would not have you distressed on her account. Well, I was captivated, but only at first, and then I felt myself bound to her. I also felt obliged to disguise my true feelings when she ended our engagement, for it does not compliment a lady to show relief! I confess, I felt it! I had become most uneasy at the prospect of marrying her, for I had discovered she was careless over certain matters of principle. I beg you will not ask me to say more!'

Much had it cost him to betray her this far, and my mind was relieved of all anxiety. 'Very well, I will not.'

He came to me, took my hand and raised it to his lips. 'Of all the ladies in the world, I am privileged to know the best of them. I can love no other. Undeserving as I know myself to be, I must, I will, press my suit. Will you remain as my wife?'

Did any lady ever receive a prettier proposal? I accepted, of course.

He sat beside me and told me of his love, and presently I remembered his uneasiness about Richard.

'You must understand, Justin, I did not conceal his presence in town, for there was nothing at all to conceal! He arrived unexpectedly, only the day before Amy — before Amy — Oh Justin! Had he not been there, I know not what I should have done!'

'Then I will not begrudge his presence, though I confess I have done so,' he said soberly. 'I should have been with you, Judith, I should have been there to help.'

'We were all helpless, even the physicians. Nothing could predict, nothing could prevent.'

We talked of Amy, sharing our grief for the first time, letting our other troubles wait. 'Always,' he said once, 'I had dismissed her as a silly girl and a confounded nuisance. She was my sister and I had a duty to her, but I cannot say I felt any deep affection for her until these last few years. Dreadful as it was to lose her, how much worse, had I never cared for her? I have you to thank for that, Judith. You taught me how to appreciate her.'

I shook my head. 'Amy taught you herself.'

I spoke of the night she died and I wept in his arms, and mangled his cravat, and smeared him with tears and ink and at last dried my eyes on his handkerchief.

'Richard was so good,' I said. 'He dealt

with everything and called in Sophie to look after Blanche and me. There was a time when he would not have been so responsible. He has improved since his marriage to Isobel.'

'Did you never wish for him, Judith?'

'Once. I was led to think I did,' I said. 'As a child. I believed Lady Hargreaves, who spoke as though it were settled. Later, I had Mrs Makepeace — Mrs Armstrong as she was then — a very wise lady. She understood his mama's manipulations and told me there was no law to say I must marry him.'

'She persuaded you against?'

'Oh no! I was merely advised to consult my own feelings without reference to Lady Hargreaves. I am attached to Richard, we have always been good friends, but I was in no hurry to marry him, which was enough to teach me I was not in love with him. But Justin, I cannot imagine how you thought it possible! Oh, before we became engaged, perhaps, but surely not afterwards? Not after I had gone so far as to propose?'

He groaned. 'Must I confess? Must I reveal how absurd I have been? What will you think of me?'

'I do not wish to reproach you, merely to understand.'

'Looking back, I now perceive I had it all

the wrong way about,' he said. 'For when I first saw him, I thought Hargreaves was resisting his mother's wishes and causing you pain by so doing. Later, I understood you had no great opinion of Lady Hargreaves: however, you appeared to know the young man's business. I knew it was no concern of mine, but I could not help teasing myself over it.'

'I wanted to make all plain, but it was difficult, for others had been hinting at an attachment between us.'

He sighed and kissed me. 'I might have seen more clearly had I not been experiencing my own difficulties. I loved you, Judith, and had no thought of winning you in my situation. I could not ask you to share such a life as I had to offer.'

'I could see no reason why not. You knew I liked you.'

He shook his head, smiling. 'I thought you very kind and of a friendly disposition,' he said. 'Never did I suspect particular interest in myself until you were so obliging as to take matters into your own hands. Do you remember the day we saw his engagement announced? You said you had been expecting it, and I wondered . . . I wondered if you had chosen our marriage because you knew he was lost and did not wish to remain in

Leicestershire and be obliged to see them together.'

'I doubt I would have chosen marriage as an escape,' I said drily. 'I had other resources.'

'Yes, and I talked sense into myself,' he assured me. 'But I was so in love with you and so happy and there were times when I was fearful it could not last. I have ways,' he admitted, 'of spoiling my own happiness, as you have so recently discovered. I am ashamed to say I allowed my own nonsense to be revived by Lady Hargreaves.'

'Oh, Justin! You knew my opinion of that!'

'Indeed I did, and again I dismissed my uneasiness. There were other occasions: you were very pressing when you asked Hargreaves and his wife to visit, and do you recall how upset you were when they left? That was because your friend Sophie had her trouble, but once again I had my own fleeting suspicion. I dismissed it, of course. And always, when these suspicions were aroused, I was assisted by your own demeanour. For you were so loving and never did you betray an inclination for him.'

I laughed. 'I could not: I had no inclination to betray.'

But I could easily comprehend him: his

suspicion was a legacy of his unhappy past: always he had reproved himself, always he had dismissed it, never had he been able to prevent it.

He was talking more painfully now: he had received the shocking news of Amy with dazed disbelief. In his first distress his thoughts had turned to me, and all his dismay and self-reproach for not being with me himself was visited upon Hugh, who should have rushed to my assistance. My brother had carelessly informed him that Richard was helping me.

'That Hargreaves should have been there, that he should have been the one to assist you, attending to all the duty that was mine! I owed him a debt of gratitude, but I begrudged it: I know I did.'

His grief over Amy had complicated his feelings, reviving his suspicions. And I was moved, for I knew how I had been grimacing even as I returned home. I had assisted his suspicion; I had pained him into a false interpretation of my expression; yet now he made no mention of it, not one word of reproach.

Instead, he told me he had reviewed the things I said to him when we quarrelled. 'For all your anger,' he said, 'your words implied you loved me! Again and again, the things you said came back to me, and I saw all your pain and knew myself responsible! I am grieved indeed, that I should have brought you to this. Such things as I said to you! Can you forgive such a poor fool? Can you bear to have him for a husband?'

'I believe I must,' I said smiling.

I slid my arms around his neck and kissed him and I was about to tell him of my discovery when he said, 'Now, I have another thing to tell you.'

I was to learn of the business which had taken him so often into Chesterfield. He had profited more this year, profited enough to repay all that remained of his debts. He smiled when I exclaimed my delight, and congratulated him.

'All that I have, I own,' he said, 'and though there is little money to spare, I could make a modest fortune should I choose to sell. I know how you have missed all the elegance of society, Judith, and it has pained me to deprive you of your pleasures. I propose we should move away from Derbyshire: I could purchase an estate somewhere closer to London, and we may go to town as often as you wish. What say you?'

'We shall do no such thing!' I said indignantly. 'Would I have you sacrifice all you have worked for?' I was upset, but moved too, that he would go so far to please me. 'You mistake me, Justin. I do not choose to be gallivanting off to town.'

'My dear, ever since your return from London . . . '

'I have looked all my disdain, all my discontent at being separated from the amusements and elegance of fashionable society,' I quoted him. 'I perfectly comprehend how you must think so. I know how my looks have pained you. This morning, my brother reproved me for regarding him in silent disgust, and only then did I become sensible there was anything in my expression to offend. And will you believe the truth, after months of suffering so? For I promise you it is quite absurd!'

'Heartburn?' Justin was so astounded when I told him he could only repeat the word helplessly. 'Heartburn?'

'I cannot tell you how it has been plaguing me,' I said happily.

'But — but heartburn? You never mentioned it.'

'After what happened to Amy, I thought it churlish indeed to trouble anyone with such a trifling complaint.'

'Aye, you would think that! And you had no notion how you looked? Judith, I cannot tell you what a lowering effect it had upon my spirits.'

'You never mentioned it.'

'No, but I thought — ' He stopped and I saw alarm cross his features. 'And do you tell me you have been experiencing heartburn constantly, this last three months? Then it is *not* a trifling complaint! We must find a doctor — '

'Five months have I been experiencing heartburn, for it began whilst I was in town, though it was by no means as severe as it has become lately,' I said. 'Now do not fuss, Justin. Doctor Bennet will visit Helen tomorrow and I shall consult him on my own account, but he will only tell me what I know.'

'Judith!' He was almost beside himself now. 'Will you have a care for yourself? All these months of suffering in silence, and heaven knows what might be amiss. You must — '

'Other symptoms have I had,' I said dreamily. 'And attributed them to various causes and not until this afternoon, when I felt a quickening within me, did I come to the truth of it all. Do you see, sir, what you have done?'

I got to my feet and stood before him and pulled my gown tight to reveal the swelling of my body. I felt the child move, and brought Justin's hand against me so that he could feel it too, and I watched his dawning comprehension.

'Well, sir, and what kind of papa will you be, I wonder? You must quickly become accustomed to the notion, I fear, for I have estimated my time will come in October.'

He was on his feet and his arms around me and tears in his eyes and strange wordless noises in his throat. 'Oh!' he gasped. 'It is too much! I cannot — Oh, Judith!'

He lifted me, sat down with me in his lap and held me against him, and for a long time he was trembling and speechless. At last he said, 'All this time, and when you needed me most, I have been too occupied with tormenting myself to pay heed! It shall not happen again, I promise. Such lessons have I learnt these last two days. Judith, my Judith, do you know how I love you?'

I sighed and settled my head comfortably against his shoulder in deep contentment. 'Suppose,' I said, 'you now tell me all about it?'